PRAISE FOR GUNNAR STAALESEN

'Staalesen is one of my very favourite Scandinavian authors and this is a series with very sharp teeth' Ian Rankin

'The Norwegian Chandler' Jo Nesbø

'A vibrant look at the life, loves and betrayals of the past and the ways in which their tentacles cling, never letting you go'
John Harvey

'Not many books hook you in the first chapter – this one did, and never let go!' Mari Hannah

'Staalesen continually reminds us he is one of the finest of Nordic novelists' *Financial Times*

'Chilling and perilous results — all told in a pleasingly dry style' *Sunday Times*

'Every inch the equal of his Nordic confreres Henning Mankell and Jo Nesbø' *Independent*

'As searing and gripping as they come' *New York Times*

'Staalesen does a masterful job of exposing the worst of Norwegian society in this highly disturbing entry' *Publishers Weekly*

'Employs Chandleresque similes with a Nordic Noir twist' *Wall Street Journal*

'Mature and captivating' *Herald Scotland*

'Well worth reading, with the rest of Staalesen's award-winning series' *New York Journal of Books*

'There are only two other writers that I know of have achieved the depth of insight in detective writing that Staalesen has: Chandler and Ross MacDonald' *Mystery Tribune*

'Almost forty years into the Varg Veum odyssey, Staalesen is at the height of his storytelling powers' Crime Fiction Lover

'Readers … will feel drawn to the characters and their intertwined lives' *Reviewing the Evidence*

'Clearly translator Don Bartlett has an excellent understanding of Staalesen's writing. Haunting, dark and totally noir, a great read' *NB Magazine*

'The godfather of Nordic Noir is on top form with an action-packed and dramatic story whose culmination blends the tragedy of two funerals tinged with the tenacious hope of a family reunion that will leave you choked up and wanting more' Crime Fiction Lover

'A masterclass in plotting, pace and characterisation … The translation by Don Bartlett is as accomplished as ever, sharing the tenor of Staalesen's voice and humour so beautifully' Raven Crime Reads

'A classic murder mystery, while also offering the reader a snapshot of Norway through the eyes of the resilient and stalwart Varg Veum. Don Bartlett's translation is excellent … Engaging. Atmospheric. Current' Swirl & Thread

'A meticulously crafted story which intelligently unfolds with some sections of high suspense where the themes of family, betrayal, revenge and environmental militancy feature prominently' Fiction from Afar

'With all of Gunnar Staalesen's hallmark storytelling, that real, authentic PI vibe, and a mixture of deception, tension and the occasional flash of high-threat action, as a fan of the series, I am left feeling very satisfied' Jen Med's Book Reviews

'Whether it's the younger Varg Veum or the more seasoned man, I know I am in for a treat when I read a book in this superbly insightful series and the intricately plotted, surprising, elegant *Bitter Flowers* is no exception. Very highly recommended' Hair Past a Freckle

'A complex, layered plot in which human tragedy and mystery combine to play out beautifully in a classic Nordic Noir with a touch of Christie' Live & Deadly

'There's a poetic, lyrical quality to Staalesen's writing, he's not all action and fast-paced plot. His ability to produce much more than a thriller, with the beautifully evocative sense of place and the masterfully created characters is a joy to read'
Random Things through My Letterbox

'A brilliant example of Nordic Noir, full of dark secrets and chilling characters' Have Books Will Read

'Hints of menace coupled with a chilling climate make this the perfect locational mystery' Bibliophile Book Club

'There are some dark and emotional twists and turns … With an addictive plot, believable and relatable characters, this is a novel I highly recommend' Hooked from Page One

'There is something just so fantastically absorbing about Staalesen's work that I'm always longing to read more … Every time I think I've read the best book I will in a year, Orenda drops a new Gunnar Staalesen that jumps straight to the top of the list' Mumbling About

'Another intriguing and entertaining read'
By the Letter Book Reviews

Mirror Image

ABOUT THE AUTHOR

One of the fathers of Nordic Noir, Gunnar Staalesen was born in Bergen, Norway, in 1947. He made his debut at the age of twenty-two with *Seasons of Innocence* and in 1977 he published the first book in the Varg Veum series. He is the author of over twenty titles, which have been published in twenty-four countries and sold over four million copies. Twelve film adaptations of his Varg Veum crime novels have appeared since 2007, starring the popular Norwegian actor Trond Espen Seim. Staalesen has won three Golden Pistols (including the Prize of Honour). *Where Roses Never Die* won the 2017 Petrona Award for Nordic Crime Fiction, and *Big Sister* was shortlisted for the award in 2019. He lives with his wife in Bergen.

ABOUT THE TRANSLATOR

Don Bartlett completed an MA in Literary Translation at the University of East Anglia in 2000 and has since worked with a wide variety of Danish and Norwegian authors, including Jo Nesbø, Karl Ove Knausgård and Kjell Ola Dahl. He has previously translated multiple titles in the Varg Veum series for Orenda Books.

Mirror Image

GUNNAR STAALESEN

Translated by Don Bartlett

ORENDA
BOOKS

Orenda Books
16 Carson Road
West Dulwich
London SE21 8HU
www.orendabooks.co.uk

First published in Norwegian as *Som i et speil* by Gyldendal, 2002
First published in English by Orenda Books, 2023
Copyright © Gunnar Staalesen 2002
English translation copyright © Don Bartlett 2023
Photograph of Varg Veum statue supplied courtesy of Augon Johnsen

Gunnar Staalesen has asserted his moral right to be identified as the author of this
work in accordance with the Copyright, Designs and Patents Act, 1988.

A catalogue record for this book is available from the British Library.
ISBN 978-1-914585-94-4
eISBN 978-1-914585-95-1

The publication of this translation has been made possible through the financial
support of NORLA, Norwegian Literature Abroad.

Typeset in Arno by typesetter.org.uk
Printed and bound by CPI Group (UK) Ltd, Croydon CR0 4YY

MIX
Paper | Supporting
responsible forestry
FSC® C171272

For sales and distribution please contact *info@orendabooks.co.uk*

Bergen, Norway

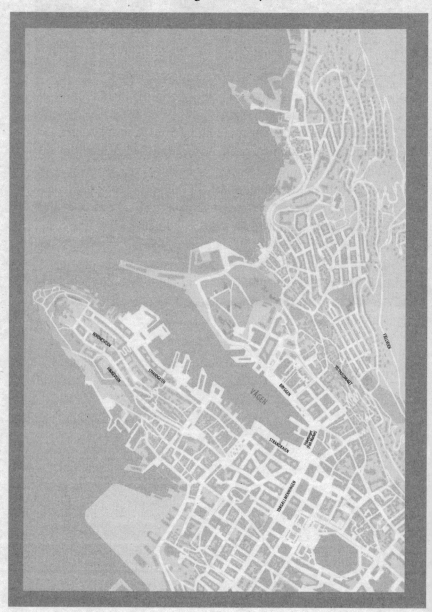

1993

1

I had seen her coming long before our paths met.

We were walking, from opposing directions, over the part of the mountain range Bergensians call The Plateau, as if it were the only one in the world. She was coming from Mount Ulriken and heading towards Mount Fløien. As for myself, I had just climbed Trappefjellet and was following the line of cairns over what was known from olden times as Alfjellet. It was a Thursday, mid-April and the thermometer was fluctuating between one- and two-figure temperatures. Down on Midtfjellet I had heard the sandpiper's characteristically sharp *wheet-wheet*. Under the drifting clouds, the first wedge of greylag geese was flying north, driven by an inexplicable longing for Møre. Spring was on the way. But there were still patches of snow lying on the plateau. In the marshes above Hyttelien you sank deep into mud if you left the path.

All of a sudden, she was gone, like the seductive forest creature of Scandinavian folklore, the *hulder*. Over the last part, where giants had been said to roam, before Borga Pass, a dip in the terrain like an enormous fingerprint, she was lost to view. For a moment I stood staring, then she reappeared on my side of the pass, climbing with great agility. I stepped off the path to let her by.

She was dressed sportily with a light rucksack on her back, brown breeches, a green anorak and a white woollen hat. As she strode past, she smiled fleetingly and called out a cheery 'Hi', the way that mountain walkers do.

'Hey,' I heard her exclaim after she had passed, 'aren't you…?'

I turned and met her gaze.

'Veum?'

'That's me.'

I speedily focused to gain an impression of her. Her eyes were bluish-green and bright. She was taller than me, more like one metre eighty-five. Yet there was something decidedly feminine about her clean-cut features, her full lips, smooth complexion, and cheeks rosy-red from the bracing mountain air. A few beads of sweat had collected in the blonde down above her top lip; otherwise she seemed surprisingly unaffected, breathing easily like a marathon runner coasting downhill.

She took a couple of steps down towards me, as if to bring us onto the same level, removed one grey knitted mitten and stretched out a hand. 'Berit Breheim.'

'Hi.' We shook hands.

'I'm a lawyer, sharing an office with, among others, Vidar Waagenes.'

'Right. But I don't think we've…'

'No, but I know who you are.'

'Shame I can't say the same.'

'Actually, I'd been thinking about ringing you.'

'Strange coincidence. Meeting here, I mean.'

She gave a wry smile. 'I often walk across the plateau if I have something serious on my mind I need to mull over.'

'And you have now?'

'I know you've been in contact with Vidar a few times.'

'You might say we've enjoyed mutual benefits.'

'I was considering offering you an assignment.'

'In connection with a case you're handling?'

'No, this is … private.'

'So long as it isn't … I mean, I don't take marital cases.'

'I'm not married,' she said, making it sound like an invitation.

'Nor me.'

'Then that makes two of us.'

'Well, not on principle…'

'No, nor me.' She smiled mischievously.

'Could you come to my office early tomorrow, at eight?'

'You're an early bird, aren't you.'

'I'm busy for the rest of the day and I'd like you to get started at once. I hope you haven't got too much else going on at the moment.'

I made a vague gesture with my hand, so as not to promise too much. But she didn't need to worry. I had zero else going on.

'Do we have a deal then?'

'So long as I hear the alarm clock.'

She smiled politely. 'Enjoy the rest of your hike then.'

'And the same to you.'

I could have walked back with her, of course. My hike would-n't have been any shorter as a result. However, she had said she had something to mull over – the following day's meeting maybe – so it was best not to disturb her. As soon as I was on the other side of Borga Pass, I turned to see how far she had walked. She did the same. With the pass between us we waved to each other before continuing in our respective directions.

It was fine. I had a few concerns of my own. Some solitude would do me good.

2

Taking a human life does something to you.

It would soon be two months since the late February evening when I despatched a man called Harry Hopland to whence he had come, yet still his final gaze was seared in my memory. He had cursed me as he plunged from the edge of the half-finished concrete building. His curse had echoed through every single hour of the sleepless nights I had endured since.

The woman in my life for the last eight years – my old friend in the national registry, Karin Bjørge – had tried to console me as far as she could:

'It wasn't your fault, Varg. It was self-defence. It was him or you.'

'But I could've saved him,' I had reasoned. 'I could've had him arrested.'

'And what then, eh? He would've probably come out of prison with the same grisly intentions as this time.'

She was right. I knew she was. Nevertheless, it had been a troublesome period. I slept badly. Harry Hopsland haunted my dreams, and when I appeared in the ante-chamber of Breheim, Lygre, Pedersen & Waagenes at one minute and thirty seconds to eight next morning I felt as if my head was full of steel wool and petrol, a grey, indefinable mass that could catch fire at any moment.

Two secretaries met me – a classic pair: one older, with an attractive network of wrinkles around her eyes, dark, elegantly coiffured hair, discreet yet tasteful clothes, light, airy glasses perched halfway down her slender nose; her colleague, twenty-something, blonde, with morning-weary eyes, far more youthfully attired: tight black trousers and a blouse so red it would have aroused even a stuffed bull. The signs on the desk apprised me of their names: Hermine Seterdal and Bente Borge.

I politely addressed the older of the two. 'I have an appoint-ment with Berit Breheim. My name's Veum.'

Her dark eyes gleamed. 'Ah, yes, you've been here before, haven't you. You saw herr Waagenes.'

For an instant I regarded her with surprise. Was this someone I had left an impression on or did she just have a good memory?

'Fru Breheim's expecting you. It's the second door on the right. You'll see her through the glass panel.'

'Thank you very much.'

I followed her instructions, tapped on the door, met Berit Breheim's eyes inside and stepped in. 'Good morning.'

She smiled. 'Good morning.'

The office furniture was simple and arranged strategically. The desk by the window, facing the door; a small nest of tables and two chairs in one corner, a bookshelf weighed down by law books in the other.

She rose and walked around her desk. 'Cup of coffee?'

'Please.'

She went to the door. 'Bente, bring us some coffee, would you?'

The younger secretary said, 'Of course', and Berit Breheim re-turned.

She was dressed soberly: cream-coloured silk blouse, black skirt and silvery stockings; she was shapely and athletic, but more discus thrower than high jumper, if you had to guess which discipline. 'I'm due in court at ten.'

'You'll win.'

She opened her mouth to answer, but at that moment Bente Borge came in with two stylish, slim, white coffee cups, a small bowl of sugar and a jug of cream, and an Italian-designed flask of coffee, all on a Merlot-red tray that matched to perfection the black wood of the table between the two red leather chairs.

Berit Breheim poured the coffee and behaved as I had ex-

6

GUNNAR STAALESEN

pected: she got straight to the point. 'As I was saying when we met yesterday, this is a private and personal assignment.'

I nodded, waiting.

'I have a sister called Bodil. She's a couple of years younger than me. Thirty-eight to be precise. She's in – how shall I put it? – a difficult marriage.'

'I hope you've remembered that I don't—'

'Yeah, yeah, Veum. But this isn't that kind of case.'

'Fine.' I splayed my hands as a sign that she should carry on.

'Fernando, her husband, is Spanish. Fernando Garrido, a marine engineer by profession and employed as an inspector in a local shipping company, TWO – short for Trans World Ocean. It used to be known as Helle Shipping.'

I leaned forward. 'Has it got anything to do with Hagbart Helle?'

'You're well informed, Veum. I like that. Yes, it has. But Hagbart Helle's dead. Think he died in 1989, and the company was sold. The owners live in London, but the company's registered in – surprise, surprise – Jersey. The branch in Bergen is run by a certain herr Halvorsen. Bernt Halvorsen, unless I'm much mistaken. Not that I have anything to do with them, but since you asked.'

'That's my style. I ask questions.'

'The problem is that they've gone missing. Both Bodil and Fernando.'

'I see. And you think there's something suspicious about that?'

'Suspicious? … Erm, well not really. If it had been, I would've gone to the police. But there are some circumstances that make me uneasy.'

'And what would they be?'

'Ten days ago, on Palm Sunday, I was summoned to Bergen Central Police Station to assist Fernando. He'd spent the night in a cell for disturbing the peace and needed legal assistance. I immediately rang Bodil to hear what she had to say.'

'And…?'

'Well, it was nothing very dramatic. At first, they'd been celebrating a wedding anniversary. They'd been married for ten years, I think.'

'Then they should've been over the seven-year itch.'

'Well, anyway, they started arguing. One thing led to another and, in the end, they were making such a din that the man in the house opposite rang the police.'

'Nosy neighbour, if you don't mind me saying so.'

'Too bloody nosy, if you ask me. What business is it of his? Cases like this are usually solved amicably. If there's someone with a bit of common sense to talk them round.'

'But the police thought there were grounds for arrest?'

'He'd become quite aggressive, they said. You know, Mediterranean temperament and all that. But I can assure you, he was pretty desperate when I saw him there, in the drunk tank.'

'But you got him out?'

'Yes, yes, no problem. I drove him home myself. But I didn't go in with him.'

'No?'

'I thought it best for them to talk things through, on their own. The two of them. I've been married. I know what such situations are like.'

'An experience shared by many.'

'You too?'

I nodded. Then I said: 'Tell me … You and your sister, how close are you?'

She shook her head. 'As close as you can expect when you live your own lives and you're preoccupied with your own things.'

'Have they got children?'

'Bodil and Fernando? No.' She grinned. 'We're not the most fertile, neither her nor me, it seems.'

'That's fine, the world being as it is. What does she do?'

'She's in insurance.'

'Not marine insurance by any chance?'

She raised her eyebrows ironically. 'How did you guess? But to my knowledge, she's stopped.'

'I see.'

'She wanted to go it alone, as a freelance consultant.'

'And how's that panning out?'

'Well, it's probably too early to say.'

'OK. So, you drove him home, on the morning of Palm Sunday? But the story doesn't end there?'

'No. I gave them a few days. And when I rang on the following Wednesday, no one answered the phone. But it was Easter week after all, so nothing strange about that.'

The family had two holiday cabins, one in Hjellestad and one in Ustaoset. To be on the safe side, she had rung there as well, to no avail. She had spent Easter in Bergen, herself.

'Actually, I had to prepare for the case I'm busy with now, but the weather was so fantastic, wasn't it, so I spent most of the days outside. I walked the plateau several times and on Good Friday I went to Gulfjellet to do some skiing.'

'Sounds sensible.'

On the Tuesday she started to become seriously concerned. By then she had rung them several times with no response.

'Where do they live?'

'In Morvik in Åsane. We'd always had a little cabin there. They'd had it pulled down after Pappa died in 1983, and built a house on the plot.'

'No shortage of holiday homes, I can see.'

'We hardly ever used the one in Morvik. It was in such a terrible state. The cabin in Hjellstad was from Mamma's family, and the one in Ustaoset they bought … in 1950. Around then anyway. But … Shall we get back to the point?'

'By all means.'

'I drove out there and rang the bell. Several times. No one answered. In the end, I went down to the boathouse. I knew they kept a spare key there. I found it and unlocked the cabin, not without some apprehension, let me tell you. But my fears were groundless. Or perhaps in fact they weren't. The cabin was empty. There wasn't a living soul in there.'

'Nor a dead one, I take it.'

'No.'

'I suppose you rang TWO and asked after Garrido?'

She sent me a patronising glare. 'Naturally. But all they could tell me was that he was away.'

I nodded. 'You still haven't contacted the police?'

'Would I be sitting here and talking to you if I had?'

'Hardly.'

'Exactly.'

'What about Spain?'

She shrugged. 'That's a possibility of course.'

'Where does your brother-in-law live?'

'Near Barcelona. His father had a little ship-building company, but he's dead now. An older brother's taken it over.'

'Have you rung them?'

'No … And I don't want to worry them either for no reason.'

'Well…' I flicked through my notes. 'So, what do you think might be going on?'

'Mm … They might be on some kind of trip, to make up, to draw a line under this episode. In which case, it would be very embarrassing if I contacted the police while they were away.'

'But you don't feel completely at ease?'

'No.' She opened a little brown envelope that had been on the desk. 'Here's the key. Go and see what you can turn up.'

'You didn't notice anything out of the ordinary when you were there?'

'No. If you don't find anything, I'll have to ask you to drive to Hjellestad and perhaps to Ustaoset, to be absolutely sure.'

'It sounds like you fear the worst?'

She hesitated. Then she seemed to take a decision. 'It wouldn't be the first time someone in our family had entered into a death pact.'

'Really?!'

'We have previous.'

'Ah, I'm beginning to understand.'

'What do you understand?'

'Well, I think it's best you tell me about that too.'

3

A black car, a 1952 Opel Olympia, two years old, was going far too fast along the winding road to Hjellestad. The tarmac was wet and black, and the rain-heavy September darkness had erased the contours of the countryside around them. The light from the headlamps reflected on the road, making the surface like a mirror, a gigantic bob run they were hurtling down with no idea of where the journey would take them.

Johan! Careful!

The man at the wheel didn't answer. The muscles in his jaw flexed and he had his eyes fixed intently on the tarmac in front of him. He was wearing a dinner jacket. On the back seat lay his musical instrument, a tenor saxophone, still not packed away in its case. The woman with the cascading, dark-red hair had mascara running down her cheeks, and the tears were still audible in her voice. Do you think he'll come after us? she sobbed, half turning her head.

Why would he? Don't you think he had his fill?

You shouldn't have punched him so hard. What if you'd...?

It was either him or me. Which of us would you prefer to have a split lip?

Blood was spurting everywhere!

Who started it?

Started it...? She gazed into the distance.

He stretched out a hand and stroked her thigh reassuringly. A shiver ran through her. They sailed round the final bend like a bobsleigh crossing the finishing line. He parked under the dark tree-tops, pulled the handbrake, turned to her and said: Journey's end, fru Breheim...

'There was never any doubt that they'd been up there,' Berit said, looking at me with a strange glow in her eyes.

'Up there?'

'In the summer cabin in Hjellestad. It's secluded, in a forest. They found … His saxophone mouthpiece was there.'

'Perhaps he'd been playing for her?'

'"The One I Love Belongs to Somebody Else"?' she said, followed by an audibly ironic question mark.

'What happened?'

'Exactly: what *did* happen? We may never know the details, but the outcome was fatal. At some point during the night they got back in the car. Whoever was driving must've been very drunk because when the car was found, a few days later, both rear wings were damaged and the full length of one side of the car was scored.'

'Where was it found?'

'In the sea at Hjellestad. A boat owner noticed a patch of oil on the water and light shining up from the bottom. He called the police. The car was hauled ashore by a crane and they were inside, my mother and … her friend, their arms wrapped around each other in a final embrace, as though neither of them had made any attempt to extricate themselves from the vehicle and swim to the surface. That was how the idea they had a death pact arose.'

'And the police were happy to accept that?'

'I never heard anything to the contrary, but I couldn't have been more than six then, and Bodil was two. We were shielded from most of it, and later … well, Pappa never talked about it.'

'What year are we talking about?'

'1957.'

'Where were you and your sister when all this took place?'

'Staying with an aunt in Nye Sandviksvei. Pappa didn't come to collect us until the Sunday evening, and I knew at once something was amiss. His top lip was swollen and I can still remember asking about Mamma. But he didn't answer, and Aunty Solveig took us home. Again and again, I've tried to recall my impressions of that day, and of the subsequent ones, but all I can see is fragments. Pappa with a swollen lip, Aunty Solveig bursting into tears, Bodil screaming and screaming and no one consoling her. I have absolutely no memory of the funeral, although I'm told I was present. The next thing I'm sure I can remember is Pappa coming home with Sara and saying they were going to get married. But that wasn't until 1958. Everything in between has gone.'

'I understand.'

'Some years later, in 1960 and then 1964, Bodil and I were joined by two half-brothers, Rune and Randolf.'

'But this death pact, as you called it, where did that come from?'

'Someone I met later. Many years later. Hallvard Hagenes. He was a nephew of the man Mamma died with, Johan Hagenes.'

'Hallvard Hagenes, the musician?'

'Yes. He plays the saxophone too. Anyway, he told me what was said about the incident in his family, even if it wasn't a topic they were fond of discussing.'

'And they called it a death pact?'

'Yes. And it struck me as I was thinking through what … Well, what else would you call it?'

'Well, if the police didn't query the death then, there's probably no reason to do so now, so many years later. But…' I leaned forward, 'however interesting this might be, is there any reason there would be a link between the events of 1957 and your sister and her husband's disappearance now, thirty-six years later?'

'No, no, no. None at all. I was only trying to explain the reasons for my concern.'

'This cabin in Hjellestad that you just asked me to go and check, is it the same one that your mother and her friend, as you called him, stayed in before they drove into the sea?'

'Yes, it is.'

'I assume you have your key too?'

'Yes.' She opened a desk drawer. 'And a key to the cabin in Ustaoset, if need be?' She took out a ring with three keys on and indicated two of them. 'This is for Hjellestad. This is for Ustaoset. And this is for the tool shed in Hjellestad.' She pushed them across the table to me and I put them in my pocket with the key to the house in Morvik that she'd handed me earlier.

'What about a photo of your sister and her husband? Have you got one?'

She nodded. 'Of course. I thought you'd ask. Here...'

She gave me an envelope. I opened it and shook out the picture inside. It was a thank-you card with a wedding photograph mounted on it. The wife had straight blonde hair, which appeared to be tied in a bun at the back. She had a classical face, pretty, slightly rounder than her sister's, perhaps, but the similarity between them was obvious. The husband was dark-haired and clean-shaven. His smile revealed white teeth, his eyes were dark. The photograph was too small to glean any sense of their personalities.

'This is all you have?'

'Yes, it's the only one I could find. We don't take many photos in our family. Perhaps because they remind us of how fragile a family portrait can be. Suddenly there's a person missing and we can't explain why.'

'Mm, I see. But how old is this one?'

'They got married in 1983.'

'Ten years ago, in other words. Maybe they haven't changed so much?'

'I doubt you'd have any problem recognising them.'

'Let's hope not.'

She snatched a hurried glance at her watch. 'Anything else you need? A small advance maybe?'

'Well, as you've brought the subject up, I do have some bills baring their teeth at me whenever I show my face in the office.'

'Five thousand kroner enough?'

'That'll cover the first few days anyway. Expenses are extra.'

'Naturally. You don't need to teach a lawyer how to write invoices.'

'I suspected as much.'

She took my account number and promised to transfer the sum at once. She had no idea what she had set in motion. The bank would reel in shock. The rates at Oslo Stock Exchange would instantly be rocketing. As soon as I was outside, I cast around for the nearest branch of my bank. I would have to withdraw the fee before it was swallowed up by an outstanding bill.

4

Outside my office window, everything was as it had been.

Spring had taken a shot across the bow. Driving rain was battering the town, a south-westerly gale at its back. The buds that only a few days ago had been ready to divest themselves of any clothing at the slightest evidence of sunshine, light-green and naked, for everyone to see, had curled up and withdrawn into themselves. Up on Rundemanen peak there was still a sparse, iridescent layer of snow staring at us coldly, as if to tell us not to sleep too soundly. Overnight frosts were not off the cards yet.

There was a message on my answerphone. *'Torunn Tafjord here. I'm a freelance journalist trying to make contact with private investigator Varg Veum. I'm calling from Anfa Hotel, Casablanca. Local time is 8.30 am. Friday. Can you phone me back on 00212 2200235?'*

'Casablanca?' I said to myself. This sounded like a joke in poor taste. I replayed the message and jotted down the number.

Torunn Tafjord? Somewhere, deep down inside my mental hard disk, I seemed to recognise her name; if not from elsewhere, then from the by-line of some reports in those national newspapers based in Akersgata and district. But from Casablanca?

I dialled the twelve numbers and waited. After three beeps she picked up. 'Hello?'

'Varg Veum here. I'm calling from Bergen. Is Rick there?'

She chuckled. 'No, he left a while ago. Thanks for ringing back so quickly.'

'How can I help?'

'You're a private investigator, aren't you?' There was an unmistakeable twang of Sunnmøre in her Norwegian, especially noticeable in her 'r's. But her accent was honed and polished, which from my experience placed her origins in Ålesund.

'I can't deny it, I suppose.'

'You've been recommended by a colleague of mine in Bergen, Ove Haugland.'

'Ah, Ove. How is he?'

'Well, I think. Recently, I've only spoken on the phone with him. Anyway, he was sure you'd be able to help me.'

'Let me hear what this is about first.'

'It's about a ship belonging originally to a company in Bergen.'

'I see.'

'The company's called Trans World Ocean.'

'I've heard of it.' I stretched out a hand for my notepad, opened it and began to make notes.

'The ship's called the *Seagull*. Right now, it's here, in Casablanca, bound for somewhere in Norway called Utvik, and coming from Conakry in Guinea.'

'Utvik in Stryn or Utvik in Sveio?'

She hesitated. 'I'm not sure. It's one of the reasons I've contacted you.'

'Would you like me to find out which?'

'Yes.'

'Can you tell me anything about what freight it's carrying?'

'Not yet. But I have my suspicions.'

'Would you like me to investigate that as well?'

She hesitated again. 'Only covertly.'

'And by that you mean I shouldn't stroll over to the Trans World Ocean offices, wherever they are, and ask them point blank?'

'I'm afraid that wouldn't be a very good idea.'

'Why not?'

'I don't think they would appreciate it, and I'd rather they didn't suspect someone was on their trail.'

I glanced at my notepad. Under 'Trans World Ocean' and 'the *Seagull*' I'd written a name. 'Now tell me, Tafjord—'

'Please call me Torunn.'

'Have you ever contacted anyone at Trans World Ocean?'

'No, never.'

'Does the name Fernando Garrido mean anything to you?'

'No. Should it?'

'I don't know. But this is the second time in very few hours that I've heard the name Trans World Ocean. Such coincidences always make me a bit – how shall I put it? – uneasy.'

'Very understandable. And what was the other time?'

'I think I should keep that to myself for the moment.'

'Right, OK. So what do you think? Can you do me this favour?'

It is a flaw in my character, I know, but I find it hard to say no to women. They didn't even have to be as nice as Torunn Tafjord. 'I can give it a go,' I said. 'Finding out which Utvik it is shouldn't be a problem. Will you be staying in Casablanca?'

'No, I'm going to follow the ship north. Don't call me, I'll call you.'

I'd heard that one before. It was how things usually finished with the women in my life. 'Don't call me, I'll call you,' they said. Then I never heard from them again.

'Do you remember what Ilse said to Rick?' I said and mumbled: 'Unless it was the other way around.'

'What's that?'

'"We'll always have Paris."'

'And what do you mean by that?'

'Don't forget to ring me when…'

We left it at that. At least we had achieved this. We would always have a phone conversation between Bergen and Casablanca.

After we had rung off, in our respective towns, I consulted the telephone directory to find out where the TWO offices were. No surprises there. The latest additions to the Bergen shipping industry were not situated by Vågen with a view of Skoltegrunn Quay and the huge cruise ships that soon would be the only ones to dock during the brief summer season from May to September. The TWO offices were in Kokstad, where they barely have a view of anything, except for evergreens, industrial buildings and planes landing at and taking off from Flesland Airport.

I made a note of the address and took it with me as I left. But first I had to head off in the opposite direction.

5

If you wanted to go to Morvik in Åsane at this hour of the day, without a definite return time in mind, you have to drive. I went up to Nedre Blekevei to get my car, a Toyota Corolla, 1989 model, which I drove around while trying to persuade my insurance company to buy me a replacement for the car I had smashed up in February. This was an event I preferred not to be reminded of. It had been a dramatic winter, even by the standards of my profession.

I followed the directions Berit Breheim had given me. The house I was looking for stood at the bottom of a steep hill, marked *PRIVATE ROAD*, a stone's throw from the sea and with a neighbour's house between it and the main road of Morvikvegen. The neighbour's house was a prefab with a white plinth and stained panelling, the type bought by half the staffrooms in every school. I glanced up as I stepped out of the car. A face quickly withdrew, but not so quickly that I didn't notice.

The house belonging to Bodil Breheim and Fernando Garrido had a little more format to it. It was on three levels and had been built in a kind of new functionalist style: box-shaped with white wood-cladding. On the eastern side there was a large terrace and, on the slope to the north, well-established snowdrops, blue and white crocuses and clusters of butter-yellow primroses. A garage had been built into the rock face. I tried the door. It was locked.

The front door was made of polished teak with dark-green leaded windows. Before I used the key, I rang the bell. No one appeared and the door remained shut. Keeping an eye on the neighbour's house, I let myself in.

I looked around. The hallway was large and light. Daylight entered through large Velux windows. On the wall opposite hung a tall, narrow picture, an explosion of colour without any obvious theme. A spiral staircase led to the first floor and a slate-tile staircase to the basement.

I felt uneasy. Walking through a house where actually I had no business to be, where I was an unbidden guest and I could never be sure what I was going to find, has always gone against the grain for me.

I searched through the house, systematically, floor by floor. I started at the bottom, where I found a rustic room with a well-stocked bar facing the terrace. Two sliding doors opened onto it when temperatures allowed. At the back of this floor there were storage rooms, a laundry, two toilets, a shower room and a sauna, all dark and closed now. Clean towels hung on hooks and everything looked ship-shape and Bergen fashion.

The sitting room on the main floor was the size of a tennis court. The whole wall facing the sea was made of glass, framed by heavy, light-green velvet curtains that could be drawn when it was dark, if they wanted to dance naked on the table. The furniture was solid enough to support them. The pictures on the walls had the same bright colours as in the hallway: gold, ochre and azure, with a sunny, Mediterranean feel to them. A top-notch B&O sound system adorned the shorter wall, and a quick glance around the room confirmed that there were at least four speakers. From the window I saw the roof of a boathouse and a concrete jetty protruding into the sea. Across the fjord lay the island of Askøy, a barrier against the sea swell.

The kitchen displayed the same elegance and the same un-constrained budget. At any rate, it wasn't a lack of means that had forced Bodil Breheim and Fernando Garrido to flee. They could live here for months; all they had to do was sell one of their frying pans.

Finally, I went up to the first floor. I started with the bedroom overlooking the sea. Inside there was a large double bed, a white dressing table with a chair in front, a portable TV on a nest of tables at the foot of the bed and two good armchairs in the corners, where they could enjoy the view if they were so inclined. I continued to the guest room, where the bed was made, in case one of them wanted to spend the night alone. Two small studies, both equipped with computers, a spacious bathroom and two separate toilets completed the picture. Everything smacked of perfectionism and orderliness.

The last room I came to was a child's room. It too faced south, and daylight flooded in. Alongside one wall was a child's bed, recently made. On the walls there were pictures of animals and flowers. But there wasn't a trace of a toy or of the child who must have lived there at one time. There was a strangely abandoned and homeless feel to the room generally, as though it actually didn't belong there.

But she had said …

I took out my latest investment, a technological development I hadn't been able to reject. The tyranny of telephone boxes was over. All good private investigators had a new friend. Now we swanned around with bulky mobile telephones attached to a belt, ready to draw them at the first beep. Mine was a Nokia 101, weighing in at around three hundred grams, with a range that increased from day to day, as mobile network coverage grew. It had no problem contacting the office of Breheim, Lygre, Pedersen & Waagenes, anyway.

It had more of a challenge with Berit Breheim though. She was in court and not available, she was afraid, said a woman I thought I recognised as the older of the two secretaries in the ante-chamber. I thanked her and rang off.

For the time being, I let the empty child's room tell its own story, as the sole anomaly in the tastefully furnished home. Before leaving the house, I checked to see if it was possible to open the garage door from inside. It was. I used the automatic switch on the wall in the hallway and the door outside swung open. But the garage was empty. All I could see inside was a set of winter tyres along one wall and a tool cabinet that was as well-equipped as the house. The garage smelt of a car, but the tools showed no sign of any use, from what I could tell. Another question I would have to ask Berit: did they have a car and, if so, where was it?

Unless there was someone else I could ask…

I closed the garage door, locked it behind me and looked up at the neighbour's house. The face was back, but this time it didn't withdraw. I nodded and indicated that I was coming up.

6

He was waiting in the doorway as I came up the gravel path. From the first moment he struck me as a man who had entered his fifties on the wrong foot. He was ungainly and thin with sharp features and a nervous smile, a man who might have been quite charming if he could be bothered to make a bit of an effort. He had an unlit fag in his mouth and stared at me with dark, almost febrile eyes.

'Who are you?' he asked. 'Are you the police?'

'No, no…' I proffered a hand. 'Veum. I'm here on behalf of the family.'

He proffered his own, warily, as though frightened what I would do with it. 'Sjøstrøm.'

'I was wondering … These neighbours of yours down there, Bodil Breheim and Fernando Garrido, do you happen to know if they are on their travels?'

He sent me a suspicious look. 'Well … I haven't seen them since Easter.'

'Ah, right. And the house is empty.'

'You've checked, have you?'

'Yes.'

'Well, as I said, the last time I saw either of them must've been … the Wednesday of Easter week.'

'And that'll be ten or so days ago.'

'Yes, it's a while.' He looked past me, as if to make sure they hadn't appeared in the meantime.

'To be frank, Sjøstrøm, the family's becoming concerned. They've employed me to do some checking. Would you be willing to answer a few questions, do you think?'

'Me?'

'Yes, as their closest neighbour you must've seen the odd thing or two?'

'Of course, by all means, if I can help at all. Would you like to come inside?'

'Thank you,' I said, and followed him in.

The contrast with his neighbours' house was striking. The hallway was dark and cold. I followed him up a staircase and through a door, and we entered his sitting room. Through the panoramic windows I could see the top part of his neighbours' house, the sea below and Askøy across the fjord. A worn old armchair was turned to face the window. Beside it was a little table and an ashtray overflowing with cigarette ends, doubtless his regular observation post.

He hadn't always lived alone. In many ways this was half a house, although he had tried to disguise the fact. He had moved the pictures around on the wall, but light patches revealed that there had been more hanging there before. Judging by those that were left, I considered her taste superior to his, unless the half remaining were hers. The only one that caught my attention was a reproduction of a tall ship in full sail against a sky of grey, drifting clouds. The furniture filled approximately half the room. The three-piece suite now consisted of only one, a sofa, and the marks on the carpet revealed where the other two had stood. But he had been allowed to keep the coffee table. It was almost a surprise that they hadn't sawn it in half while they were dividing up their assets.

Two solitary dining-room chairs and a wealth of floor space made me feel as though I was back in the dance class of my childhood, standing by the wall like a castaway with an ocean between the girls and us. A lone fish swam around in a big aquarium. On the floor where there had once been a partition, he had placed a radiogram and a pile of LPs. Obviously, she had taken the CD player and TV with her. His window on the world was a small portable TV in the corner. It was on, of course, but with the volume turned down, showing what seemed to be a

Brazilian soap opera, with temperamental women silently erupting in emotional outbursts on the tiny screen. He made no move to switch it off, and all the time I was there, his eyes kept veering to the side, as if to make sure he didn't miss anything important.

'A fifty/fifty split, I see,' I commented.

He eyed me sullenly. 'She got first choice, as was her wont.'

'That was how she got you, wasn't it.'

He sniffed and moved one of the dining-room chairs to the coffee table. Then he sat down on the sofa. 'What do you want to know?' he asked with an expectant expression on his face.

'As I've already mentioned, we're not at all sure how serious this is. But the fact is that your neighbours have been gone since Easter, and the family's started to worry. How do you get on with them?'

'With them down there?' His face reddened. 'Well, I'm going to be absolutely frank with you, Veum. We've always got on badly.'

'I see. Any special reason?'

He got up with difficulty and beckoned me over to the window. 'Just look.' He pointed downward. 'When my wife and I moved here in 1978, there was only a little cabin there. We could see right down to the fjord. You could follow every boat that passed. Some of us derive great pleasure from that. Following the traffic on the sea. The Hurtigruten ship. The Westamaran hydrofoils. The cargo boats. But then – in 1983 – they took over, demolished the cabin and over a few years they had that skyscraper erected in its place. Bye-bye, view. Bye-bye, boats.'

'But they gave you notice, I suppose?'

'Notice? I suppose you think they needed to, do you?' He rubbed his thumb against his first two fingers. 'With money you can buy exemption from the rules. Any idiot knows that.'

'Well…' I imagined a textbook fallout between Norwegian

neighbours here. 'So, in other words, your relationship wasn't the best?'

'Damn right it wasn't. They are, excuse my Bergensian, a couple of real arseholes, both of them.' With that, he turned his back on the window and slumped back down on the sofa.

I followed him. 'Anyway, back to the fact that they're missing. You said yourself you hadn't seen them since the Wednesday of Easter week, didn't you?'

'Yes, it must've been Wednesday. They drove off in their car.'

'Right. I noticed the garage was empty. Do you know what make of car they drive?'

'A BMW 520, pretty new.'

'That's detailed.'

'I know a bit about cars.'

'Colour?'

'Dark blue.'

'Do you know the number as well?'

He thought for a couple of seconds. Then he gave it to me.

I wrote it down in my little notepad. 'Did you notice if they had any luggage with them?'

He sent me a disgruntled look. 'I don't hang out of the window watching their every movement, you know.'

'No, no. So, in other words…'

'No, I didn't notice if they had any luggage with them.'

'But you did see both of them leave?'

He hesitated for a moment. 'I can't be sure. He was definitely driving. I'm certain of that.'

'You were on holiday yourself, were you?'

'Not in the usual sense. I've taken early retirement. Heart trouble, you know. About four years ago I had a serious heart attack. The doctor was convinced my divorce caused it.'

'So, you had more than enough opportunity to follow what was going on?'

'You mean...' He nodded towards the window. 'Down there?'

'That too.'

'Yes ... But I don't exactly keep a log.'

'No, no,' I hastened to add. 'I didn't mean ... But it's true that it was you who rang the police when there was some commotion down there that Palm Sunday weekend.'

'Yes, I felt it was my duty.'

'What had been the problem? Loud music?'

'Music? I would've coped with that. They were having one hell of a ding-dong. The way she was howling, you would've thought he was killing her.'

'And, of course, you have no idea what the row was about?'

'Don't I now?' He sent me an eloquent look. 'What do you think?'

'Well, you're probably the only person who can answer that question.'

'Another man, obviously.'

'Whom you'd seen out here?'

'It's no secret that she's very...' He formed two pairs of rabbit ears with his fingers. Air quotes. '"Alone". Garrido is away a lot, travelling, inspecting ships all over the world, from what I gather. And she has the occasional visitor.'

'I see.'

'I've observed at least two different men down there while Garrido was away. What happened on the Saturday before Palm Sunday, in my view, is that Garrido came home unexpectedly, a day early.'

'Oh, yes?'

'I could hear their voices from right up here.'

'You're still talking about the evening?'

'No, no. This was mid-morning. I heard the loud voices and went to the window. Garrido and this guy were standing outside the house and shouting at each other. No idea what the problem was, but they definitely weren't of one mind.' A broad grin spread across his face as if to say it was better entertainment than the TV. 'And that night the racket started again.'

'But by then the other man was long gone, I assume?'

'Yes, yes. Garrido was on the point of chasing him up the hill, I can tell you.'

'This man ... Do you have any idea who he was?'

He shook his head slowly. 'A fancy pants. Well dressed with a trim beard and a red Ferrari, which he usually parks up by the main road when he visits.'

'Age?'

'Same as Garrido. Mid-thirties.'

'And he was often there?'

'Well, often ... He'd definitely been there several times before. What do I know? Perhaps he had other irons in the fire too.'

'You've mentioned one man. But didn't you say there was another?'

He nodded. 'The other one plays the saxophone.'

I sat up straight. 'Saxophone? How do you know?'

'I've heard him. He played for her when he came round.'

'Not exactly softly if you could hear him all the way up here?'

'Veum, it was at night and I always sleep with the window open. Even in February. And their house is not that far away.'

'No, OK. February this year?'

He nodded. 'Yes.'

'And what did this guy look like?'

'You'll have to find that out for yourself.'

'You only heard him?'

'No, but I know his name.' When I didn't answer, he continued: 'I saw him in the paper, a picture of the band he played in.'

'And you noted his name.'

'Well, I recognised him, didn't I. You never know what might come in handy one day. Such as now for example.'

'Forward-looking of you. And what's his name?'

'Hallvard Hagenes.'

A chill ran down between my shoulder blades. For the sake of appearance, I wrote down his name. I should have been surprised perhaps. However, for some reason I was not.

7

In the very old days, it would have taken me a good day to travel from Morvik in Åsane to Hjellestad in Fana. Even by car I would have had to reckon on a few hours of winding roads. That was until parts of this stretch were upgraded to motorway standard in the 1980s. Now I drove on autopilot with a tiny delay at the toll booths in Helleveien; then it was through the Fløifjell Tunnel and out the other side of Bergen. In the last bit, after the Blomsterdalen turn-off, the road bore some similarity with the bad old days, and I had to slow down and drive with increased caution.

By the marina in Kviturspollen there was feverish activity. The sailing community had defied the rain storms and the biting wind. Now it was all about getting ready for the first of May, when all leisure-boat owners were going to sail their boats in procession across By fjord to demonstrate against high taxes and the increase in VAT.

I stopped a couple of times and had to consult Berit Breheim's directions before I found the small, demarcated parking spot, not so far from Bergen Sailing Association. From there I followed her route through the forest to the cabin. The path was easy to find through the blueberry shrubs and the dark-green moss. In the trees above, the season's first sopranos were singing their arias with gusto. Between the trunks I glimpsed Raunde fjord and the mountains on the island of Sotra.

Then the cabin emerged from the woods, red with blue wooden trim and frames. The window panes were black and empty. Under the west-facing terrace birch logs had been stacked, and the flowerbeds looked overgrown and untended. The east-facing tool shed looked equally abandoned.

I walked around the cabin. Everything seemed so quiet and peaceful. The twitter of small birds was the only noise. I estab-

lished that the front door was locked. So I took out the bunch
of keys I had been given by Berit Breheim, inserted the correct
one and turned. Gently, I pushed the door. No cooped-up
animal leapt up at my face. All that met me was the stale, clammy
smell of winter confinement.

'Hello?' I called into the dark hallway. No answer.

I went through the cabin assiduously, room by room, across
the main floor and up into the attic. There were four bedrooms,
one of them with a double bed. In two others there were bunk
beds. None of them was made up.

I turned on the taps, but either the stopcock was off or the
pipes had frozen. At any rate, no water came out. But the fridge
was on. I had a look inside. There were only a few jars of jam,
half a tube of caviar, a jar of olives and a couple of bottles of
mineral water.

The cabin was well furnished, if not luxurious, with a radio,
TV, fridge and stove. On the walls hung a variety of landscapes,
some in oils, others photographs, a couple of which were of
Hjellestad in the 1940s, judging by the costumes. In one corner
of the sitting room there was a wood-burner. I leaned forward
and checked the ash. It was cold and grey, like abandoned
remains in a crematorium. A shotgun hung from the wall above
the wood-burner. For a moment I stood staring at it, then I
slowly tore myself out of my reverie and devoted my attention
to the rest of the room.

On a small table there was a cabin scrapbook. I picked it up
and thumbed through. The first entry was from 1960. Pictures
had been glued in, mostly of children, the oldest in black and
white, the latest in colour. I thought I recognised Berit and her
sister in some of them.

I leafed through to the last note, dated less than six months
ago:

12.12.1992
Have tidied up and prepped the place for winter. Always sad.
Going to pick up F from the airport.
Bodil

I made a mental note of the content and jotted down the date in my notepad. Afterwards, I stood looking around.

An eerie sensation shivered through my body. So, this was where they had spent their last night in 1957, Tordis Breheim and Johan Hagenes. What had they done? Had he taken out his saxophone and played 'I'm in the Mood for Love' to her? Had they made love for the very last time? How much had they drunk? And what had made them get into the car, drive to Hjellestad quay and plunge into 'the deep, blue sea' without so much as a bass line as accompaniment? Had they found peace down there in the depths? Or were they wandering around up here as spirits? Did the echo of his very last saxophone solo resound in the streets at midnight on the anniversary of their dramatic deaths? Was she symbolically clapping her hands from the Beyond? Or...

Something startled me. I turned to the door. Wasn't that the sound of ... footsteps?

I walked over to the window.

Berit Breheim was warily approaching the hut from outside. She placed her face against what must have been her own reflection in the window pane, saw mine and immediately recoiled. She held her hand to her mouth in shock.

I waved reassuringly through the window and walked towards the open door. We met in the doorway.

'I had no idea ... I thought one of the neighbours had got out of his car over there.'

'You couldn't wait for my report?'

'No, no, I finished in court earlier than I'd expected and as it was Friday anyway...'

'Well, come in. Perhaps you can see if anyone's been here. It doesn't seem like it to me.'

'I rarely come here. Bodil and Fernando are the ones who use it. I've always preferred the mountains, myself.'

'So, the cabin in Ustaoset is more to your taste?'

'You could put it like that. Besides...'

'Yes?'

'No.' She looked around and shuddered. 'I can never come here without thinking about my mother and what happened to her and that man back in 1957. I've never understood how Pappa could return here. Nor could Sara.'

'I didn't quite ... When did you say your father died?'

'In 1983.'

'But your stepmother's alive?'

'Still going strong. After all, she's not a day over sixty.'

'And, your two half-brothers, do you have any contact with them?'

'Not much. Sara was fantastic with us. There was no evil stepmother syndrome or anything, if that's what you're thinking. But it was Pappa who held us together, and when he was gone there was nothing left. We usually meet for one day over Christmas. That's all.'

'Do all three of them live in this district?'

'Randolf doesn't. He's in Svalbard of all places. But I see Rune now and then. He's in insurance, too.'

'Like Bodil, you mean?'

'Yes, but not in the same company.'

'Is it likely that she may have contacted them for some reason or other?'

'I find that hard to believe. And I'd rather you didn't ... You understand – I mean with our past. If Sara suspects that Bodil has done what Mamma, I just can't imagine...'

'Let's cross that bridge when or if we come to it.'

'So, tell me where they are then.' For the first time I sensed an undertone of hysteria in her voice.

'Well…' I gestured expansively with my arms and cast around. 'Can you see anything that suggests they've been here?'

'No.'

'Erm, you mentioned that you knew – or had met – a musician called Hallvard Hagenes.'

'Yes, I did.'

'Did you meet him through Bodil?'

She tossed her head. 'Through Bodil? How do you mean?'

'Well, I was just wondering, did she have any contact with him, do you think?'

'With Hallvard Hagenes? You … I'm talking about something that happened twenty years go. He talked about this with … my uncle and Mamma.'

'So, none of you had any further contact with him?'

'I didn't anyway.' Then I saw a reaction in her face. 'You don't mean that something was going on between Bodil and Hallvard Hagenes?'

I tipped my head vaguely.

She appeared affronted. 'Fate cannot be that cruel. Surely life cannot go in circles like that? Or can it?'

'You can turn up the strangest things once you start digging.'

'Is that the private investigator's motto?' she said with sudden sarcasm.

'Maybe.' I held her gaze. 'There's another matter I'd like to ask you about.'

'Mhm?'

'When I was walking through the house in Morvik I came across what looked a lot like a child's room…'

She went pale. 'Oh, my God.' Again she raised her hands to her mouth. 'Don't say that. Where?'

'On the first floor. Does that come as a surprise to you?'

'A surprise?'

'You've never seen it?'

'No, why would I…? There are just bedrooms up there. But I would never have thought in my wildest dreams that they'd keep it.'

'I think perhaps you should explain.'

She nodded, ran a hand across her brow and looked at me with a kind of distant gaze, as though she had just come to after fainting.

'Yes, I'll…' She swallowed. 'It must've been 1986, three years after they got married. Bodil was expecting and they were very happy. I tried to warn her, reminded her of what I'd been through myself, told her not to take anything for granted. But they didn't listen to me. They bought baby equipment, she knitted clothes, they even prepared a room for the little one. And then she lost it. Just as I'd lost … all mine.' She flapped one arm. 'Afterwards she never fell pregnant again, not to my knowledge anyway. But fancy not doing something about the room. They've turned it into a kind of … what's it called? A mausoleum. For an unborn child.'

'So, to be clear, no child has ever slept in that bed?'

'No.'

We stared at one another, each seeming to see the surprise on our own face mirrored by the other's. Eventually she tore her eyes away and cast a final gaze around.

'Well,' she said, 'there's nothing here anyway.'

'No. Doesn't seem to be.'

We went outside and I locked up. Between the trees to the west of the cabin I saw the lid of an old well. It was a square, solid wooden lid, attached to the framework by large hinges. There was a weighty padlock that held the lid in place and several of the boards had been replaced with new ones, not that long ago apparently.

'The well's no longer used, is that right?'

'That's correct.'

'But the lock looks new.'

'That's something to do with security. There are children in the area, you know. It would be a catastrophe if one of them fell in.'

'Of course.' Once again I shook off a sense of unease. 'So…'

'Let's go,' she said, her voice trembling.

Together we walked through the trees and down to our cars. She drove a metallic-grey Mitsubishi Galant, and we went in convoy as far as Flyplassvegen. There, she branched off while I drove up towards Kokstad. It was time to pay Trans World Ocean a visit.

8

Trans World Ocean was based in a metallic-grey building that could also have been designed by Mitsubishi. The front entrance was constructed from glass and blue steel. Two flags adorned the drive, one in Norwegian colours, the other with the company's logo on a white background: a Viking ship in full sail, formed into the letters TWO, passing through a blue and green circle.

The first thing I saw as I entered the concourse was the same symbolic circle on the back wall and a stylised long ship cast in iron and suspended from the ceiling as a reminder of past maritime glories; the days when seafarers from the north crossed the great ocean between what they then called Norveg and Vinland, built castles in Katanes and Dubh Linn, sailed up the rivers to Holmgard and Tuskaland, staked their claims to any agricultural land they could find and beheaded anyone who protested.

The well-built guard behind the counter by the security channel appeared to have descended directly from the same seafarers, except that his hair had been cropped close to his skull and he hadn't gone to the trouble of growing a beard. His light-blue shirt bore the shipping company's logo on the upper arm and had been ironed with such ferocity that I wouldn't have liked to have the crease held to my throat.

I was at my very politest as I explained the purpose of my visit. 'May I speak to Fernando Garrido please?'

Initially he seemed friendly and obliging. 'Have you got an appointment?'

'No.'

He didn't even check his screen. 'Garrido isn't here.'

'Isn't he? Will he be away long?'

He sent me a probing look. 'That depends on your point of view.'

'Pardon?'

'According to the information I've been given, he no longer works for us.'

'I see. I had no idea.'

'Yes, it's all a bit sudden. Even for us.'

'Who can I speak to then?'

'What's it about?'

'It's too complicated to explain, but surely you can get someone who worked with him, can't you?'

'Mm.' For the first time he shifted his gaze to the screen, carefully manoeuvred the mouse across the pad and acted as if he was considering who that might be. 'Kristoffersen, maybe. He's probably the closest.'

'Then I'll try him.'

'If he's here, that is.' My friend behind the counter raised his voice sufficiently to make it clear who was in charge.

I kept my mouth shut and let him work it out on his own. It is important not to tread on the toes of administrators. They hold the whole wide world in their hands.

He nodded silently, banged a number on the keyboard and waited for a few seconds before speaking into the microphone on the collar around his neck. 'There's someone here asking after Garrido.' Silence while he listened. 'But now he's asked to talk to you.' Another silence. 'No, it was me who—' He was interrupted. I couldn't hear a sound from his headset, but his face had gone a very deep red.

He turned back to me. 'What was the name?' he snapped.

'Veum.'

He conveyed this information without getting much of response and directed his gaze at me again. 'The name means nothing to him.'

I was beginning to become impatient. 'Tell him his name means nothing to me either, but if he prefers to speak to the police, he's cordially invited to do so.'

'The police?'

'Yes.'

He eyed me sardonically before passing on the message, not without some schadenfreude. He listened to the response, grunted back and rang off. 'He's coming down.'

'Hallelujah, Brother. Down from the heavens…'

One and a half minutes later Kristoffersen announced his arrival. He filled his double-breasted jacket without a millimetre to spare, but was still conspicuously light on his feet, like a sumo wrestler on speed. His dark hair was combed back and to the sides from what resembled a sabre slash to his scalp.

He may have looked like a teddy bear, but his temperament left something to be desired. The look he sent me was like a gale warning. 'What's all this then?' he growled.

'Could we speak privately?' I said, motioning towards the guard.

Kristoffersen snorted and beckoned me through to his side of the security channel. The guard pressed a button in front of him, the two plastic saloon doors opened and I stepped through.

I held out a hand. 'My name's Veum. This is about Garrido.'

He ignored my hand. 'Over here.'

He led me behind a partition and to a minimal lounge, sited next to tall glass walls looking out at the atrium where it would probably have been enjoyable to sit and have a coffee on a midsummer lunch break. There was no one there now. And I wasn't offered a cup of coffee either.

He motioned me to sit down. However, he chose to stay on his feet – a sign that this was not going to take long. So I didn't sit down either.

'What's this about?'

'Garrido no longer works here, I've been told, by the guard.'

'Yes. So what?' The angry look he sent the guard didn't bode well for his future company prospects.

'Do you know where he is?'

'Who? Garrido?' He glared at me. 'Have you tried his house?'

'That's precisely the problem. He's nowhere to be found.'

'He's probably gone on holiday then.' Before I could answer, he continued. 'Tell me, who actually are you? What do you want?'

'I'm a private investigator.'

He snorted. 'And what was all that about the police?'

'If Garrido doesn't turn up soon, this will become a police matter.'

He looked at me more and more impatiently. 'And then what? What on earth has that got to do with us?'

I raised my voice slightly. 'The fact that he worked here until a few days before his disappearance, surely that should make you at least a little concerned?'

'Tell me, Veum, are you suggesting something criminal may've happened to Garrido?'

'His wife's missing too.'

'Bodil? And what do you mean by "disappearance"? They're on holiday, I keep telling you.'

'I heard you. But I'm not convinced they are.'

We stood weighing each other up. He reached a hand into his inside pocket, took out a packet of cigarettes, without even so much as giving me the chance to decline his offer, and lit a fag with a small, gilt lighter. He inhaled the smoke so deeply that I thought I could see it curling through his bronchial tubes. Then he was racked by a violent cough; it sounded as if it came from the bottom of a lift shaft. 'He must've needed a good rest after the recent shocks.'

'By which you mean…?'

He waved his cigarette hand. 'It's no secret that he's been on a crash course with the rest of the management team recently, including me.'

'And what was it you disagreed about?'

'That's company business, Mr Private Dick. We see no reason to broadcast our concerns via casual visitors.'

'So that's why he chose to leave then?'

'Interpret it any way you like,' he said sullenly, slowly exhaling the smoke through his nostrils.

I gambled on a shot in the dark. 'Did it perhaps have something to do with the *Seagull*?'

His eyes took on a two-ton dead-weight look. 'The *Seagull*?'

'Yes?'

'What…?' He bit his tongue. 'As I said, we don't discuss company business.'

'I'd better ask Garrido then, when I find him.'

'You do that, Veum. You do that. And say hello from me, won't you. Tell him we haven't missed him for a second, from the moment he left through that door.' He nodded towards the exit and began to walk in that direction himself. 'If there's nothing else…' As he passed me, he brutally stubbed the cigarette out in a standing ashtray.

Reluctantly, I followed him.

Coming in through the security channel was an elegantly dressed man in a light-coloured coat. He was in his thirties, very blond, had had a recent trip to the hairdresser and wore an extremely trim beard. He had regular features, cool, bluish-green eyes, and the faint reddish tone of his sensitive skin lent him a vaguely feminine air. Hence the beard, I guessed.

He nodded to Kristoffersen and eyed me inquisitively.

'Are you on your way out, Kristoffersen?'

'No, no. I'm going up.'

'Good.'

He continued up the stairs to the office floor. I watched him until he was out of sight. This was a man I had never seen before. But he reminded me greatly of someone Fernando Garrido's neighbour had described to me.

'Who was that?' I asked.

'Our CEO, Bernt Halvorsen,' Kristoffersen said.

'Does he drive a Ferrari?'

'Yes, but...' Once again, I had the pleasure of seeing him bite his tongue, at least mentally. From hereon he didn't say another word. When I was on the other side of the security channel, he growled something or other, turned his back on me and left.

'A red Ferrari, if I'm not much mistaken,' I said to the guard.

'Exactly,' he said, probably as he had nothing left to lose.

Before signing off for the evening, I drove out to Flesland Airport, parked as conscientiously as I could and then checked off every single vehicle in the long-stay car park against the number of Garrido's BMW 520. In the end, I was able to establish with one-hundred-per cent certainty that it was not there.

But where was it then? That I still had to discover. There was no shortage of possibilities, from the northern cape to Lindesnes in the south. The only question was: where to begin?

9

Going to a jazz café at twelve noon on a Saturday morning felt continental and un-Norwegian. While the rest of the population was cleaning and hoovering, before tucking into rice pudding and listening to the radio's regular crime play, unless they were already out on the week's longest compass-free hike from shop to shop, jazz fans were gathering in dark, smoke-filled rooms, where they listened to driving swing and bitter-sweet blues, performed largely by local artistes ranging from twenty to well over sixty years of age, their eyes veiled in a haze, their tongues wagging to excess, driven by a form of cheerful melancholy, the jazz club's prime motor.

The jazz and blues café that the Den Stundenløse hostelry had founded this winter, in the basement of what had once been the Ole Bull cinema, but which now was a combined discotheque and bars, was the latest blossom to emerge on Bergen's relatively fertile jazz scene.

I met Karin on the pavement outside just before noon. According to the poster by the entrance, Tydal Jazz Company was doing the honours this Saturday. We went downstairs into the subterranean room, I ordered half a litre of beer, she ordered a glass of white wine, and I made a first attempt to spot any familiar faces in the already smoky room. On stage, the musicians had already set up their gear. Now they were sitting at a small table in a corner drinking coffee, except for the leader, Lasse Tydal, who was standing at the bar with a beer in his hand.

He nodded casually as I approached. 'A good morning to you,' he said in an imitation of standard Norwegian before reverting to his sedate Bergensian. 'Out to lubricate the works, eh?'

'Never miss an opportunity. And your lungs are in good shape?'

'I stick to ballads now, you know. But I still have some puff in my chops. You'll see…'

Lasse Tydal was well into his sixties with a high forehead and thick, grey hair over his ears. Some of the power behind his puff clearly came from the midriff area, which had increased in girth, presumably to accommodate powerful bellows.

'I was wondering … A younger colleague of yours. Hallvard Hagenes, do you know anything about him?'

'Hallvard, oh, yes. Talented young tenor player once.' He scanned the room. 'Sometimes he drops in, but I can't see him today. Not yet anyway. He drives a taxi to make ends meet. It's never been easy to survive as a jazz musician, but nowadays it's nigh on impossible unless you're among the absolute top performers.'

'And he isn't?'

'Not the way the market is in Norway anyway. Have you got a job for him perhaps?'

'Afraid not. I just wanted to ask him a question.'

'Tore Lude and Reidar Rongved over there have worked with him on some trio gigs. I can introduce you to them in the first interval if you like. We're about to start now.'

'Where would you place him on the local scene?'

'Oh, you know, there are several good tenor players in the district. Søbstad's still going strong. The Hystad brothers. Olav Dale. But Hagenes is no slouch. He can play everything from free jazz to standards. It's in his genes, you know. I remember his uncle, Johan Hagenes. The local answer to Lester Young when he was at his peak.'

'Did you know him?'

'Of course. But … We have to get going now. Talk later.'

Taking his beer with him, he walked over to the stage, where the other musicians were now taking up their positions: Tore Lude on piano, Reidar Rongved on bass and Mons Midtbøe on drums, while Terje Tornøe was carefully trying out the mouthpiece on his trumpet. Lasse Tydal mumbled a few words to the others, put his beer down on a small table behind him and

placed the strap of his copper-coloured sax around his neck. I
went back to Karen.

She looked up curiously. 'You took your time.'

'I was chatting to someone.'

'You're working, are you?'

'I need some information.'

I didn't get a chance to expatiate, as a management rep
stepped up onto the stage to introduce today's guests, and then
Tydal Jazz Company burst into a stomping version of 'Tiger Rag',
with Terje Tornøe taking the hottest solos, a crystal-clear trumpet
tone that wove silver patterns through the cigarette smoke and
brought the conversations at the tables around us to a halt.

The previous evening, I had rounded off the day deep in concentration as I pored over the telephone directory. I had
discovered where Bernt Halvorsen and Hallvard Hagenes lived:
the former in Hopsneset and the latter in Rosegrenden. Also, out
of sheer curiosity, I had looked up Berit Breheim, who lived in
Fantoft, not so far from the stave church that had burned down,
destroyed by an arsonist less than a year ago.

Tydal Jazz Company were working their way through the
century. After the opener Tor Lude took the star role in several
ragtime numbers. Now it was Lasse Tydal's tenor in the spotlight, full and breathily warm in Ellington's immortal 'All Too
Soon', one of Ben Webster's old tours de force.

'I may have to go to Ustaoset tomorrow,' I said to Karin.
'Want to join me?'

'Me? Skiing?' She smiled gently.

'That's an idea. Perhaps I should take skis.'

'You could always do a little training session for the Skarve
race. Isn't that next weekend? Some girls at work are going up.'

'Not you?'

'No. Not me.'

The first set closed with a climax, another classic:

'Whispering'. After the musicians had sat down at their table and refilled their cups and glasses, I made my apologies to Karin and strolled over to them. Lasse Tydal had obviously forgotten his offer, but when he saw me, he banged on the table to get his band members' attention. 'Tore, Reidar – this is Veum, an old pal of mine. He needs some info about Hallvard Hagenes.'

The two musicians sent me sceptical looks. Tore Lude was in his early forties, his hair a mass of greying curls, his body compact with a slight stoop. Reidar Rongved was the youngest in the group, still in his thirties, with shoulder-length dark-blond hair and thick glasses.

'Info?' Tore Lude queried.

'Yes, nothing special,' I said, with a faint smile. 'His name appeared in connection with a case I'm investigating.'

'Case? Are you a cop or what?'

'I'm a what. A private investigator.'

Mons Midtbøe, the kindly, red-haired bass player, let out a long whistle. '*Bang bang,*' he said, his hand shaped like a gun. Terje Tornøe stood up with a world-weary expression on his face and repaired to the toilet.

'I can't think of anyone less worth investigating than Hallvard Hagenes,' Tore Lude said curtly. 'Music is all he lives for. He drives a taxi to survive.'

'Family?'

'Not even so much as a woman, I don't think.'

'Really?'

Lude looked around the table. 'Not that I know of, anyway. Anyone know any different?'

The others confirmed his impression with a shake of the head. 'He's not gay either,' Reidar Rongved added. 'We've shared so many hotel rooms, on tours and so on, I would've noticed if he'd had other tendencies.'

'A burnt child shies the fire, as the saying goes,' Lasse Tydal said.

I stared at him. 'Which, in this particular case, means…?'

Tydal looked across at Lude. 'Wasn't there a time when he was pretty down?'

'Yes, I think there was,' Tore Lude answered. 'But for as long as I can remember, his well had run dry, if I can put it like that.'

'Perhaps he was frightened by what happened to his uncle,' Lasse Tydal added, with a glance in my direction. 'I don't know if you've heard about how Johan Hagenes ended his days?'

'Yes, I have. But surely you don't mean…'

'Talk of the devil,' said Mons Midtbøe. 'He's just walked in. Over there.'

I turned in the direction he indicated. 'Who is it?'

'The tall guy making for the bar,' Lasse said. Then he motioned to the band to get back on stage.

Terje Tornøe passed Hallvard Hagenes on the way up. I went back to Karin while keeping an eye on Hagenes. He paid for a beer and stood at the bar, looking round for a free chair with people he knew. Evidently he didn't find anyone, so he settled at the bar and concentrated on the band, who were about to start the second set.

They were still sticking to the forties and fifties. Classics such as 'Night and Day', 'Prelude to a Kiss' and 'Over the Rainbow' filled the room with cool improvisations on the themes. Lasse Tydal had a wonderfully full tone, consciously low and romantic. Terje Tornøe was responsible for high energy on the trumpet, while Tore Lude, with his light, playful touch on the keyboard, was undoubtedly the greatest talent among them. Reidar Rongved and Mons Midtbøe made up the accompaniment and for the duration only had a token solo each, Rongved on 'Prelude to a Kiss' and Midtbøe on 'Pick Yourself Up'.

Hallvard Hagenes followed the music with a tiny smile on his lips while discreetly tapping the beat with his free hand. In the other, he had his glass of beer, which he sipped at tentatively. He was tall, lanky, with a somewhat bony face, a pronounced nose and small chin. At regular intervals, with a toss of his head or a stroke of his hand, he swept the dark fringe from his brow.

The basement was filling up, and many had to content themselves with standing room. Those who had been doing their weekend shopping would pop into Den Stundenløse with all their bags and parcels, in the hope of finding somewhere to take the weight off their feet. Though they would be disappointed if there was no one familiar they could squeeze in next to. However, the music from the stage perked most of them up.

When the second set finished, I got up from the bench to try and introduce myself to Hallvard Hagenes, but I was thwarted in this attempt. Beside me, Karin sighed pointedly when she saw Paul Finckel, the journalist, making a beeline for our table, beer in hand and a lit cigarette in the corner of his mouth. My old school pal from Nordnes had a tendency to repeat the same old, moth-eaten childhood memories she had heard many times before. The fact that, as far as I could judge, he was going through one of his boozier phases didn't improve matters.

Few people I knew had gone through as many physical changes as Paul Finckel: fat, thin; long hair, cropped skull; clean-shaven, bearded, and all stations in between, always slightly behind the fashion as he consistently did his clothes-shopping the following year in the sales. Nevertheless, he was far more up to date than I would ever be. It was all, I had learned, a reflection of where he was relationship-wise: in, out, *hors de combat*. Now he was definitely out and he had been for a good while, judging by his *embonpoint* and the unappetising stubble on his face.

'Wolfie is taking out his blonde?' he growled genially as he squeezed himself down beside me, without so much as a by-your-leave.

'Or is she taking him out?' Karin replied astringently.

His eyes were watery. 'Exactly.'

'And you?' I said, as politely as old friendship and present utility demanded.

'Well, there's been so much rock'n'roll in my life recently, I realised it was time to embrocate my body and soul with some golden tones.' He held his glass in the air as though it was there the golden tones were to be found.

Karin got up and nodded towards the toilet. 'I'll be back.'

'I certainly hope so.'

She put on a bitter-sweet smile and rolled her eyes in Paul Finckel's direction.

I concentrated on the intruder. 'Tell me, Paul, now that I have you here – does Trans World Ocean mean anything to you?'

'TWO, yes. Changed their name from Helle Shipping. Good timing. In the red, I've heard. But who isn't at the moment? They should see my bank account. That would make them feel better.'

'In the red? Really?'

He sank forward, not necessarily to be discreet, but because he couldn't sit up straight any longer. 'We'll only find out when someone in the know decides to leak – either that or there's a solemn press conference announcing an orderly liquidation.'

'That bad?'

'No, no. They're just examples.'

'What kind of goods do they transport?'

'Everything under the sun, Wolfie. You name it, they trans-port it – to the end of the world, if that's what you want. Go for the money, that's always been their motto. You know what their roots are, don't you?'

'Hagbart Helle & Co Ltd.'

'Right. Norwegian shipping's master crook. Others find themselves up in court – I won't mention any names…' He beamed, as if there were some Bergensians who were unaware of who he had in mind. 'But Hagbart Helle went to his grave an honourable man, his reputation intact, with a sculpture erected

in the main office of the Norwegian Shipowners' Association
and his name in gold letters on a hospital wing in Nassau.'

'Do any of his heirs run TWO?'

'To my knowledge, there are no family connections anymore.
The owners are foreign. The branch here is run by one Bernt
Halvorsen. A typical grasping businessman, if you ask me.'

I noticed that Karin had stopped to chat with someone she
knew. Hallvard Hagenes had taken the opportunity to wander
over to the musicians. When Lasse Tydal said something to him
and pointed to me, I raised a hand in an inconspicuous wave.
Hagenes nodded quickly as if to say he had seen me. Then he
turned his back and continued to talk to the others.

'A boat called the *Seagull*. Does that mean anything to you?'
I asked Paul.

He shook his head. 'Negative. Nothing.'

'What about Utvik in Stryn or perhaps more likely in Sveio?
Do you know any of the harbours where TWO docks?'

'Not a clue. Nothing at all, Wolfie.'

'Well, if you hear anything, you know where to find me.'

He looked at me a little peeved. 'I wasn't thinking of going
for a while yet.'

'No, but we might have to.'

Tydal Jazz Company started their third set with a finger-snap-
ping, upbeat version of 'I Got Rhythm'. When I looked around
for Hallvard Hagenes, he had gone. I half stood and scanned the
audience, but couldn't see him anywhere. I looked up at Lasse
Tydal, who openly shrugged his shoulders, then returned to his
playing.

He had simply vanished. Karin, on the other hand, you could
trust. She returned, brave woman that she was, and patiently
conversed with Paul Finckel until the last note had been played,
the band were packing up their instruments and the room was
slowly emptying. Afterwards, we went home.

10

Hardanger plateau was closed for the winter. To get to Ustaoset as quickly as possible, I had booked a seat on the first express train east, at seven-thirty on Sunday morning.

At ten-twenty I alighted from the train. The light sleet and the bitter westerly sweeping in over Lake Uste made me pull my woollen hat from my anorak pocket and yank it right down over my ears. I looked in the direction Berit Breheim had described. She hadn't sold me a pup. The cabin was easily recognisable.

I had rung her at home the night before. When I told her Garrido had stopped working at TWO she had reacted with astonishment. 'I had no idea.'

'Could that be why he was out of sorts on Palm Sunday, do you think?'

'It's possible, of course.'

'He didn't say anything to you about it?'

'Not a word.'

'Strange. This Hallvard Hagenes…'

'Yes?'

'I tried to talk to him earlier today, but he didn't seem to want to talk to me.'

'No?'

'Don't you think that's odd?'

'Did you have a chance to explain what you wanted to talk about?'

'No.'

'Well, you're the detective, not me.'

'So, how are you going to spend Sunday?'

'Why do you ask?'

'I was thinking of going to Ustaoset tomorrow. Would you like to join me?'

'I can't. I'm in court on Monday and have to prepare. If I'd had the time to travel up there myself, I wouldn't have needed to engage you, would I.'

'This cabin, is it hard to find?'

'No. Are you going by train?'

'Yes.'

'You'll see it from the station. A log cabin with a blue door, roof ridge and shutters. Just follow the road east of the hotel.'

At first, I felt like Spencer Tracy in *Bad Day at Black Rock*. Then I started walking. Ustaoset was dead for most of the year, but at Easter it was quite crowded. In a five-kilometre radius from the station there was perhaps the greatest concentration of cabins in Norway. In the section nearest the station there was less space between them than between downpours in Bergen.

The road up had been cleared and sand had been strewn so that owners could drive all the way to their cabins in their urban tractors, if they so desired; and they did. But not many had taken the opportunity on this doldrum weekend between Easter and the Skarve cross-country ski race. Greyish-white smoke rose from one of the neighbouring cabins. That was the only sign of life I could discern.

The log cabin I was making for lay deep in snow, with all the cogged corner joints filled in with swirling powder. The path to the front door had been dug clear and there were half-covered boot-prints on the way down. I gently tried the door handle, but it didn't open. So, I took out the key Berit Breheim had given me, unlocked the door and stepped inside.

I groped around on the wall for a light switch. I found one, and the ceiling lamp came on. I was in a small porch with several pairs of skis around me. On a couple of hooks there were some well-worn outdoor jackets. A rose-painted door led into the cabin. I entered, located another switch and turned on the light there too.

I had entered a large, cosy sitting room with tables and

benches made from varnished wood, black-and-white nature photographs on the walls and reindeer antlers over both doors. But no one had lit the fire and there was no one relaxing in the chairs in front of it. It felt like a cold-storage facility. Vapour was coming off my clothes and out of my mouth.

Before I'd had a good look around, I heard heavy footsteps outside. I turned to the porch and met the sharp gaze of a man in the doorway. 'Who are you, may I ask, and what are you doing here?'

He was taller than me – well over one-eighty – lean and broad-shouldered, with a sun-tanned, wrinkled face that revealed many years of fresh mountain air. His eyes were blue, his nose was narrow and pointed, and there was something surprisingly sensitive and feminine about his mouth.

'The name's Veum and I'm here on behalf of Berit Breheim.'

'Oh, yes?' He eyed me sceptically. Then he came inside and proffered a hand. 'Harald Larsen. I live next door. We have an agreement that I keep an eye on the cabin when they're not here.'

'I see,' I said, shaking his hand.

'Mountain folk are used to helping each other, even if we come from opposite sides of the country. I've known Berit from when she was small.'

'And Bodil…?'

'Bodil too, of course. But it's a long time since I've seen her here. After she married that foreigner…'

'Garrido.'

'Exactly. He's in shipping, isn't he?'

'Yes, he is.'

'I was in shipping myself before I retired.'

'But not in Bergen.'

'No, no. Oslo.'

'Have you seen them recently?'

'You mean…?'

'Bodil and her husband.'

'Oh, my goodness, it must be years now. When they were newly-weds, I think. It's hardly surprising though. He wasn't much of a skier. Berit's used the cabin most. But not so much in recent years. This year she hasn't been here at all, even though the weather was a dream this Easter.'

'So, the footsteps outside…'

'They're probably mine. I like to keep myself busy, and as I'm here anyway, I often clear the path to their front door too. Then it's not such a hassle for her if she suddenly decides to come up.'

'You spend a lot of your time here then, since you retired?'

'As much as I can. I've had enough of city life. I don't hanker for foreign trips either anymore. And I was widowed four years ago. In the mountains I feel free, summer and winter. I relax, find myself and confront the Beyond, if I may be a little earnest.'

'You said … Did you also know Berit and Bodil's parents?'

'Indeed I did. We came here at about the same time. 1950, in the autumn. Ansgar and Tordis bought their cabin finished, but it was no more than a couple of years old – from 1947 or '48, as far as I remember. I built mine myself. The year after Berit was born.'

'You have a good memory.'

'We were good friends. We did a lot together. Svanhild, my wife, and Tordis became really good friends. It wasn't the same – afterwards.'

'You're referring to when Breheim remarried?'

'Yes, his new wife, Sara. Well, she definitely wasn't the mountain type. It would've had to be the hottest summer for her to come. She didn't like snow. So they began to use the cabin less and less. Ansgar often came on his own. We had a few great autumn walks, he and I did, hunting birds. But he never talked about his marriage. Nor about Tordis and not about Sara. And I didn't broach the subject. We talked about other things. Our jobs, the world, the countryside, hunting. Where the best chances were of finding grouse. That sort of stuff.'

'And the two sons?'

'We hardly ever saw them. As rarely as Sara.'

'Even after they grew up?'

'I think the cabin was left to the two girls from his first marriage, and as I said, in recent years only Berit has come up. Do you know why she wasn't here at Easter?'

'Well, my understanding was she was simply too busy.'

'Mhm.' He looked around. 'So, what were you supposed to check? That everything was in order?'

'Yes…' I hesitated. 'The situation is this: Bodil and her husband have been away for a while now, without telling anyone where, so as I was coming by anyway…'

'Surely she didn't think they were here?'

I shrugged. 'I don't know how much you know – if you know about the old family story…'

He nodded gloomily. 'Ah, now I'm getting the picture.' He sent me a concerned look. 'But she doesn't think that Bodil and … that, so to speak, she's going to follow in her mother's footsteps, does she?'

'That's precisely why she wanted to make sure that they … that no one was here.'

'But they were completely different times. Completely different people. Tordis, she…'

'Yes?'

'Well, I can remember when she met him.'

'Met who?'

'This saxophonist she had a death pact with.'

'Oh, yes?'

'It was Easter Saturday, 1956. The night we always used to go down to the mountain hotel. Tordis with her husband, Svanhild with me. The weather was disappointing, I remember. It had been wonderful on Maundy Thursday and Good Friday, but on the Saturday it clouded over, and up here gale-force winds were blowing. Usually there were torches lit in front of the hotel, but that year they gave them a miss.'

They had handed their outdoor gear to the cloakroom lady and changed into indoor shoes: the men's, black and polished, the women's, elegant and with heels. The hotel manager had accompanied them to their table in person. He had held out a chair for Tordis, as he did for Svanhild. The table they had reserved was by the window, as usual, so that they could see across the railway line to Lake Uste.

It was hardly a surprise that it was Tordis who attracted the manager's attention. With her flame-red hair, high bosom and glittering eyes, she naturally became an object of admiration and envy from all corners of the dining room. And not so much as a split hem on her tight-fitting, daringly low-cut, ice-green dress revealed that she was a mother of two, the latter born barely a year before. Her husband Ansgar – dark-blond hair, well built and himself elegantly attired – tried with a mixture of composure and irritation to ignore the admiring gazes that followed his wife. He clearly had every intention of holding his innate jealousy in check, on this evening, as on others. Tordis was flirtatious by nature, but to Harald Larsen's knowledge, she had never let her nature go beyond what was good manners. He feared how Ansgar might react if that were to happen.

You look so pensive, Ansgar, he remarked. Is something bothering you?

No, no, Ansgar answered with a strained smile. It's just – what is it we say – melancholy born of the moment?

Born? Svanhild queried, with a coquettish smile.

And who is the we? Tordis commented, with arched eyebrows. Mm…

He surveyed the other tables, nodded to people he knew and mentally sorted the hotel guests from the cabin-owners. But to no avail.

It made no difference where he looked, his eyes returned to exactly the same place, just above the smooth, ivory-white shoulders of Tordis Breheim.

What a sight she was. Not that there was anything wrong with Svanhild, apart from her somewhat short body, like a doll that had been left in a child's room. But Tordis ... Beside her, Svanhild walked through life invisible. Tordis was a magnet for men's eyes. And not only his...

'So, what happened?'

'After the meal there was a dance. The hotel had booked a band from Bergen for Easter. Don't ask me what they were called, but I remember the saxophonist as if it was yesterday.'

'Johan Hagenes?'

'Yes, I found out later.'

'Was he that good?'

'That's not why I remember him.'

Dancing with Tordis was quite different from dancing with Svanhild. She had always been a heavy weight in his arms, as if she were an item that had to be transported across the dance floor, come what may. Tordis, on the other hand, floated, like a cork on a tranquil current, a feather on a breath of air, a cloud drifting across the sky. With her head at a slight angle and her supple body arched against his lean, sinewy torso she fixed her green eyes on his, a promise of something that in reality was unattainable, a contract that would never be signed.

But she had been different on this evening, she had been inattentive, distracted, and when he had tried to follow her gaze to where it was constantly headed, it landed on the stage. There was a high-tension cable running between the saxophonist and her, with messages flying to and fro, faster than the musician's fingers on the keys of his instrument. On behalf of Ansgar, and – he had to confess

– of himself too, he felt a sudden, uncontrollable feeling grip him, deep pangs of jealousy, stronger than he had ever known. Later he thought he had never really escaped from the shadow this jealousy cast. Not least with respect to everything that followed.

Afterwards he had tried to understand what might have lain under the surface. Had she met this man before? Or had she been seized by some momentary insanity? Could there have been anything else behind it, something between Ansgar and her he would not have known about? He would never find out; he had come to terms with that long ago.

He had danced with Svanhild again and with a woman from one of the other cabins up the slope, without taking his eyes off Tordis as she glided across the floor, floated and glided, watching the saxophonist as he played 'The One I Love Belongs to Someone Else', 'I'll Be Seeing You' and other sentimental standards from their dance-band repertoire.

The first time he noticed that she wasn't there was when the band had an interval, but it was still so early in the evening that he assumed she was powdering her nose, as women put it. But she was away a conspicuously long time, and her nose wasn't that large. Ansgar was standing at the bar, drinking harder than he usually did, and was remarkably quiet.

Then the band reassembled on stage, and suddenly she was back, her cheeks a trifle redder than usual, and when he invited her to dance again, he felt a touch of frost in her fingers, as though she had been outside in the cold.

Have you been out for a breath of fresh air?

Mhm.

The same happened in the next interval, but now Ansgar was gone too. With an expression of astonishment on her face, Svanhild looked through the smoke of the cigarette he had just lit.

Where have they gone, Harald?

Where have who gone?

Tordis and Ansgar, of course.

She rolled her eyes, but not long afterwards they had the answer. Loud voices reached their ears from the lobby. Through the racket they recognised Ansgar's voice, repeatedly rising to a falsetto. When they followed the noise and went out, they found Tordis and Ansgar in a heated argument; him still screaming at her, while she was doing everything she could to make him lower his voice.

It wasn't what you think.

Oh, no? Didn't I see you with my own eyes? You were kissing him. Keep your voice…

Desperate, she looked around. He met her eyes, took a step forward, but Svanhild held him back.

Don't. They have to…

Ansgar gestured to the cloakroom lady, who had already given them their coats. He grabbed the warm garments, put them over his arm, kicked their boots towards the exit and shoved Tordis in the same direction.

Ansgar! My God, how can you be so—?

Out! Ooouuut!

The hotel manager scuttled after them with a despairing glance at the other guests. He bent down, picked up the boots and followed them into the entrance area. They stood there getting dressed. Tordis was still scouring the lobby, in such a state of distress that he took another step forward.

He had looked at Svanhild.

Shouldn't we go with them? What do you think?

No, Harald. This is nothing to do with us. They'll have to sort this out themselves, she had answered, before definitively pulling him back into the dining room, to the window table, which suddenly seemed like a deserted island in the Pacific, surrounded as they were by silent but eloquent glances and so alone for the rest of this bizarre evening.

After a while the band returned to the stage, the saxophonist the last to appear, too late for the intro to the first tune after the break.

When he and Svanhild drove back up, after midnight, Tordis and Ansgar's cabin was dark. On Easter Sunday, they met them on the slopes leading to Skarvet as though nothing had happened, and the episode was never mentioned again, by any of them; until the tragic events of 1957, when Svanhild and he exchanged glances over the breakfast table after reading the headline in the newspaper.

Oh, my goodness, isn't that the saxophonist?

Yes…

'Does that mean that … Breheim never gave you any explanation?'

'We never talked about it, Veum. Not a word passed our lips.'

'So, you know nothing about what might've happened between Easter Saturday 1956 and that September day in 1957?'

'No. What could there be to know? We can all imagine the end of the story.'

'What about Easter that year? In 1957, I mean.'

His eyes became distant. 'I remember it vaguely, but … There was a different band down at the hotel, and Tordis and Ansgar stayed in their cabin that Saturday evening. Neither of them felt any obligation to explain why they'd broken our tradition. It wasn't necessary anyway.'

'Right.'

I looked around the empty cabin. So, they had been here then, on Easter Saturday 1957. Perhaps they had shared a bottle of wine. Ansgar had had a tumbler or two of whisky, she'd had something not quite so strong while they tried to think as little as possible about what had happened the year before and what – for all I knew – was still going on between Johan Hagenes and her. The classic love triangle, one vertex pointing somewhere into the dark. Six months later two of them were dead.

'Well?' said Harald Larsen, looking at me inquisitorially.

'Well, obviously there's no one here.'

'So…?'

Once again, I looked around, but I didn't have the impression he was going to leave me alone here. Perhaps my mere presence was obstructing the memories he had of the people who had once lived here.

In the end, I shrugged. 'Well, nothing left to do but go.'

He nodded, seemingly satisfied with this conclusion.

We turned off the light and stepped outside. He stood watching as I locked up. Some scattered snowflakes landed on my shoulders like dandruff. The sky over Ustaoset was grey and wan. It was time to go to the station.

'That cabin over there is ours,' he said when we had walked down and reached the main road. He pointed to a low, tar-coloured log cabin, not unlike the one belonging to the Breheim family.

'She was a strong personality, Tordis Breheim, was she?' I asked before we went our separate ways.

Again his eyes took on their distant look, as if an invisible breeze was caressing his skin. 'I can tell you one thing, Veum: I lived for the whole of my adult life with Svanhild, but even now, after both of them have gone – Tordis thirty-six years ago, what's more – but it's still her I think about mostly – Tordis, I mean.'

I stared at him in silence, waiting for more.

His eyes had gone moist. But he didn't say anything else, and with a firm handshake we parted company. He went back to his cabin; I went down to the station.

11

Being the unenlightened person I was, I had been looking forward to sitting in the restaurant car on the journey back to Bergen. But it no longer existed on day-time trains, and the strongest drink the trolley had to offer was Coke. I took a cardboard cup of coffee as well; a drink in each hand has always been my idea of a balanced diet. I arrived home stone-cold sober and with the world's best conscience. To make up for it, I poured myself a glass of aquavit, then called Berit Breheim again.

She picked up quickly. 'Hello?'

'Veum here.'

'And?'

'They weren't in Ustaoset either.'

She didn't answer.

'And you still haven't heard anything?'

'No.'

'Isn't it time to contact the police then?'

'We've been through this before, Veum. I have no intention of making a fool of myself, least of all with the police.'

'What about…? She must have some good friends. Some women she would confide in?'

'Bodil?'

'Yes.'

'Well, she might have. But no one I've been introduced to. We were, as I've tried to explain to you, not that close generally.'

'No, I'm beginning to get the picture. But your stepmother or one of your half-brothers? They might know something.'

'I doubt it.'

'Do you mean I shouldn't even try?'

She hesitated. 'Only if you feel you have to.'

'In a way it's you who should. I'm just trying to do the job you've given me.'

'Yes, I … Sorry, Veum, but I'm … Right now, my mind's else-where. It's this case I'm working on. It's not simple, I can assure you, for a woman.'

'No?'

'No. But you do what you want and contact me as soon as you have something.'

I raised my glass in a silent toast. 'Then I wish you luck with your case.'

'Thank you. Goodnight.'

'Goodnight.'

She rang off. I drank up.

I slept badly that night. A few kilometres away, Karin Bjørge was sleeping in her own flat. I was fifty-one years old, father of a son of almost twenty-two who lived with a girl from Løten, but I myself hadn't lived with anyone since Beata left me in 1973. Karin and I had developed a life of the kind that trend re-searchers called LAT – living apart together. It was a relationship that suited us both. She didn't have to wash my dirty laundry and I had no other bills to pay but my own.

On the other hand, on nights like this, with the rain lashing against the window and my head full of confusing thoughts, it might have been good to have a nice, warm, round back to cuddle up to, another body to wrap my arms around and a neck to breathe onto, gently, so as not to wake her.

Cupid is an inept planner, an impulsive scatterbrain and, by the grace of God, a capricious archer. When you are young, his shooting is wild, random and unceasing, until you resemble a pin cushion bombarded with errant arrows. This lusty whelp has a piece of cloth tied around his eyes and cottonwool in his ears. He can neither see where he is aiming nor hear the screams of pain caused by his indiscriminate unleashing of pro-jectiles. At a more mature age, Cupid's arrows are further apart in time. You are no longer a prime target in Love's flurried assault, but when he strikes – blindfolded as always – it can be all the more painful. Was that what had happened to Tordis Breheim and Johan Hagenes? Was it pain such as this that had lured them into what Berit Breheim had called a death pact? A last resort, a leap into the eternal void, where everything or nothing welcomed them? Had this episode cast such long shadows that it had consequences thirty-six years later for Tordis Breheim's daughter, Bodil, and her husband, Fernando Garrido?

Should I question my sources for more facts about what happened that September night in 1957? Was one of these sources perhaps Hallvard Hagenes? Were the police sitting on any documents related to this case? Were there any other people I could ask? What about the other job I had, also with a connection to Trans World Ocean? Was this just a coincidence or did it have something to do with the disappearance of Fernando Garrido and Bodil Breheim? But, above all, where on earth were the pair of them? Was there something I had missed? In their house? In the cabins in Hjellestad and Ustaoset?

At four I got up, went into the kitchen, poured myself a glass of water, walked over to the window and stood looking out. A dark shadow was sneaking along the wall across the alley: a cat out courting or Cupid in disguise?

A conspicuous calm had settled over the town, an illusion that would soon be broken; if not before, then definitely when the first buses began to roll through the streets and the morning traffic washed through the centre like a melancholic swell, a tide that took everything with it: sombre memories, unpleasant thoughts and sleepless nights...

I went back to bed and finally got some dreamless sleep. Hours later, when I moved down to my office, I just had to admit it: this was one of those Mondays when you looked at life through a grey filter and with a chafed soul.

I had two names on my notepad: Bernt Halvorsen and Hallvard Hagenes.

I brewed a pot of strong, freshly ground coffee. After drinking the first cup, I felt as though heavy-duty steel mesh was wrapping itself around my singed, sleep-deprived nerves. I got up from my chair and paced the floor restlessly, tearing at my hair, my eyes darting in all directions. I went to my desk and opened the bottom drawer on the left. There it lay, the shiny bottle of aquavit rolling around, the only contents of this drawer. I gulped. The choice was simple. It was that or the car.

Perhaps it was a sign of my maturity that I overcame my worst proclivities. I chose the car and drove to Trans World Ocean in Kokstad without an appointment. A shot in the dark, some might say. But then I was in good company. Cupid and I had previous.

12

The same security guard was on duty. His wary eyes revealed that he hadn't forgotten me, and this time he wouldn't give anything away. Furthermore, there was no one around with the time to talk to me, least of all the CEO.

I leaned over the barrier confidentially. 'Had garlic in your dinner yesterday, did you?'

'Eh?' That was all it took to wrong-foot him.

'Be so kind as to tell herr Halvorsen the same as you told herr Kristoffersen on Friday. If he doesn't want to talk to me, he can expect a visit from the police. His Ferrari's been seen, you can tell him.'

'His Ferrari's been seen?'

'Too much info, was it?'

He glared at me, dialled an internal number and passed on the message. 'Mhm? Mhm,' he answered into the receiver. After ringing off, he focused on me again. 'CEO Halvorsen has requested that you wait. Then he'll see…'

'See? See what?'

With a meek smile he nodded to a leather suite beyond the security channel. On the table there was a selection of journals and newspapers about shipping and finance. That was as far from my favourite reading as it was possible to be, but I sat down anyway, grabbed the nearest reading matter and started to flick through it. When I came to what looked like a stock exchange review, I searched for shipping shares and Trans World Ocean. As far as I could make out, the rate was way under par. I assumed that meant it was doing badly. Then I read an article about which shares I should take a punt on, if I had anything to invest. Were they thinking about the paltry 1,500 kroner I had made in the previous year's accounts, I wondered.

I heaved a heavy sigh and looked around. Not much happening. I got up and went over to the reception desk again. If nothing else, I could see how far I could push the guard. 'Tell me…'

He glared up from Bergen's local tabloid, where he was immersing himself in the first of the day's ten pages about FC Brann.

'What's holding the CEO up? Is he trying to address last year's operating losses or is he launching a new deficit?'

He stifled a yawn. 'He was going to see when he had time,' he said.'

'Fine, but he must've bloody seen by now. Ring him, say hello from me and tell him Brann's shit this season. He can put down the paper now.'

'Do you think so?'

'Think what?'

'That this season's going to be shit too?' He looked as if I had told him his grandmother was on her death bed.

'They lost 2-1 to Fyllingen yesterday, didn't they? Do you need a more convincing sign?' I pointed to the telephone. 'Dial, dial. Ring, ring.'

Strangely enough, he did what I asked. But nothing good came of it, for him or for me. 'But it wasn't me who…' he said, trying to stem Halvorsen's flood of abuse. 'I've told him … Alright then.'

He slammed the receiver down, his face flushed a deep red. Before saying a word, he visibly pulled himself together, breathed in several times – as had been recommended by a business psychologist – and concentrated on not smashing up the central switchboard. When he finally spoke, it was through gritted teeth. 'Veum…'

'That's me.'

'CEO Halvorsen has asked me to pass on the following message: as you're clearly in a hurry, he felt obliged to ask you to come another day.'

'He preferred the police then, in other words?'

'He said nothing about that.'

I cursed inwardly. Either he was simply too busy or he had seen through my ruse. What evidence did I have to take to the police?

I immediately tried a different tack. 'Answer me this then.'

He eyed me dismissively. 'And what would that be?'

'When's the *Seagull* due in Utvik?'

'The *Seagull*?' He pressed a few keys and looked at the screen. Then he remembered his new resolution, bit his tongue and went as quiet as a soap dish.

I seized the only cake of soap there. 'Utvik in Sveio.'

'Yeah, yeah. That's what I thought you meant.'

I wallowed in the triumph of the moment. Now at least I had something for Torunn Tafjord.

He glowered at me. 'You know very well that I can't give you any information.'

'And why not?'

'We don't give info to just anyone.'

'But if you're probably going to be looking for another job anyway...'

'Out!' Again he was on the point of exploding. The business psychologist had a bit more work to do with him before she could feel happy with the result. He drew himself up to his full height and pointed to the foyer. 'The door's over there.'

'Are you coming with me? I could give you some good advice...'

He looked as if he was going to vault the barrier, and it occurred to me that I still had a few jobs to do today. There would be no point spending it in A&E.

I raised my hand in a defensive gesture. 'Just get in touch. I've got some good contacts in the Employment Office.'

But I didn't hang around for an answer. I was already on my way out.

13

April is an unpredictable month. There can be days when the air shimmers like silver. There can be days as clear and transparent as if they were made of glass, with the sun reflecting on window panes. There can be days of frost and snow, which turns quickly into rain, and bitingly cold northerlies that whistle round houses and chill you to the bone. And there can be days like today, with a searing sun and clouds that frolic like new-born lambs across the pastures above.

The Rosegrenden district is like a little conservation area of white nineteenth-century houses, down towards the busy traffic on Sjøgaten. An old country road had once led through this cluster of houses from Helleneset and the districts north of Bergen, when people walked or used a horse and cart to get to town. There hadn't been any big roads to shout about. Most people travelled by boat anyway.

The tiny quarter consisted of small wooden houses, but it wasn't the rose bushes decorating the walls of some of the houses that had given rise to the name Rosegrenden. It was a reference to Frederik D. Rose, the skipper, who at the end of the 1820s had built one of the houses up in Sandviksveien.

The house where Hallvard Hagenes lived lay midway down Rosesmuget. The front door was black. His name was fixed behind a small plastic disc by the doorbell. From outside I could hear the sound of his saxophone. I stood listening for a while without being quite able to identify the tune. It sounded like free improvisation, but the basic theme was clear enough, and occasionally there were snatches that seemed familiar.

I waited for a break in his improvisations. At the lower end of the street there was a mixture of restored warehouses and newer industrial buildings. A steady stream of cars and buses flowed through Sjøgaten, but there wasn't much activity to be

seen on the fjord. A lot had changed since the first days of
Rosegrenden.

When Hallvard Hagenes finally found the time right to have
a break, I leaned on the bell. Straight afterwards he filled the
doorway with his full height. 'Yes?'

I could see that he was trying to work out where he had seen
my face before, without success. 'I'm Varg Veum. You may've
seen me at Den Stundenløse on Saturday.'

'Oh yes ... right.' I could see the memory slowly dawning on
him. 'And how can I help you?'

'I'm a private investigator and I'm trying to find out what's
happened to Bodil Breheim and her husband, Fernando
Garrido.'

'Bodil? What's that supposed to mean – "trying to find out
what's happened"?'

'Shall we talk about this inside?'

He looked at his watch. 'My shift starts soon. I'm a taxi driver.'

'Until then?'

'Alright.' He stepped back into the narrow hallway and led me
quickly past a kitchen and into a sitting room. Through a door I
saw an adjacent bedroom, which was evidently being used as a
makeshift office. Lit up by a computer screen. On what was func-
tioning as a desk I saw piles of unpaid bills, sheet music, some
books and a handful of newspaper cuttings, which, judging by
the top one, were reviews of gigs. In the hall I had noticed a
narrow staircase going up to the loft. I assumed this was where
he had his actual bedroom. There wasn't a lot of space, especially
for a man of his dimensions. And definitely not for a partner.

He showed me to one of the old-fashioned armchairs, shifted
his saxophone from the other one and placed it on the small
sofa, which together with another, dark-brown desk and a round
table constituted the sum of the furniture. 'I'm afraid there isn't
time to put any coffee on.'

'That's fine. We can get straight down to brass tacks. How do you know Bodil Breheim?'

'Know her…?' He ran his hand through his hair and his nostrils flared. 'Actually it was her sister I … A long time ago.'

'Berit?'

'Yes, in 1972. We were both active in the anti-EEC movement and … well.'

Berit Breheim had been an attractive, red-haired law student of twenty-one. He himself had been a lanky seventeen-year-old schoolboy who played sax as the fifth member of the rock group Fiskerjenten – 'Fisher Girl', named after the female vocalist, Astrid Hauso, who came from Nautnes on the island of Øygarden and studied arts at school. She was the one who wrote the lyrics, in halting rhyme but broad dialect, and as anti-EEC as was de rigueur at that time: EEC, why are your sheep dying? EEC, why are your livestock rotting? When are you going to open your eyes? Can anyone tell me that?

He had met her for the first time during a demonstration in September when they were standing side by side in the market square while Arthur Berg, Hallvard Bakke and Rune Fredh each delivered their brief appeal. He'd had his saxophone in its case over his shoulder because the Fiskerjenten were playing at the gathering in the old Folkets Hus after the demonstration, and between a couple of the speeches she had nudged his case and asked:

What have you got in there, a machine gun?

A saxophone.

As gauche as ever, he had held out his hand: Hallvard Hagenes. Hi.

She had looked at him in astonishment. What did you say? Hagenes?

Yes?

Nothing, I was just struck by…

Afterwards he had felt her eyes on him the whole time, but when

he turned to her, she looked away, and later – in the Folkets Hus –
he had seen her in the audience while they were playing, and after-
wards, when they had finished, she had waved to him from a distance
as he stood drinking a beer at the back of the room. A few days later
he had bumped into her at the anti-EEC headquarters, where she
was lying on the floor writing posters with a felt pen for the day's
demos. Fancy giving me a hand? She had looked up at him with her
big, blue-and-green eyes and he had nodded. He did.

'From then on, we were together.'

'Berit Breheim and you?'

'Yes.'

'You were seventeen and she was twenty-one?'

'You can imagine what it was like. Twenty-one! Seen from my
perspective, she was a mature woman and … she was my first.'

'You slept together?'

He nodded. 'Everyone did in those days, didn't they?'

'N … yes … maybe.'

'You were probably too old for that.'

'I was past the whelp stage, yes, let me put it like that.'

'But now I have to…' He pointed to the clock and rose to his
full height.

'But we haven't even … Where's your car?'

'Down in the centre. I have to go down there anyway. Trond,
the other driver with the firm, is probably already waiting for me
so he can finish his shift. The boss checks up on me regularly,
and if I'm not punctual he gets annoyed,' he explained as he led
me out. 'We can finish our conversation down there. I don't
always get a ride straight away.' He locked the door behind us
and we walked to Sandvikstorget.

It was him who changed the topic of conversation. 'But you
were saying when you arrived … Has Bodil gone missing?'

'She's not around at any rate. When did you meet her?'

'First meet her?'

'Yes.'

'Oh, my goodness, ages ago.'

'Really?'

'Nothing happened, if that's what you're thinking.'

'I don't think anything.'

'That was … sometime later.'

'We're still in 1972?'

'Yes, Berit and I had been together for a couple of months already and … It had been quite a busy time, I can tell you. After the EEC battle was over, she had even more time for us. Or me, that is. With school work and Fiskerjenten on top … I was in my penultimate year and I wasn't always getting the sleep I needed. At any rate, my grades sank like a stone.'

*It was just before Christmas and she had looked at him solemnly:
You're invited to lunch with us on Sunday.*

Eh? Lunch?

Yes, do you think that's a bad idea?

No, not bad, but … To meet your parents, do you mean?

My father and my stepmother.

Your mother's dead?

She had looked at him strangely: Didn't you know?

No. You didn't tell me.

But I asked you about your uncle, didn't I. Who also played the saxophone.

Uncle Johan, yes.

Who died…

In a car accident.

My mother was in the same car.

What? Was it your mother who…?

She had fixed her eyes on him: Have your parents never told you what happened?

Yes, but they didn't … They didn't mention any names. They called it a death pact, between Uncle Johan and a woman he'd become … he knew.

A death pact! Is that how they explained it?

Yes, a double suicide, carried out by two people who'd gone off the rails.

A death pact…

We had reached Sandvikstorget, where a black Mercedes with a taxi sign on the roof stood waiting. Hallvard Hagenes exchanged a few words with his colleague, a fat guy with a very creased, baggy face, after driving for far too many hours with black coffee and acrid cigarettes as the only stimulants. Then Hallvard got behind the wheel, logged on to the system and motioned me to sit beside him.

'So that was the first time you realised she knew more about you than you imagined?'

He nodded.

'What effect did that have on you?'

'It was a shocking story, wasn't it. The double suicide, I mean.'

'Yes.'

'Well, of course, I had to ask if that was why she'd been interested in me. When she first heard my name.'

'And she said?'

'Yes. She admitted it. That was how it'd been at the beginning. But later what she liked was … me.'

'How was it meeting her father and stepmother?'

'It was a bizarre experience…'

He had felt like a beginner at a dancing-school ball. The Breheim family had lived in a luxurious house in Sudmanns vei and her two half-brothers, twelve and eight years old, had run around the large garden like chimps, yelling and laughing when they saw him. They

*could barely sit still at the lunch table. Her sister, Bodil, had stayed
in her room and only came down for the meal with great reluctance.
At the table she sat sullenly staring at her plate the whole time; he
had hardly met her eyes a single time that Sunday. Breheim himself
didn't appear to have much time for this boy his elder daughter had
brought to the house, while the stepmother – a dark-haired woman
with sweet, almost doll-like expressions – did her best to keep the
conversation flowing, without much response from any of them. Fru
Breheim wasn't yet forty; she was seven years younger than her
husband and 'more like an older sister than a mother to me', Berit
had told him. While they were eating, he hadn't even managed to
catch Berit's eye either. She had kept looking in her father's direction
as though expecting a reaction. The whole meal seemed like a nightmare to him. He had broken into a cold sweat; the steak had gone
hard and dry in his mouth and he only managed to swallow it with
an effort. When at last they left, several hours later, he had sworn to
himself: never again … Never again!*

'And in a way I was proved right. I never saw any of them
again. Apart from Berit, that is. And then Bodil. But that was…'

Suddenly his computer uttered a sound. A message came
through on the roll of paper. He waited until the message had
finished, tore it off and read it. 'OK, Veum. I've got a ride.' He
typed in a confirmation and nodded to the door on my side.

'Have you got a phone number I can contact you on later?
We haven't really got to the heart of the matter.'

He pushed the gear stick into first and eyed me impatiently.
'To the stuff about Bodil, you mean? I know nothing about it.'

I returned his gaze. 'No?'

'OK, right.' He scribbled down a number. 'This is to the car.
Try it.'

I opened the door and stepped out. Before closing it, I leaned
down and said: 'Just one more thing. You couldn't give me a

name, could you, from the jazz circle? Someone I could talk to about your uncle?'

He gave the matter some consideration. 'Call Lasse Tydal. He may be able to help you. But now I have to be off, Veum.'

'Away you go.'

I shut the door and he turned quickly out of the car park. Before I had reversed my car out of the space, he was gone. I drove to the town centre, parked in Markeveien and found my way back to my office. I still had the same names on my notepad.

14

Lasse Tydal, I said to myself. What on earth did he do when he wasn't playing the sax? And on a Monday morning?

I consulted the telephone directory and rang on the off-chance he was at home. I was out of luck. But his wife was there. 'Lasse? He's in the office,' she said.

'And which office would that be?'

'Bergen Tax Office.'

Oh, shit. Who would have guessed...?

'He's a tax inspector,' she added, as if that would make him sound less dangerous.

'Thank you.'

I opened the lowest drawer on the left, took out the bottle, unscrewed the top and drew the unmistakeable aroma of caraway down deep into my lungs, to summon up the necessary courage to dial the Tax Office number. But I could have relaxed. First, I had to wait in a queue for ten minutes before I was finally put through to a living human being. And then the woman I got on the line was so obviously one of Bergen's kindest, and she had absolutely no hesitation in connecting me.

'Tydal.'

'Veum.'

'On a Monday...?'

'I liked what I heard on Saturday.'

'Kind of you to say so, Veum. How can I help you today?'

'You said you knew Johan Hagenes.'

'Knew ... hmm, well, yes. We were about the same age and a couple of times we played in the same band. In Kjell Tombra's sax group in the 1950s when we were barely into our twenties. But then we went separate ways. We played in a variety of outfits, him mostly with something called Blåmanden, me with all sorts at The Golden Club in the Industrihus. Then all the stuff with

Johan and this woman happened, and I crossed the Scandes mountains to Sweden and tried my luck there. Didn't come back home until 1977.'

'And straight into the Tax Office?'

'I'd trained for it already. I worked here before I went to Sweden too.'

'What do you know about Johan Hagenes and what happened to him and this woman in 1957?'

He remembered it as if it were yesterday. He had been nursing a beer in the Norge Hotel bar one Tuesday evening when Bjørn Heggelund, who played the bass in Blåmanden, came in, looked around, recognised him and hurried over.

He wasn't sure that he was happy to be interrupted. One of the town's most attractive actresses, sporting a very elegant, velvet hat at a jaunty angle, was sitting at the table next to his, drinking champagne and being courted by two polite businessmen. He had been sitting with his eyes half closed, dreaming that it was him she was sending the veiled glances to, and not the two with the silver-tongued wallets, whose tax returns he had decided he would send for immediate reassessment the following day.

Have you heard? burst out Bjørn Heggelund, as he sat down and waved to the waiter for a beer, who nodded back discreetly.

Heard what?

About Johan Hagenes.

No…

The waiter elegantly set the beer on the white cloth. He seized the opportunity to order another, then Bjørn Heggelund carried on:

Just listen. There was this woman in the audience, at one of the tables in front of the stage. A real looker, if you ask me. Tall, red-haired and a body Marilyn Monroe would've envied.

Oh, yes? You were wearing your glasses, were you?

He straightened them and nodded:

Of course, it's not that unusual for there to be some, erm, eye contact between us in the band and some of the audience. You know that yourself. And when Johan played 'All of Me' as the last number in the first set it was as if he was giving her his undivided attention. The rest of us noticed. In the interval Johan was nowhere to be seen. When he did finally turn up and we asked him where he'd been, he just shrugged. The first number in the second set was 'When I Fall in Love' and the contact between the tenor player and the lady in question was no less intense. The problem, however, was that she had her husband with her. He was sitting on the side-lines and fuming, as acutely aware of what was going on –in their heads at least – as we were. I said to myself: Bloody hell, I'm going to have to talk to him about this. To Johan, I mean. You can't behave like that. But there won't be a chance now.

What do you mean? What happened?

The beautiful actress's laughter rippled past, but he was no longer looking in her direction. He was too immersed in what Bjørn was telling him:

When the second set finished and we were leaving the stage, the husband charged over, grabbed Johan by the lapels and started yelling at him. And a fight broke out – the husband threw a punch, Johan ducked and retaliated with a perfect upper cut, straight to the jaw. The guy bit his lip and blood flowed. It was a terrible scene. The waiters piled in, and the maître d'hôtel, and it was only when things calmed down that we realised that Johan had left, and the lady with him.

Oh, shit.

The guy went mad, as you can imagine, threatening to smash up the whole place and if he got his hands on the two of them … there was no telling what he would do.

And what did he do?

Bjørn Heggelund gesticulated:

Well … I've just heard this afternoon that Johan's dead.

What?! Dead?

Hauled out of the sea at Hjellestad. He drove in there with the redhead at his side. A beautiful death, some might say, but I wouldn't have bloody chosen it, he said with a grim expression on his face.

There was silence at the other end of the telephone line.

'And then?' I asked.

Lasse Tydal cleared his throat. 'Well, there wasn't anymore. It never became a case, as far as I know. Not long afterwards I went to Sweden, as I said, and all I saw later was the attractive actress. In the weekly magazines, that is.'

'And Bjørn Heggelund?'

'Gone as well. Carried out on a stretcher when Miles Davis played Grieg Hall sometime in the eighties. The new style was too much for him, they said.'

'Right. Do you reckon anyone else would know anything? One of the others in Blåmanden, for example?'

'You could try Truls Bredenbekk, the pianist. He's played with most, and I wouldn't be surprised if he was in Blåmanden at the time.'

'And where will I find him, d'you think?'

'If I were you, I'd start with the phone book.'

'The private investigator's best friend. Thanks, Tydal. And…'

'Yes?'

'If you should come across my tax return, could you just quietly let it through?'

'That's not how we do things here, Veum.'

'No, I've noticed.'

15

I rang Breheim, Lygre, Pedersen & Waagenes and asked for Berit. She was in court, I was informed.

So I got out the telephone directory and started thumbing through.

I found Truls Bredenbekk. He had an address in Roald Amundsens vei, a shanked kick from FC Brann's stadium.

While I had the directory in my hands, I decided to look up 'Breheim, Sara,' as well. She lived in Starefossveien. Not a bad address either. I found 'Breheim, Rune' as well, the half-brother, who was in insurance. He didn't live in quite such elegant surroundings, but in a typical new-build district, in Bønes. Everyone was within easy reach.

Not the half-brother in Svalbard, though. And anyway, what did these people have to do with the disappearance of Berit Breheim and Fernando Garrido? What was the point of raking up the tragic deaths of 1957, if it wasn't because they kept appearing of their own accord wherever I turned.

I activated the answerphone, locked the office door and repaired to the courthouse in the hope of exchanging a few words with Berit Breheim before resuming my investigation.

The front of Bergen Courthouse is massive, guarded by the four cardinal sins carved in stone. They subject all those who visit the building to a stern examination, whether charged with a crime or not. Even those who only go there to get married might find it unnerving; perhaps not such a bad thing, bearing in mind the rising divorce rate.

I climbed the stairs to the second floor. A court official explained to me where Berit's case was being held. I opened the door carefully, stuck my head in, quickly took my bearings and then found a seat on one of the rear benches among the handful of spectators.

Berit Breheim was in mid-plea, and not the slightest flicker betrayed that she had observed my arrival. 'Ladies and gentlemen,' she said in a clear, pure voice. 'The facts of the case are not in dispute. There can be no doubt that the defendant of her own accord and volition invited the accused to her home. And she did not invite him only for coffee; she served spirits, even home-made blackcurrant liqueur, we have been told, and let me remind you of the outfit she was wearing that evening: a very short, black leather skirt and a tight-fitting red top with a plunging neckline, so deep that her black brassiere was visible.'

In the dock, the approximately thirty-year-old man, the corners of his lips extending into a smile, nodded in support. The young, male police prosecutor on the opposite side of the room, with a face like a newly qualified theology student, coughed admonishingly and looked at the judge. A female counsel with blonde hair and narrow glasses leaned over to her client and made an inaudible comment. The plaintiff was in her mid-twenties and dressed in a grey jumper and a dark suit jacket. She stared wanly at Berit Breheim.

'Is it any wonder, may I venture to ask, honourable ladies and gentlemen, that my client construed this as a clear invitation? Is it any wonder that he, intoxicated by the blackcurrant liqueur she had herself served him, did not quite appreciate that she had suddenly changed her mind about what was going to happen?'

The police prosecutor jumped up. 'Your Honour, I object to the notion that my client "had suddenly changed her mind". It's clear from the proceedings that the plaintiff had never – I repeat, never – intended to invite the accused to anything more than a cup of coffee and a glass of liqueur to round off an otherwise pleasant evening.'

The judge ran a hand through his thinning, grey hair and nodded wearily. 'Counsel for the Defence, may I ask you to re-formulate your last comments.'

Berit Breheim smiled sarcastically and nodded eloquently to the panel of judges. 'Let me reformulate ... The plaintiff didn't change her mind at all. There was never any doubt regarding the nature of her invitation. May I remind you about the report from the medical experts? Yes, intercourse had taken place. No, there were no visible signs of violence. The plaintiff's swollen upper lip was a result, as my client has explained, of them accidentally banging heads during their love-making. At the time they had both laughed.'

She paused for dramatic effect, then continued: 'My conclusion is therefore as follows. According to the facts of this case, there is only one plea possible, and it is this: we are asking for a full acquittal. In our opinion the accusation is without grounds. We will later ask for my client to be awarded full compensation for all the costs he has had to bear as a result of this extremely unpleasant case, in addition to the restitution of his reputation after what we consider to be a false and unjustified accusation.'

The police prosecutor shook his head demonstratively. With a serious expression on her face, Berit Breheim gathered together the papers she had on the table in front of her, fixed her gaze sternly on the plaintiff and walked over and sat down next to her client, who leaned against her with a grateful smile. The young woman on the opposite side of the room burst into tears and hid her face in her hands. The female counsel wrapped an arm around her reassuringly while staring at Berit Breheim with evident disapproval.

The judge cast a quick glance at his watch. 'The court will adjourn for twenty minutes.' He banged his gavel, nodded, stood up and made for the side door. Everyone stood up.

I caught Berit's eye. If she was surprised to see me there, she hid it well. She nodded towards the door and indicated that we could chat there.

A natural consequence of the narrow corridors and the

gallery looking out onto the large central hall of the courthouse was that people immediately collected in groups, often at opposite ends of the gallery, where they could observe each other from a distance and confer with their own without any danger of being overheard by the opposition. That was how it was this time too.

The plaintiff had retreated as far from the courtroom door as she could without losing sight of it. She had sat down on a bench and was staring rigidly at the floor while her defence counsel and a woman I identified as a girlfriend or sister sat talking to her in a low voice. Downcast eyes and an expressionless face were all they received in return.

The accused had a handful of male friends, a woman who might have been his mother, and a few journalists around him. He was in high spirits and talking and making jokes left, right and centre. Their outbursts regularly wafted over towards the plaintiff, who literally ducked as every new gale of laughter reached her ears.

The police prosecutor and Berit Breheim exchanged a few words on their way out of the room. Berit nodded in my direction, they concluded their conversation, and the police prosecutor continued around the corner in the direction of the gentlemen's lavatory. She came over to me and formally shook hands while looking at me inquisitorially. The black gown suited her. The contrast with her red hair and light skin lent her a classical touch, enhanced by her height. She could have walked out of a court painting by a new classicist: *Woman in the Service of Law*.

'Veum, what brings you here?'

'There was something I wanted to ask about before continuing.'

'OK, I didn't think you were here to while away the time.'

'No. You mentioned the name Hallvard Hagenes. But you

didn't say that you used to be an item – not even when I brought his name up a second time.'

She blushed. 'Well, I'm not sure about an item. Firstly, it's a long time ago, and what's more, it didn't last long.'

'No?'

'Did he say anything to the contrary?'

'No, we … didn't really finish the conversation.'

'But you've met him, I can hear.'

'Yes.'

'And Bodil? Did he know anything about her?'

'Not even that she was missing.'

'Well.' She threw up her arms.

'The other matter I was wondering about … back in 1957…'

'I should never have mentioned it.'

'No?'

'It obviously can't have anything to do with this. The only reason I brought it up was that I thought that it might tell us something about Bodil's – how shall I put it? – state of mind.'

'And by that you mean…?'

'That you find yourself ultimately in a situation – as my mother must have done – where death is the only way out. That all hope has gone. A form of self-destructive defeatism.'

'And you think you observed that in your sister?'

She looked resigned. 'How well did I know her, actually? These things are not exactly what we go around talking about, are they.'

'No,' I said. Then added: 'Not with just anyone. But maybe with your sister?'

A court official came into the corridor and announced: 'We're ready to resume.'

Quickly I said: 'By the way, I hadn't expected to see you on that side of the courtroom.' I nodded towards the accused, who was beaming with confidence at his tall defence counsel.

She arched her brows. 'No?'

'I mean, the arguments you used…'

'Yes? You don't think they hold water?'

'I just can't understand why you'd take on such a case. As a woman, I mean.'

She sent me a ferocious look. 'My job as defending counsel is not to be a woman, Veum. It's to ensure that my client receives the fairest possible treatment, that Norwegian law is followed and that there are no miscarriages of justice. Don't forget that everyone should be allowed the benefit of the doubt until the contrary has been proven.'

'OK, OK,' I gestured defensively. 'Forget it. I'm not a lawyer.'

'Evidently not.' She sent me a measured smile and was one of the last to enter the courtroom.

I didn't follow her in. Before I knew what was going on, someone might begin to suspect me too, and I was not at all sure that I would be given the benefit of the doubt, however good my defence counsel was or whatever gender they were.

16

In my line of business, there are two possible ways to approach people. You can ring them beforehand, state who you are and, in all probability, find yourself rejected outright. Or you can visit them personally, at home or at work. Where they always find it more difficult to say no.

I knew nothing about Sara Breheim except that she lived in Starefossveien, had two sons with the late Asgar Breheim, had been a 'great' stepmother and was, according to Harald Larsen in Ustaoset, definitely no 'mountain type'. Nevertheless, she had settled down on a mountainside above Bergen, close to the Starefossen waterfall, and with the whole of Mount Fløien as her back garden, in a duplex house, occupying the south-facing part with a view of Mount Ulriken.

The woman who opened the door when I rang reinforced my impression of Ansgar Breheim's good taste in and success with women. If the beautiful and much-admired Tordis Breheim had been difficult to rein in, his second wife wasn't a bad replacement. The sixty-year-old, dark-haired woman with a slight, but decorative, streak of grey in her hair was still an unalloyed beauty. Her face was oval and soft, and she radiated a charming blend of assurance and grace. Wearing a plain black dress with a salt-and-pepper jacket hanging loose over her shoulders, such discreetly applied make-up that you barely noticed it, and a cheery glint in her dark-blue eyes, she made me automatically straighten up and pull my stomach in. 'Sara Breheim?'

'Yes?'

'My name's Veum. Varg Veum. I've been hired by Berit, your stepdaughter. To help me with her assignment, I'd be obliged if we could have a chat.'

'Hired?'

'Yes, I'm a private investigator. Your other stepdaughter, Bodil, has gone missing.'

'Missing?' She looked at me with horror. 'What do you mean, gone missing? Come in, come in.'

She led me through a hallway and up a staircase. The room we entered was an example of solid elegance, with dark leather furniture, polished writing desks, Royal Danish porcelain behind vitrine doors and shelves of leather-bound books. In recesses there were lit candles and in the white hearth a faint glow came from some burning logs. Through a tripartite window framed by potted plants climbing, hanging and standing, I glimpsed the characteristic silhouette of Mount Ulriken as one of the two cable cars was leaving the station at the top with a little jerk of its belly-heavy gondola.

'Take a seat,' Sara Breheim said, directing me to a leather sofa of the kind it is hard to disengage yourself from once you are ensconced. 'May I offer you something?'

I immediately registered that she retained the polite form of address in Norwegian at least ten years after it had gone out of fashion. 'No, thank you. I...'

'A glass of mineral water then, at least?'

I nodded. She fetched a bottle and had an opportunity to show off two slender, chased glasses from her collection. The shiny, mineral water fizzed quietly.

She sat down. 'Now you have to tell me more. Gone missing, you said. Bodil?'

'Is it a long time since you last saw her, fru Breheim?'

'Mm, Christmas, I think. When we were all together, except for Randolf, that is, who's in Spitsbergen.'

'Svalbard.'

'Yes, I call it Spitsbergen, as in the olden days.'

'What's he doing up there?'

'He's an engineer. Employed by Store Norske.' She smiled. 'I'm actually expecting him home this weekend.'

'I see. Any particular occasion?'

'No, no. He was owed a week's holiday and as he wasn't home at Christmas. He must've thought it was time to see his old mother.'

I accepted the challenge with relish. 'Old? You aren't—'

'Thank you, herr Veum. At any rate I'm not too old for flattery, I notice.'

For an instant our eyes met, and there was a tiny pause before I took up the reins again. 'This Christmas visit…'

'This year we were at Rune's. He's got such a lot of room now in his new detached house. Berit, Bodil and Fernando, Rune and his family were there. And me of course. There aren't many of us.'

'Only Rune has children?'

'Yes. Three delightful grandchildren, I can tell you. You can see them in the photos on the sideboard.'

I followed the finger she was pointing. There was a line of framed photographs, some clearly taken at a professional photographer's, others enlargements of private snaps.

'So, this was the last time you saw your stepdaughter, at the Christmas festivities?'

'Yes, I suppose it was. And now it's April already. How time flies.' She smiled sweetly, as if to emphasise how little any of us could do about that.

'And nothing dramatic happened that day?'

'Dramatic? What drama could there be? I can promise you, herr Veum, there is nothing in our family but peace and goodwill. Right from the very start I did everything in my power to make sure the two young girls didn't feel marginalised by Rune and Randolf, when they came, and I think I succeeded.'

'No one has claimed anything different.'

'I'm glad to hear that. And I would've been an equally good grandmother to Berit and Bodil's children, if they'd had any, as I've been to Rune's. But you still haven't told me … What about Bodil? Is she supposed to have disappeared? What about Fernando?'

'He's gone missing too.'

I gave her a brief outline of events. She listened with a serious expression on her face.

After I had finished, she said: 'But this is just so ... over the top. She and Fernando must've gone on holiday. Berit and Bodil don't exactly see each other that much anyway.'

'Don't they?'

'No. I mean, not as rarely as all of us meet, of course, but they haven't had a close relationship for many years.'

'No? Why not?'

'Well ... first there was the business with that boy.'

'Which boy?'

'A boyfriend Berit brought home whom Bodil fell head over heels in love with. And then it turned out it was mutual.'

'Are you talking about Hallvard Hagenes?'

'Hallvard, yes. After that they were like cat and dog – for many years, Bodil and Berit. And the situation didn't get any better when they started arguing about the plot in Morvik.'

'They argued?'

'Yes, but it was Ansgar's decision. If Berit and Rolf hadn't divorced, it would've ended up in court. Then there was a kind of reconciliation, and Berit was bought out.'

'How did your husband take this?'

'He was dead, of course. That's why the whole business blew up. Before he died, nobody had said a word.'

'That was in 1983, wasn't it?'

'When Ansgar died? Yes. He had cancer – prostate cancer – and when they discovered it, it was too far advanced.'

'I'm sorry to hear that.'

'Thank you. It can happen to the best.' She subjected me to a stern look, as if to say: 'No one is safe, not even you.'

'Did you know him at the time his first wife died?'

'Did I know him? What do you mean?'

'I mean, he married you the year after she died, didn't he?'

'Yes, but a whole year had passed and … he wasn't the kind to cope with living alone. How would he be able to look after two small girls while running a business?'

'I obviously hadn't picked up on that. What business was he in?'

'Gentlemen's outfitting. I thought you knew that. But we sold up when Ansgar died. Now a Swedish chain's taken it over.'

'Were you involved in the business as well?'

Her gaze hung in the air without meeting mine. 'I was working in the shop at the time. That was how we got to know each other.'

'So, in other words … You *had* met him before his first wife died?'

'Yes.'

Tordis Breheim had swept in from the street, as gorgeous as ever, her red hair cascading down onto her shoulders, a jauntily elegant little hat, fur coat and sophisticated shoes.

Good morning, frøken Taraldsen. Is my husband around?

Sara herself, dark-haired with white skin, had been wearing an eggshell blouse with an open neck and a tight, black skirt.

You'll find him in the office, fru Breheim.

Bitter-sweet smile: Thank you.

Not at all.

Later the same day she was called to Breheim's office. He had looked at her with those lingeringly observant eyes that made her melt inside every single time.

This time he had stood up behind his desk then walked over to her. He had leaned back, to get a clearer view, while lightly stroking her shoulder, as if to brush away a stray hair.

My wife thinks the blouse you're wearing today is a little too brazen, frøken Taraldsen.

Oh dear.

Without realising, she had tears in her eyes, but whether they were tears of annoyance or shock, or because she suddenly feared for her job, she couldn't say.

Now, now. Don't take it amiss. She didn't mean it like that. But you could bear that in mind in future, couldn't you, so that we don't annoy her unnecessarily?

Yes, yes, of course, herr Breheim. I'll change as soon as I … I promise, you won't ever see me in it again.

Don't take on so, frøken Taraldsen. Personally, I think you look captivating in that blouse, I…

And then, without further ado, he had placed a finger under her chin, raised her head, leaned forward and kissed her lightly on the mouth. Confused and blushing, she had tumbled out of his office and back down to her own department, and…

She swore that was all there had been.

'By all means, fru Breheim. I'm not suggesting anything—'

'If you only knew … He was just so unhappy afterwards. When she was dead, I mean. Everyone felt sorry for him, and I … Of course, he already knew me. He felt he could confide in me. And that was how we became a couple … after all.'

'After all?'

'Yes, because I couldn't believe … He'd been married to a beauty, as you know.'

'Well, you weren't so bad yourself, were you.'

'Mm…' She was actually blushing. 'Thank you, once again, but as I said … Beside her, everyone paled by comparison.'

'Dare I ask how old you were then?'

'I can hear you do dare,' she said, with affected irritation in her voice. 'But as you asked so nicely … I was twenty-four, so now you can work out how old I am.'

'Age doesn't interest me that much.'

'No? An unusual man, I see.'

'I don't know about that.'

'But Ansgar had only just turned thirty, so there wasn't much of an age gap.'

'No, she was young, Tordis Breheim, when she died.'

'Yes, much too young, of course.'

'The circumstances that led to the accident, do you know anything about them?'

Her eyes went walkabout, and an odd, almost youthful expression spread across her face. 'I was myself a kind of witness to the occasion.'

'Right, you mean…?'

She hesitated. 'There was never any point telling the young girls this, I think. But I was there when it happened.'

'Where are you saying you were?'

'At Norge Hotel, when Ansgar and this musician came to blows.'

'You hadn't gone there with Breheim, though, had you?'

'No, no, I told you. I was there with someone else.'

Nevertheless, she hadn't said no when Ansgar Breheim invited her to a slow foxtrot, and she hadn't argued when he pulled her close while they were dancing, as though *they* were the couple and not Tordis and him.

Afterwards she had thought: was that perhaps why Tordis had behaved as she did with this musician? So that Ansgar had been forced to react … But Ansgar had rejected the idea: No, no, Sara. This was something that had been going on for a long time…

She could still see the scene. Ansgar grabbing the musician's jacket and pulling him down from the stage, the loud altercation and the set-to … When it was all over, she saw Tordis dash for the door, closely followed by the incensed musician, while Ansgar was sitting on the floor with his back to the stage, a serviette held to his lip and blood spurting out over his shirt and dark suit.

What happened? asked one of the guests, who had just arrived.

He was punched by one of the musicians, a waiter answered, helping Ansgar to his feet. He'll never get a job here again, I'll see to that.

The head waiter was white with fury: Do you know him? CEO Breheim, I mean?

No.

Sara had leaned forward: I do. My ... and I, we're his employees, both of us.

The waiter looked relieved. Then I think you should ... someone at any rate has to accompany him home or to a first-aid post.

Ansgar's vision was blurry and it took him a while to focus on her.

S-S-Sara? he mumbled, and she could smell the strong smell of alcohol on his breath.

Yes, it's me, herr ... We'll get you home, we ... Don't worry.

'And you did?'

'What else could I do?'

'And your escort for the evening, what did he do?'

'He came with us of course.'

'And at casualty, or the first-aid post, as you called it...?'

'Well, there wasn't much to do. There was more blood than damage, so he was sent home.'

'And you organised that? You and your partner?'

'Yes. We took him home, unlocked the door and put him to bed.'

'Was he alone?'

'Yes. The girls were with Solveig, his sister. No one else was there.'

'And after you and your friend had helped Ansgar Breheim indoors and put him to bed, what happened then?'

'Nothing. Not for us, I mean. We went home – to our separate homes. All very proper. There was nothing going on.'

'Has he got a name, this friend of yours?'

'He does, but I can't see it has any relevance to what you're investigating today, many years later. In general, I can't see what the connection is here.'

'I'd like to know his name.'

She fixed me with a stare. 'And I have no intention of telling you.'

'Why not?'

'Because it's none of your business. You concentrate on finding Bodil, if it's true that she's gone missing.'

'You don't believe it is?'

'I won't until I read about it in the newspaper.'

'Alright.'

I don't know what had occasioned this, but somehow we had veered off course. What had started as a relatively amiable conversation had hit a cold, unfriendly stand-off, and I could see no reason to force a resolution.

'Have you got what you came for, herr Veum?'

'Sort of.'

'Then it will give me great pleasure to accompany you to the door.'

'The pleasure is all yours, so to speak.'

But it wasn't a great pleasure, judging by her expression. She accompanied me all the way out and, as I sat in my car, I could see she was keeping an eye on me from the large window, as if to be sure I wasn't waiting in case a jilted lover from 1957 turned up, thirty-six years too late.

17

From Starefossveien I took the shortest route to Roald Amundsens vei. On the Nymark pitch a number of scattered football players were putting in the day's first training shift, divided into two teams with the help of hi-vis vests and watched over by a grim-faced coach. I didn't stop to watch. Their nerves were already on edge after the weekend's miserable performance against Fyllingen.

Truls Bredenbekk turned out to be surprisingly sprightly for a man well over seventy. 'Johan Hagenes? Of course. Come on in,' he said once I had explained the reason for my visit, and to emphasise how fit he was, he grabbed hold of the chrome steel pipe screwed to the ceiling in his hallway and did a couple of quick arm lifts – up, down, up, down – before gracefully letting go, walking on and opening the sitting-room door without any sign of breathlessness. Impressed, I followed him in.

'It's about keeping your arms active,' he explained. 'Although it's rare I play now.' Nevertheless, he sat down at the piano by one wall and rattled off the opening to 'If You Knew Susie', then jumped up, launched himself at a chair, part of the bluish-green three-piece suite, and pulled it over for me. 'Coffee?'

I quickly realised he was the type who found it difficult to sit still and do nothing. 'Yes, please.'

With that he was up again and off into the kitchen. The sound of running water and cups rattling on saucers reached me in the sitting room, and while he was waiting for the water to boil, he paced back and forth to ask me if I took milk or cream (no, thank you, neither), if I played an instrument too (only mouth organ) and whether I'd ever heard Johan Hagenes play.

'I'm afraid not. I was fifteen when he died.'

'Ah, OK,' he said absent-mindedly, as if he was going to repeat the same question a minute later.

The dark sitting room was small and compact, with a prominent, old-fashioned radiogram cabinet containing a record-player, a cassette and CD player, and a large selection of LPs and CDs. Squeezed into a corner was a small TV, and facing the screen was a keep-fit bike. The tired-looking suite, the low coffee table and a dining table turned the rest of the floor into an obstacle course you had to cross with the greatest care. Through the windows came the thwack of leather footballs, shrill whistles and angry shouting.

Truls Bredenbekk dashed in, set the table with a sweep of his arms and rushed back into the kitchen to filter the coffee. He was small and light, with straight, combed-back hair, light brown with thick streaks of grey. His fingers were surprisingly short and chubby, but that clearly didn't affect his mastery of the piano keyboard.

'At last,' he said as he poured the coffee and sat down, for ten seconds, only to jump up again and run into the kitchen for a plate of pastries and biscuits, and a bowl of strawberry jam.

Back again, he fixed his steely gaze on me. 'Out with it, Veum. What do you want to know?'

I waited for a moment or two to see if he was really intending to stay put. When it looked as if he was, I said: 'Right, first – what was Johan Hagenes like? As a person, I mean.'

'As a person? Hm. I knew him mostly as a musician, you know. He was a pretty good saxophonist. At the time Stan Getz was the big name. Him and Al Cohn and Zoot Sims. He tried to play that style. Cool. But in reality he came from the Lester Young school, a drier tone with controlled, precise improvisation. We didn't usually meet privately, although we did bump into each other occasionally at gigs. When other musicians were playing, I mean.'

'And otherwise? Was he a skirt-chaser?'

'Skirt-chaser? Johan Hagenes? No. He was like me. I never married either.'

'By which you mean...?'

He shifted uneasily, as though he had already been seated for too long. 'I don't know if that was a loss for him. I mean, children and that sort of responsibility. It's always a struggle if you have to try and live off music, and I suppose he would've wanted to go to Stockholm or Copenhagen, like so many of us. That's where the big jobs were – recording contracts too, if you were lucky. But he didn't get any further than Bergen either. Well, there were a few guest appearances in Oslo, of course, and Stavanger and Haugesund, and so on.'

'In other words, all the big towns.'

'And he was pretty darn good. He reminded me of Leif Pedersen, who had a solid reputation locally, in the thirties and forties.'

'How long did you play together?'

'Well, apart from sporadic guest spots, we were in Blåmanden first, which we started in 1953…'

He suddenly stood up, rushed over to the piano, sat on the stool and played a few verses of Bergen's version of 'Blue Moon' while singing in recitative style: *Blåmanden, you have stars on your back, you always make me so happy and glad, when I see your slopes.* Not great poetry exactly, but an established standard we made into our own home-made signature tune, and which we all sang on the rare occasions we didn't have a vocalist. I was the oldest, about ten years older than the others – Johan, Bjørn Heggelund on bass and Helge Bystøl on drums.'

'So, you were the prime mover then?'

'In a way I probably was. The arrangements were mine. I organised most of our gigs, but it was Helge who took care of the ladies.' He played a few bars of Benny Goodman's 'Whispering' and sang a verse of the popular Norwegian translation: '*Elskede, kom i mine arme…*'

'On one occasion, Johan's beloved must've come into his arms too?'

He nodded, amused. 'You're referring to what led to his death?'

'Kind of.'

He continued playing without looking at the keys. 'It wasn't the first time he'd met that woman.'

'So I've heard.'

The job in Ustaoset over Easter 1956 had come as manna from heaven, he said. He could remember the excitement they felt as they stepped off the train with all their instruments and baggage. They were picked up at the station by car and driven the five hundred metres to the hotel. Afterwards they were shown their rooms, two men to each, down the end of a corridor and at the top of the rear building. They played in the evenings; in the mornings they could go skiing, those of them who were that way inclined. In reality, that came down to Helge Bystøl, who had spent his Easter holidays in Kvamskogen when he was growing up and was an experienced skier. Helge claimed, quite credibly, that if he had met any available women earlier in the day, on the ski slopes down to Skarvet or Tuva, he had an extra advantage in the evening. Helge Bystøl was the skirt-chaser among them, sitting behind his array of drums, with his charming smile and bright eyes. But it was all about Johan Hagenes that Easter.

'You've heard about love at first sight, haven't you, Veum?'

'"Heard about it" is a perfect description.'

'I think something like that must've happened to Johan and this woman.'

They couldn't help but notice. From the moment the two couples, the redhead the natural centre of attention, entered the room, it was like Johan's saxophone tone acquired an extra sensuality, and he himself had never heard 'Polka Dots and Moonbeams' played with such verve – it was as though he could hear the lyrics in his inner ear:

There were questions in the eyes of other dancers as we floated over the floor.

The woman with the red hair had raised her head. She sat listening, as still as an ivory sculpture in the dimmed, yellowish lighting, and the gaze she sent Johan was both surprised and direct: There were questions but my heart knew all the answers and perhaps a few things more.

By chance he had passed them in the lobby during the break. He had never found out who had introduced them or whether it had been an evil caprice of fate, but as he walked past he had heard the very first words they exchanged:

Breheim.

Johan Hagenes.

You're from Bergen too?

Yes, I…

Then he was out of hearing range.

When they came onto the stage after the interval, he noticed that Johan seemed excited and his cheeks were flushed, as though he had been outside.

Where were you? he asked.

I needed a bit of fresh air, the saxophonist answered, without looking at him.

His eyes were already across the dance floor, on one of the window tables, where the woman called something-or-other Breheim had returned to her seat. Aptly enough, the first tune in the second set was 'The One I Love Belongs to Somebody Else'.

'It was in the next interval that the row broke out.'

'What happened?'

He waved his arms. 'Christ knows. We didn't see him in that break either.'

In the same way that he had illustrated his narrative with brief, expressive snatches from the relevant tunes – 'Polka Dots

and Moonbeams' and 'The One I Love Belongs to Someone
Else' – he suddenly burst into a few spirited bars of what I eventually recognised as 'But Not for Me'. His eyes, though, were far,
far away.

*When people were on their way back after the second interval,
their attention was drawn to a furious uproar by the reception area.
The woman with the red hair was being guided, shouting, to the exit
by her husband, who was right behind her, carrying their coats over
his arm, and behind him again trooped the hotel manager with their
boots in his hands, as if to make sure nothing was left behind.*

There's a limit to how much I can put up with, the husband said.

It wasn't what you think.

Oh, no?

It was something very different.

*I'll give you something very different. I will, you'll see. And you'll
feel it.*

The hotel manager had tried to arbitrate: Herr Breheim, please!

*The angry man had turned on the manager at once: And you
shut your mouth. Is this how you treat your guests? When I tell my
business colleagues about this…*

But herr direktør…

You can shove your herr direktør.

*Breheim had opened the hotel door and left snorting with fury,
and when the hotel manager caught sight of Helge Bystøl, Bjørn
Heggelund and himself, they found themselves the subject of even
more fury:*

*And you lot are catching the night train. Tonight. And you'll pay
for this.*

Us? Helge said.

What the hell have we done? Bjørn chimed in.

*They couldn't see Johan anywhere, until he rushed on the stage
in the middle of the intro, and when Helge asked him where he had*

been, he had merely answered with a pained expression: In the toilet.

Do you realise the mayhem you've caused?

Caused?

'The manager was livid, I'm telling you, Veum. We were put on the midnight train and sent home like parcel freight, and we never got any more gigs at Ustaoset Hotel.'

'And all because…'

'I think … It was as if they couldn't keep away from each other from the very first moment. They were irresistibly drawn to each other.'

'Then, when it all ended as it did, eighteen months later…'

He nodded. 'Mm. It didn't exactly come as a surprise, but of course no one could've predicted that it would end so dramatically.'

'No. Did you ever talk to Johan about it? About his relationship with Tordis Breheim, I mean?'

He got up from the piano stool, walked over to the wall, ran a finger over the spines of his LP collection, as though searching for something he couldn't seem to find. Then he turned to me again. 'Once he told me … It was late at night. We were sitting in our room at the Alexandra in Loen, where we were playing one May weekend that year.'

'1957?'

'Yes. He told me that this woman – Tordis Breheim – he'd never met anyone who'd had such a strong effect on him as her. He didn't know how he could live without her. But she had two small children – two girls, unless I'm mistaken – whom she couldn't in all conscience bring herself to leave, although her feelings for him were just as strong. I think…'

'Yes?'

'I think she was quite simply the love of his life.'

'I've heard big doses of most things can kill.'

Suddenly he was quiet. Completely quiet. So quiet it was conspicuous.

Through the windows I could hear heated shouting. The coach was losing his temper.

'Yes, you may be right about that,' he said. 'Cod liver oil and vitamins and love…'

'The evening they died – do you remember anything special about it?'

'No, I…'

They had played two sets of standards, mainly upbeat dance music, as the hotel had requested. Quite early in the first set he had noticed that the Breheims were in the room, and when he glanced over at Johan, he was already in some kind of trance, like a doomed rodent hypnotised by a snake. It had struck him that even though he had never met Tordis Breheim face to face, he was convinced she would have green eyes, like an incarnation of Olga Barcowa, from the detective magazines he had read as a boy: Olga Barcowa, 'the green menace'.

The hotel was big, with salons and corridors, rear staircases and closets, and he had no idea where Johan Hagenes had spent the interval between the first and the second sets, but when he returned to the stage, it was too late to stop him before the spotlight revealed – at least to those standing close to him – the unmistakeable imprint of bright red lipstick on his collar.

The other musicians exchanged glances, half envious, half resigned. The lack of discretion had slowly become obvious and when Johan and Breheim had started brawling after the second set, no one was in the least bit surprised.

It had been worthy of a scene from an American melodrama. Lying in the arms of a waiter, blood pouring from a deep cut to his top lip, Breheim had angrily watched Johan Hagenes follow Tordis

Breheim to the exit, Johan with an apologetic glance at his Blåmanden colleagues, Tordis staring at her husband with a mixture of fear and despair.

That this was to be the last time they would see them, never crossed their minds. It would never have occurred to them in their wildest dreams. Anyway, they had more than enough to do rearranging the third set. Now the piano was the only solo instrument and consequently they had to rejig their repertoire.

'I didn't hear what'd happened until Tuesday afternoon, when Bjørn Heggelund rang to tell me that both Johan and Tordis were dead.'

'Were any of you summoned to a police interview?'

'Yes, but I don't think they listened very carefully. They didn't seem very interested, let me put it like that.'

'So long afterwards, I don't suppose you remember who led the investigation?'

'In fact I do, yes. Because he lived in our street when I was a boy. PC Neumann, we called him. Hans Jacob Neumann.'

'And how old would he be if he were still alive?'

'Over ninety at least. And he is alive. I know he is. Try the Cathedral Old People's Home. I saw him there the last time I visited my Aunt Edel.'

'Well, I never, you really have got your finger on the pulse.'

'No more than is normal for my age.'

He struck up a last tune on the piano, to bring the proceedings to a natural conclusion: 'They Can't Take That Away from Me'.

18

In the early 1960s, when it was built, the Cathedral Old People's Home was a temporary replacement for the venerable old Norge Hotel, which had been demolished while a new one was being erected on a site by Ole Bulls plass. Norge Apartment Hotel they had called it then. It was nicely set back from the traffic in Kong Oscars gate, with St Jakob's cemetery as a buffer zone, lushly planted with linden, beech and horse-chestnut trees.

The old man in the wheelchair who the woman in reception had said would be *so* pleased to have a visitor occupied a room on the seventh floor. He was asleep with a blanket over his legs when I arrived, but the nurse who accompanied me went over and shook him. 'Hans Jacob. Wake up. You've got a visitor.'

'Eh? Who?' He raised his head and looked around. Catching sight of me, he gave a broad grin, as though I were one of his best friends from years back.

'He's a bit hard of hearing, but otherwise he's in fine fettle,' the nurse said – a small, dark-haired woman, who, despite her unmistakeable Bergen dialect, came from quite different latitudes than these.

Hans Jacob Neumann had the appearance of a tame bird of prey, sitting in the wheelchair with a crooked back. His forehead was high and his pate bald, except for a transparent white wreath of hair growing untidily from the back and, in the light from the west-facing window, forming a kind of halo around his head. Through the window I could see the glass dome of the railway station, Bergen College of Art, which had taken over the handsome building that was formerly the old people's home, on the corner of Kaigaten, and the frivolous Lysverket building with its Stalinist façade, which always made me want to sing the Beatles' 'Back in the USSR'.

I walked over to him and held out a hand. 'Hello, herr Neumann.'

He shook hands. 'Yes, thank you. I'm fine. Are you the new priest?'

'No, no. My name's Veum. I'm a sort of detective.'

'Mentally defective?'

'De-Tective.'

'Ah, I see.' His eyes cleared. 'How's it going at my old workplace?'

'Er…'

'You have a new chief constable, I see.'

'Yes, they…'

'Impressive bow-tie,' he chuckled.

'Now, I work for myself.'

'Yes, I did too, for all those years.'

'Oh, yes?'

'No one complained. I can still remember … it was some time in the thirties. A small boy had vanished into thin air. Turned out he'd cleared off in the middle of a lesson because the teacher had been persecuting him. Teachers in those days, Bruun. They could be real tyrants. Well, we started a huge search for him, and do you know what?'

'No. What?'

'Two days later our colleagues in Oslo found him. He was sleeping on a park bench. He'd simply got on a train, down here, and travelled the whole way alone, and no one so much as asked to see a ticket. Those were the days, they were. Now you can't even go to the toilet without someone wanting money off you.'

'Not here though, surely?'

'Down there,' he said, pointing to the railway station. 'But he was as proud as a peacock when I met him. You see, they sent me to bring him safely home. I was only a constable then, but I still remember the train trip over the mountains. In fact, it was my first time in Oslo, Bruun.'

I nodded exaggeratedly, confident at least he would understand that.

'I'm on an investigation,' I started, then raised my voice considerably. 'An old case.'

'Oh, yes?' He looked at me, interested.

His face was narrow, nose large, eyes blue and moist. His chest was concave and there weren't many muscles left in his frail body. You would need quite a bit of imagination to visualise him thirty-five or thirty-six years ago, tall, agile and running full tilt up and down the stairs in what used to be the main police station in Bergen, which had occupied an old workhouse building in Allehelgens gate, long gone now.

'A couple who were found in the sea. In a car. At Hjellestad.'

He nodded slowly, and his lips moved silently until words emerged, like in a badly synchronised news programme on TV. 'I remember it. It was so – what shall I say? – unusual that it's etched itself up here.' With a little effort he raised one arm, and pointed a finger at his head, as if to make sure I wouldn't misunderstand. 'At the end of the fifties, wasn't it?'

I nodded. '1957.'

'I remember. There was something that bothered us. The autopsy showed the man was probably unconscious before the car entered the water. There were marks from a punch to the face and one to here...' He indicated his temple. 'But when we made further enquiries, it turned out he'd been in a fight with the woman's husband the night before, at the dance hall in Norge Hotel. And he could've got the blow to the head when they drove into the sea.'

'Did you investigate this then?' I shouted.

He stared at me in astonishment. 'Of course.'

'And what conclusions did you draw?'

'What?'

'Conclusions.'

'Erm…' He smiled and nodded. 'The husband had a sort of alibi, if not a completely solid one. He'd been hurt in the brawl too, and there was a young couple he knew who'd accompanied him to the hospital and then home. They both maintained he wouldn't have been able to drive. He'd been drinking. It was Sunday evening before he turned up at his sister's. Their two children had been staying over with her.'

'I'm impressed by how well you remember it.'

'I had two daughters myself, and I remember thinking how awful it must've been for them to lose their mother in that way.'

'I see. So how did you first hear about the deaths. Were you looking for her – for fru Breheim?'

'No. A boat-owner in Hjellestad discovered the car – on the Tuesday around lunchtime, if my memory serves me well. Yes, Breheim they were called. The husband hadn't come to see us at the station. As dramatic as her exit from the Norge had been, in a way he knew where she was – or at least who she was with. But he could never have imagined something so terrible would happen to them.'

'No?'

'A grisly sight. I'll never forget it.'

A heavy-duty crane on a truck had lifted the black Opel out of the sea. A cold wind had been blowing in from Raunefjord and a handful of police officers stood gloomily watching the water cascade out of the car as if it were a broken aquarium. It was only when it was placed on the quay that they saw them clearly, two figures clinging to each other in the driver's seat, her behind the wheel, her eyes staring and glassy, him with his face against her chest as if asleep. No one said anything. All they heard was the seemingly endless flow of water, and the gulls screaming like carrion birds above them: death's creditors, ever alert, ever present.

I looked at him. So he had been present on the Tuesday in September 1957 when Tordis Breheim and Johan Hagenes were pulled out of the sea. He had been standing there on the quay and had seen them as the car doors were opened and the two dead bodies were brought out, laid on stretchers and despatched to Gades Institute to be autopsied, while the car was taken to the police impound for a thorough forensic examination.

He had been standing there on the quay, Hans Jacob Neumann. But did he have any information to pass on? Anything that might cast more light on the events?

'Did you examine the cabin?!' I shouted.

'Yes, yes. We found the fingerprints of the two deceased – and of several other people of course. Herr Breheim's, naturally enough. After all, it was him and his wife who owned the cabin. The fingerprints of the man in the car...'

'Hagenes.'

'Hansen?'

'Hagenes.'

'Yes. On a red-wine bottle and some glasses and a couple of other places. As well as a number of other prints we neither had the time nor the opportunity to identify.'

'Was there anything to suggest that any other people had been present? Apart from fru Breheim and Hagenes?'

'In the cabin?' He angled his head and grimaced. 'Hm. Impossible to say. But there were only two glasses and, on the bottle, there were only fru Breheim's and this – Hageset's – dabs.'

'You mentioned a young couple – who'd accompanied Breheim home from the hospital. Do you remember their names?'

'No, I'm afraid not. Names are not my strong suit, Bruun. Sorry.'

I smiled and nodded, and gestured that it didn't matter. 'Did you discover anything else? When you examined the vehicle?'

He gazed into the distance. 'All I can remember is … one rear door wasn't properly closed. If it had been a newer car, I suppose a light would've shown up on the dashboard.'

'In other words, there could've been a third person in the car, who jumped out?'

He gawped at me.

'A third person – who jumped out?'

Again he made a gesture: who knows? But then he added: 'The man's saxophone was on the back seat. I think we concluded he'd put it there and not closed the door properly. That can happen in the heat of the moment.'

'Yes, it can happen in the heat of the moment,' I mumbled. 'It would be bloody difficult to claim anything different so many years later anyway.'

'What surprised us was … the mouthpiece was missing.'

'It was back in the cabin, I heard.'

He looked at me as if from a distance. 'Oh, yes? Well, that's probably right if you say so. But it suggested they were in a hurry when they left.'

'It does,' I said, nodding my head as far as it would go so that he could see I agreed.

Hans Jacob Neumann nodded and smiled. 'Is he getting on alright, the new police chief?'

'I'll try to remember to ask next time I meet him.'

'Yes, it's always like that,' Neumann said, in a chatty tone, as though we had bumped into each other at one of the home's cocktail parties or an Oldies But Goodies do, as they called it in this home.

I stayed for a while longer, and he told me some, to varying degrees, coherent anecdotes from his long career as one of the law-enforcement officers in the town between the approximately seven mountains, because not even the police had ever established which of the six, seven or eight were the real ones.

As I left, he took my hand and looked me straight in the eye. 'Say hello to all of them from me, Bruun. And come again soon. Nothing cheers me up quite like a chat with good colleagues.'

I nodded and smiled, and found my way back down to street level, though not without a tiny prick of conscience. What was I actually doing? Wasn't it time to return to the present instead of getting ensnared in a long-shelved case from 1957? Or were its shadows really as long as they seemed to be?

Before getting in my car, I stood looking at the old graves in St Jakob's cemetery. So many dead people, so many secrets, gone to their graves for ever…

19

When I returned to my office, there was a message on my answerphone: 'Hello, Veum. This is Torunn Tafjord. I'm calling from Hamburg. Can you ring me as soon as convenient?' She left me her telephone number and concluded the message: 'Bye.'

I considered the request for five seconds. Then I shrugged and dialled the number.

She answered at once. 'Torunn here.'

'Veum.'

'Great. Thanks for calling. Have you found out any more about what I asked?'

'As far as I can make out, this is about Utvik in Sveio. I don't have much more to tell you.'

'Right. What about the case you were investigating?'

'What about it?'

'Well, I just meant have you got any further?'

'Not much. I'm afraid my reputation as an investigator is receiving a real battering.'

'Mm—' she said.

'But,' I interrupted.

'Sorry…'

'No, no, I was just wondering … What are you doing in Hamburg?'

'The *Seagull* has docked here, waiting for better times.'

'Which means?'

'They seem to be waiting for something. Instructions, I reckon. The mood on board seems pretty tense, from what I've been able to establish. Among the officers at any rate.'

'They're still intending to go to Utvik though?'

'I think so. They took a container on board in Casablanca, and they're not planning to unload it here, at least.'

'Carrying what?'

'That's the question, Veum. I have no idea. But there's something else I was going to ask you.'

'Fire away.'

'Does the name Birger Bjelland mean anything to you?'

I went quiet.

'Hello? Are you still there?'

'Yes.'

'Did you hear my question?'

'Yes. He's in prison.'

'Is he? That might be the reason then.'

'The reason for what?'

'For them to be moored here.'

'Possible, but if they're intending to wait until Birger Bjelland gets out, they could be there a while.'

'Tell me about him.'

'Where to start? Let's be polite: he's a businessman. Involved in a variety of organised crimes, others might say. That's why he's banged up. Among other things. A nationwide prostitution ring, which I played a part in uncovering.'

'Not bad.'

'Fortunately, mafia activities are only in their early stages in Norway. We just have to hope they never develop into anything bigger. By European standards Bjelland is a dwarf, but at home he's probably had a finger in a lot of pies. Grey money, tax evasion, the dark side of betting and, as I've just said, prostitution.'

'Could he have anything to do with TWO?'

'An interesting thought, I have to say. It's something I'd very much like to ask CEO Halvorsen about the next time he refuses to speak to me.'

'Have you had trouble getting to see him?'

'Trouble isn't the half of it, my friend.'

'Hm.'

'How did you run across him, or his name?'

'I happened to overhear a conversation between two officers.'

'Happened to?'

'Yes.'

'You have your methods, I can hear.'

'As you have yours.'

I nodded, as if she could see me. 'Perhaps I should…?'

'Yes?'

'I can make a couple of calls. And I could drive to Sveio and see if I can find anything out there. If nothing else turns up, I can go down tomorrow. Would that be of any use to you?'

'Very much so.'

'In return…'

'Uhuh?' She almost sounded as if she was expecting me to make an indecent proposal.

'Well, if the name Fernando Garrido comes up, don't hesitate for a moment. Call me, whatever time of day.'

She chuckled. 'Will do, Boss.'

'No one has ever called me that before.'

'There's a first time for everything, isn't there.'

'Indeed.'

'Take care then. Bye.'

'Bye.'

I rang off and sat looking at the phone, half expecting her to call back.

She didn't, so I took out my road atlas and flicked through the pages to find Utvik in Sveio. Then I rang Bodil Breheim and Fernando Garrido's number. Still no answer. I didn't ring Berit Breheim. I planned to speak to her personally, on her home ground this time.

20

Stavkirkeveien was off the beaten track, a cul-de-sac with an assortment of detached houses on the hills between Fantoft and Paradis. The name – literally Stave Church Way – was misleading, because if you wanted to go to the burned-down church, you would have to leave the road and follow the path through the forest. All Stavkirkeveien led to was Fana Tennis Club, which no one had ever considered worth setting fire to. Though it had also definitely seen better days.

The house where Berit Breheim lived was discreetly set back behind a green wire fence and a continuous hedge of large rhododendron bushes covered in buds. When I opened the black wrought-iron gate, I heard a ringing noise inside the house, and as I climbed the steps to the front door a loudspeaker next to it crackled: 'Hello?'

'Veum here.'

'Just a moment.'

Thirty seconds later I heard her footsteps inside. The light inside the hallway was switched on and brightened the matt, yellow panes in the door. She opened up with an inquiring expression on her face. 'Have you found them?'

'No, I'm afraid not.'

She was wearing tight-fitting, dark-green satin trousers with a loose top, a shade lighter. 'What's this about then?'

'May I come in for a moment?'

She didn't seem keen.

'I have a few additional questions.'

She forced a smile. 'OK, then. I hope this won't take long.'

'I thought your case finished today.'

'There are always new cases waiting,' she said irritably.

'Yes, of course … However, it wasn't me who engaged my services.'

'Yes, I apologise.' She had to force another smile, more re-signed this time. 'I'm always a bit tense when a case has finished and all that remains is the sentencing. You put so much into what … well, it's not always easy to justify to yourself how you spend your time.'

'Ah…'

'I've been thinking about what you said this morning when we met in the courthouse. You have to remember, we have a legal system to maintain. Even the worst criminal has a right to fair treatment.'

'Naturally. I didn't really mean to…'

'No, one never does, does one?' she retorted, ironically, as if she were still in court. 'But, what was it you wanted to ask about?'

I looked around. We were in the hallway. The walls were dark red with a tinge of burgundy. There were pictures of animals on the walls: a couple of hunting dogs scenting prey and one with a partridge in its jaws, some cats playing with a ball of yarn. Harmless pictures with no evidence of a human in them, except for the painter.

She looked at her wristwatch. 'Right, come on in.'

'Are you expecting someone?'

'I'm expecting a … friend. But not for a good while yet.'

I nodded and followed her up a few steps into the sitting room. It faced away from the road, onto a little garden with fruit trees, rose bushes and flower beds. A sliding door led onto a flag-stoned terrace with elegant white garden furniture, from neither IKEA nor Bohus, as far as I could judge. But the door was closed. It still wasn't the right temperature for tête-à-têtes outside. Instead she had set a little table by the window: two placemats, plates, cutlery, wine glasses and candles – as yet unlit.

I raised an eyebrow. 'Looks like you have something to cel-ebrate.'

She sent me a resigned look. 'The case is finished.'

'Have you invited the judge?'

She gave me a bitter-sweet smile. 'Could we get to the point? The point of your visit, I mean.'

I nodded, and she added: 'Take a seat.'

I sat down on a solid, bull-hide sofa, dark brown with golden undertones. I took in the art on the walls with one sweeping glance. It was still nature that dominated, but this time it was fields of flowers and trees that were the priority, except for a dramatic picture of a harpooned whale being hauled ashore by a group of whalers in costumes from the early 1800s. The seascape was overwhelming; it could have been a Johan Christian Dahl print for all I knew. The maritime theme ended in a large aquarium, illuminated from behind, a judicious selection of decorative fish gliding elegantly through the water.

She sighed aloud and coughed impatiently.

'Oh, yes, sorry, I was just so taken by your pictures. They give a sense of your personality – which certainly doesn't come out in court.'

'You haven't come here to advance dubious theories about my personality, I assume?' She put a hand through her red hair, attractively untidy now she was on home territory.

'No, I'd like to come back to this love triangle of several years ago.'

She glared at me dismissively. 'Tell me, are you going to talk about my mother and her affairs again?'

'No, not this time. This is about you, your sister and Hallvard Hagenes – in 1972, wasn't it?'

'I see. What is that now? Twenty-one years ago?'

I nodded. 'Long enough in anyone's life.'

'And what's that supposed to mean?'

'But not so long that you can't bear a grudge.'

'Listen here, Veum…'

I raised a hand. 'I've been speaking to your stepmother.'

'Sara? Ah, and what did she have to say?'

'The following: that what happened when Hallvard Hagenes left you for Bodil had left deep scars…'

She opened her mouth and snorted aloud, an indignant expression on her face.

'And that you'd been like cat and dog, to use her own simile, you and Bodil, for many years afterwards.'

'That's the most stupid thing I've ever heard. I was at their wedding. We met – on family occasions.'

'How often was that?'

'Often enough.'

'Not only that, she told me about the row over the Morvik property.'

'She's really lost it now. We settled that matter ages ago.'

I leaned forward. 'Tell me, Berit, how often did you see Bodil and her husband?'

She flapped her hands about. 'Often enough, I've told you. Do I have to account for every single occasion? What's this got to do with them disappearing?'

'If they don't make an appearance soon, you'll have to go to the police. A missing-person article in the press would be far more effective than me going round investigating people only tenuously connected with this business.'

'No police until we're sure, I told you.'

'Sure about what?'

'That they really have disappeared.'

'Back to … When was the last time you saw her?'

'Bodil?' She stared into middle distance, thinking.

'When you drove Fernando home from the police station that Sunday, you didn't see her, did you?'

'No, I told you. I just dropped him off. But I'd spoken with her on the phone. I told you I had.'

'Your stepmother mentioned something about a Christmas visit to one of your half-brothers. Rune, was it?'

She nodded.

'She hadn't seen either Bodil or you since then. What about you? Have you seen your sister since Christmas?'

Her eyes clouded over. 'Well, we've both been busy with our own things.'

'When your brother-in-law was done for breach of the peace, why did he ask for you as his lawyer?'

'He probably didn't know anyone else.'

'Really? In his line of business?'

'It wasn't exactly a business lawyer he required.'

'No, but … When you talked, did he mention anything about what had caused the row?'

'No. Not a word. And I didn't ask him either.'

'Why not?'

'They have nothing to do with my private life, so…'

'…you don't have anything to do with theirs?'

'Exactly.'

'But you want me to find them?'

'I want to know that nothing has happened to them.'

'Right.' After a short pause, I added: 'What about your private life twenty-one years ago? Can we perhaps talk about that?'

'No, because it has nothing to do with this.'

'But you met Hallvard Hagenes first?'

'I don't want to talk about it, I told you.'

'Is it a long time since you last saw him?'

Her face was flushed now. 'How many times do I have to tell you?'

'Listen. Let me repeat what I said before: You engaged me. You yourself alluded to this Hallvard Hagenes.'

'I happened to mention his name, yes. In connection with what happened to my mother and his uncle.'

'But then his name came up in another connection. This one. But not even then would you admit that you'd been lovers once.'

'Admit? There was nothing to … It was a matter of little consequence, Veum. And it happened a long, long time ago.'

'I may have to speak to him again, so if you give me your version first, then…'

'Jesus!' Again she looked at her watch. 'What do you want to know? A young girl's confidences? Or rather, a young woman's.'

A woman who fell in love for the first time.

That is what she had been. In love. And he had been untrue to her, with her own sister.

'What shall I say? How much is there to tell?' Her tone sounded almost absent-minded. 'Hallvard and I were going out together. Then there was an incident…'

She remembered.

Or did she?

The first glances over lunch? Laughter in the garden while she went indoors for juice and water? Hurried footsteps moving apart when she came round the corner of the house where Hallvard and Bodil…?

But it hadn't been a figment of her imagination. It had been the onset of something, like an illness, before they were all suddenly well again and Hallvard was out of their lives, it was as simple as that.

She remembered…

They had been to Hjellestad, and she had to stay in bed because she had been running a temperature while Hallvard joined Bodil and 'some girlfriends' in Grønneviken to go swimming.

She remembered it as if it were yesterday.

She had been indoors while the light outside was strong and bright. In the distance she heard the sounds of children playing, an outboard motor in the fjord, a radio blaring.

She felt marginalised, so outside of all life that she had ignored her temperature, put on jeans, a T-shirt, gym shoes, and walked through the forest to Store Milde, followed the path from there into Grønneviken and the newly planted arboretum. She had passed the public toilets and walked down to the sea without seeing them anywhere. Then, on an impulse, she had crossed the rocks and gone through the trees, where people often sunbathed.

Then she saw them.

She stopped in her tracks, she froze, and that was how she felt too, like a block of ice, from top to toe, with hoarfrost around her heart. Hallvard … and Bodil…

They had been lying on a blanket, and she couldn't see any girl-friends there. Bodil was on her back, wearing her yellow bikini, her legs slightly apart. He was lying on his side, leaning over her. He was stroking her hips with one hand. Supporting his head on his elbow with the other. Bodil was winding his long hair around her fingers. Then she pulled him down to her and it was as though they merged into one in an unending, enervating kiss.

She had stood there, in the shadow of the canopy of trees.

Hallvard and Bodil kept on kissing.

Without saying a word, without revealing her presence, she walked back, but when they returned to the cabin several hours later, Bodil's cheeks were flushed and Hallvard's eyes were evasive – they must have realised she knew. Did you see us? Bodil had asked in a showdown several months later. Were you there when we did it? Did what, my little sister? What did you do?

'Are you happy now, Veum?' She sent me a death stare, as if it had been me who hurt her. 'Does it turn you on to hear women telling stories like that?'

I shook my head, and she returned to what she had been saying.

'They were together for a short while, Bodil and him. Then it finished too. I think she'd achieved what she'd been after. She just wanted to make her mark, in a way. Show that she was the equal of her big sister, that she was grown up now too. And Hallvard…' She shrugged. 'There were other men.'

'Yes?'

'Yes,' she said curtly. 'I really don't have any more time now, Veum. I have to get some food ready.'

'Yes, I'm sorry.' I stood up. 'Your ex-husband, Rolf…'

'He's definitely got nothing to do with this.' Her face was red. 'I thought you didn't take that type of case?'

'True, but…'

'Then I'd recommend you keep to your word. Rolf was an arsehole, the worst mistake of my life, and if you mention his name one more time in my presence … I'm just warning you, Veum. Don't do it.'

'Alright.' I held up my palms. 'But I think I've come to the end of the line with this. I simply don't know what to do next. Tomorrow I'll try a different angle: Trans World Ocean. There might be a connection, although I can't see what.'

'But he stopped working there, you said.'

'Yes. Just quit, I was told.'

She gave a look of surprise. 'Don't you think…? It almost looks as if this is something they've planned right from the off, doesn't it?'

'What makes you say that?'

'First Bodil leaves her job, and then starts up on her own. Then he leaves his. It's as though they were putting a stop to everything.'

'In a way, it does, yes.'

She stared solemnly into the air, and I could see what she was thinking, it was like a shadow over her face: the death pact in 1957, if that was what it had been.

She accompanied me to the door and stood on the step until

I had closed the gate behind me. From inside the house I heard the ringing again. I got into my car, drove to the end of the road, turned round and drove slowly back down. Just before the turn-off for Storetveitveien I pulled in and took out my mobile. I tapped in the number Hallvard Hagenes had given me for his car. No answer. I dialled his home number. No answer there either. Perhaps he had a gig. Unless he had been invited to an evening meal with a mutual acquaintance.

What to do? I could wait of course. Or I could return in an hour's time, ring Berit Breheim's doorbell once again and be fired from the job. I could try to go through the hedge, creep round the house and take a peep through the sitting-room window. But if she had an alarm system attached to the gate, perhaps she had other security measures too. I could wait in the car until her guest came out – later that evening, in the wee hours or at the crack of dawn.

I decided I needed my beauty sleep, so I drove home. My plan was to get up early. Between me and Utvik in Sveio there were two ferry crossings and a two-to-three-hour drive each way.

Early Tuesday morning I got into my car and set out for Halhjem, with NRK Hordaland on the radio and nothing of any value in my head either.

21

Norwegian National Highways were still clinging on to the dream of a ferry-free trunk road from Stavanger to Trondheim. The road tunnel under Bjørnafjord was light years away yet, but the politicians had given their blessing to the triangle link in Sunnhordland, so motorists could already look forward to increased ferry prices as an advance on the toll money to pay for the project. From what the newspapers were saying, there was still a long time to wait before even the blasting work could begin. The state mill churned as slowly in Sunnhordland as everywhere else.

Two ferry crossings and four cups of coffee later, I was on my way down through Sveioland, on the R47 towards Haugesund. At the community centre in Sveio I branched off again and followed the signs towards the coast. In the end I had to consult the map to find my way over the last part.

A broad tarmac road down to the sea was blocked by a solid gate. Around the property rose a three-metre-high fence with barbed wire at the top. On the gate was a sign saying: *NO ADMITTANCE. INDUSTRIAL SITE.*

I got out of the car and approached warily. On the other side of the gate, the road led down to a natural dip in the terrain and out of my field of vision. I shook the gate. It was locked in the usual way and additionally secured with a solid chain and padlock. To open it required better tools than I had at my disposal.

Instead, I scanned the surroundings. Behind the property, I could just make out the sea. On both sides of the dip there was thick vegetation, but it was low, shaped by the strong winds that so often raged along this stretch of coast. My guess was that it might be possible to scramble up onto one of the rocks outside the fence for a better view.

I reversed the car up the road and parked so far to the side that even a cement lorry would be able to pass. Then I worked out where the nearest vantage point was and entered the scrub alongside the road. After ten minutes of ploughing through scrub and climbing, I emerged onto a weather-beaten, wind-blown rock. From here I could see straight over to the Sletta waters, where the sea rolled up its shirtsleeves and seagulls dived low over the crests of the waves that resembled floes of foam. To the south I had Ryvarden lighthouse. To the north-west I saw the southern point of Bømlo municipality.

Immediately below me lay the buildings of what once must have been an active coastal industry. Now it seemed abandoned. The winches on the quay had long gone, many of the window panes were smashed, and there were no boats docked. The only thing that looked as if it had been upgraded was the broad strip of tarmac road leading to the quay area.

The rock I was standing on sloped steeply down to the wire netting fence barring the way to unauthorised personnel on this side as well. If I ever came back, I would have to bring bolt-cutters. I saw no reason to try and tackle the fence now.

For a little while longer I stood gazing across the sea. The view was powerful and impressive. You didn't need much im-agination to see the long ships along the coast, from the days of Harald Fairhair to the golden age of the kingdom of Norway under Håkon Håkonsson and Magnus Lagabøte. Times had changed. Now the long ships had been replaced by cruisers and speedboats, and right out there, behind the horizon, it wasn't Iceland waiting but the oil platforms in the North Sea.

I tore myself away and walked back down to my car. A kilo-metre or two back down the road I had passed a general store. On my return I popped in.

The shop was down-at-heel and only partially modernised. However, it wasn't so old-fashioned that there was a merchant standing behind the counter. The goods were on shelves and there was a cash desk by the exit. The choice was fairly limited, as far as I could judge, but then the cabin folk in the area hadn't moved in for the summer yet.

A chubby, fair-haired woman in her fifties was tidying the shelves. She looked up, her eyes alert and inquiring. I looked around. 'A bar of milk chocolate and a bottle of mineral water, please. Thank you.'

'No need for thanks. That's what we're here for,' the woman said, taking the biggest bar she could find. 'Will this do?'

'Yes, thank you.'

'Sparkling or still?'

'Sparkling.'

After I had paid and she was putting my bulk purchase in a plastic bag for me, I asked, as casually as I could: 'Tell me, the industrial site down by the sea, is anything happening there at the moment?'

She looked at me, still holding my items, as though now she didn't want to hand them over. 'The industrial site? Old Starfish, you mean?'

'Yes, probably.' I pointed in the appropriate direction. 'Behind a gate, down to the sea.'

'Then the answer is: yes and no.'

'What do you mean?'

'They went bankrupt in 1989. It had been going since the early 1920s until that point. Then they called in some yuppies, who took over, and two years later they closed up, and it was all over. My daughter worked down there. Now she's moved to Haugesund.'

'Now you've explained the "no" part.'

'Exactly. The "yes" is because the quay is still in use, though I don't know what for.'

'Oh?'

'Vehicles arrive at regular intervals. At all sorts of times, very often at night.'

'What kind of vehicles?'

'I think I'd probably call them tankers. My son-in-law thinks it's something to do with the dumping of waste.'

'I see.'

'But I don't know. I don't have a clue about that sort of thing.'

'Well, it doesn't sound like an unreasonable guess. Toxic waste, I'd say, which has to be shipped out.'

'He said something like that too.'

'But you never see them? They don't stop and do some shopping?'

'They do, if they come during the day, but that's rare. For cigarettes mostly. Or they want something to drink. Coke or mineral water. But I've never asked them anything. I'm not the kind to ask awkward questions.'

'No?'

'It's got nothing to do with me. I'm glad of the little turnover I get. I'm telling you, there was more life in Utvik in the old days. You should hear the old folks talking, you should, about the herring years.'

'That's a long time ago now.'

'Yes, much too long, if you ask me. Much too long.'

After we had established that we agreed about that too, there was apparently little more I could get out of her. Finally, she considered the time ripe to hand me the chocolate and mineral water, as if I deserved it now, after long and faithful service. I thanked her, left, got in my car and pointed its nose back northwards.

More ferry crossings awaited, more cups of coffee that had spent too long in the machine, and the same old sailors with narrowed eyes from gauging clearances. This had been the Vestlander's world ever since they had decided to settle on the edge of a country that mainly consisted of scattered islands, high mountains and deep fjords. A chief highway engineer's nightmare; a normal day for almost everyone else.

I had to wait half an hour in Valevåg. By the time the ferry at last manoeuvred its way through the narrow sound, I had almost fallen asleep.

22

On the ferry between Sandvikvåg and Halhjem I had a hot meal: rissoles in gravy. From Halhjem I rang Hallvard Hagenes. He was at the airport waiting for a punter, he said. I could try again when I was closer to Bergen. At the top of the Valla mountain ridge I pulled in. The whole of the Bergen valley unfolded in front of me, adorned, as it were, with glitter in the hazy blue twilight. I rang again. He had a ride, to Åsane.

'How long will it take?'

'A little break would be handy after this trip, Veum. Café Caroline at the railway station. We can meet there in about half an hour.'

'Great.'

He kept his word, with a minor delay of five minutes. I had found a seat by the window. Through the tall glass panes facing Kaigaten I saw the little chapel that had once belonged to Nonneseter convent. Not so long ago it was revealed that there was a brothel in the adjacent building, or a 'massage parlour' as such establishments like to call themselves nowadays.

Hallvard Hagenes got himself a cup of coffee and a waffle and sat down across from me.

'We didn't quite finish our conversation yesterday,' I started.

He had put some jam on his waffle from a mini-pot. 'Didn't we?'

'There's some fuzziness at various points, if I can put it like that.'

He folded the waffle heart and pushed it bit by bit into his mouth. 'Oh, yes?' he mumbled between two mouthfuls.

'Let's begin at the beginning. You probably don't know much about what happened between Tordis Breheim and your uncle in 1957…'

'Much? Barely the actual circumstances. There was this talk

of a death pact, which I mentioned to you yesterday. But otherwise … It wasn't exactly the sort of thing you talked about with
small children present, and I was about two years old at the time.
Later it was never much more than a vague event in the past,
briefly recalled when I met Berit.'

'Alright, let's come to the next point then. When you left Berit
for her sister, Bodil.'

He glared at me. For a moment he stopped chewing. 'I didn't
really leave her. It was her who—'

'But the two of you were caught in the act, weren't you? You
and Bodil?'

'Caught in the act? What are you talking about?'

'In Grønneviken.'

'Tell me, who've you been…? Is this Berit?'

'Grønneviken, late May, 1973…?'

*Yes, he had to admit it. Berit's little sister had him wrapped
around her little finger with her provocative eyes, captivating smile
and supple body.*

*When Berit had had to stay in bed with a fever, he didn't have
the slightest objection to going with Bodil to the beach, where,
between the trees, on a blanket they had spread out on the ground,
they had kissed, their bodies still wet from swimming, their tanned
skin still covered with drops of salty water like small pearls. He had
seen the outline of her nipples through the bikini top, as hard as
pebbles, and she hadn't moved his hand when he gently stroked
them; on the contrary, she had pressed her groin against his, gazed
into his eyes as deeply as she could, smiled engagingly, placed her
hands around his neck and pulled him down.*

'She never said anything…'

'Didn't she?' I said.

So, it hadn't been his imagination after all. Someone had *seen them. He had felt it from the moment they crossed the threshold of the cabin. He had seen it in her eyes, understood her sullen expression, the sudden stiffness of her body and the cold shoulder she had shown him, the following day, when she was back on her feet and they were on the bus to Bergen, while Bodil stayed in the cabin with a girlfriend who had come, too late to avert what had already taken place.*

'It wasn't long before I realised it was over, and it was only then that I got together with Bodil.'

'Really? Let's take this step by step. Berit finished with you…'

'Yes, without saying a word. She just rejected me, said she had other things going on, never had any time for me, and then it was simply over.'

'So, in other words, the two of you might still be together?'

He gaped at me. 'Still? What do you mean?'

'Well, not really. But there was never a decisive break? That's what I mean.'

'No.'

He had met Bodil in Torgalmenningen in town, it had been July, he had a summer job at Hansa brewery, but was on the evening shift that day, and she was alone in Bergen. He could see it now: she was wearing a short, stone-washed denim skirt, white blouse, so flimsy that the flower pattern of her bra was visible through it. After a long, rainy July the sun had finally broken through the clouds, and the rays reflected on her blonde hair and dazzled him. She was laughing. Was that perhaps the reason why?

So you and Berit aren't together anymore? Is that right?

Doesn't seem so.

Spontaneously, she had reached out to him and kissed him on the cheek. Oh, we'll have to celebrate this then. Do you want to come with me? Home?

He did. They had sat in the garden in Sudmanns vei, drinking white wine from tall glasses, and she had smiled and laughed at everything he said. With a mischievous smirk she had taken off her blouse, then encouraged him to do the same, caressed his chest and looked at him with that strange, compelling gaze that turned him to butter that melted in the sun. They had gone into the big house, to where it was cool, up under the roof, stylishly furnished and with polished woodwork. In her parents' bed – Mine is so narrow, she had said, undoing her skirt from the side – they had made love without inhibition, and with an intensity so febrile that his memories of Berit paled from congress to congress, the first, second, third … Afterwards they walked naked through the rooms as if they were alone in the world, touching each other, tempting each other, playing with each other…

'Yes, I fell headlong. I met Bodil in town, one day in the middle of summer, went back to her house, and we…' He flapped his hands. 'You know. We were young and impetuous.'

'And afterwards it was the two of you?'

'Mm.'

He remembered more. Later the same day, when he had to go to work, she had looked at him strangely. But do you have to go?

It's my summer job. I need the money.

Today of all days?

She wrapped herself around him, held him tight, she was like the kind of rubber toy that sticks to you and you can't get it off.

I'm sorry, Bodil. I have to go. They're waiting for me.

When he left, she was wearing an injured expression, and he knew – in retrospect – that already then he had known this wasn't going to last, that this was a tiny insight into something overwhelming and incomprehensible that he was still too young to appreciate.

'Right? Would you say she was uncontrollable?'

'Well … in those days. Then…'

All night, he had stood next to the conveyor belt at Hansa in a trance, blinded by the darkness, a sense of something momentous and irreversible inside his chest. Afterwards he had often thought that the summer of 1973 was the one he had lived transfixed by a sunbeam. Whenever he grabbed his saxophone, it was as though a new tone had grown inside him, something the tenor was unable to express, a wild jubilation he needed an alto for, like Charlie Parker on 'How High the Moon'.

Bodil and he – they had been two precocious children teetering on a precipice over the void that would constitute the rest of their lives. When September came, it was suddenly over. She, like a butterfly, fluttered on to new stamens; he immersed himself in music: I Can't Give You Anything But Love, Baby.

'We were two eighteen-year-olds who barely knew what to do with the feelings we held in our hands. I mean, we simply weren't grown-up enough, and so we drifted apart. By autumn it was over.' He grinned wryly. '"September Song". One of my favourites.'

'But not for ever, eh?'

'Not for ever, eh, *what*?'

'You met her again.'

'Which one?'

'Which one would you like to talk about first?'

'I don't know what you're driving at, Veum.'

I didn't answer. To tell the truth, I wasn't sure myself. 'Let's start with Bodil. Since she's the one who's disappeared.'

His cheeks burned. 'I don't know anything about that.' And added weakly: 'No more than you told me yesterday.'

'Then we're back where I started. You met her again.'

He looked at me defiantly. 'This town is too small for us to avoid each other for years, Veum. Yes, I've met both Bodil and Berit again, as you put it. But that's a long way from claiming…'

'Long way from claiming…?'

'Listen, Veum. Give me one good reason why I should sit here and tell you … It's nothing to do with you. Who I've met and who I might be having a relationship with is simply none of your business.'

'It isn't, you're right.' I leaned forward. 'But you were definitely playing your horn at Bodil's house as late as February this year.'

He stared at me pallidly. 'How do you know?'

'Do you deny it?'

He didn't answer.

'Well?'

'OK then. I was at hers and I played a song or two for her, but it was a … chance encounter, a … Isn't there a novel entitled *Rendezvous with Lost Years*?'

'I think it's *Rendezvous with Forgotten Years*.'

'Anyhow, that's how it was. A rendezvous with what had been, a failed reprise. Or to put it in the music idiom, a new recording that was nowhere near as good as the original.'

'You two didn't play the whole repertoire?'

'No, we didn't.'

He had been out having a couple of beers after a gig at Den Stundenløse, and while he was waiting for another at the bar, she was suddenly standing beside him…

Hallvard?

Bodil.

For a moment they had stared at each other. Yes, she had lost some of her lustre too, crow's feet around her eyes, furrows around her mouth, but she made them look good, and the sensual gaze was still there, with an undertone of melancholy.

*Then she leaned forward, like a silhouette from the summer's day
in Torgalmenningen in 1973, kissed him on the cheek and said: How
are you?*

Good, I think.

She had looked over her shoulder at him: Are you alone?

I'm with some colleagues. Musicians. And you?

Fernando's away.

Fernando?

*As in 1973, he went home with her. They each had a drink from
the well-stocked bar. She told him about the joys and woes in her life
and she eventually asked him to play for her:*

*Hallvard, play how you did all those years ago. Play 'Yesterday'
for me…*

'Yesterday'?

Like a memorial to what our lives have become: Yesterday all
my troubles seemed so far away…

*He had assembled his saxophone for her. Standing on the floor
in her large sitting-room he had played 'Yesterday' for her, then 'Time
after Time' and finally 'September Song'.*

'But we'd had our fingers burned before, Veum, and so badly that
we weren't going to fall into that trap a second time. Neither of us.'

I looked at him. There was something he wasn't telling me. I
could see it in his face.

'But you went back?'

'No. Whether you believe me or not, that was the last time I
saw her.'

'And you didn't even get so much as a kiss?'

'No, I did. I did get a kiss.'

*They had stood in the doorway. Afterwards he had thought: we
were standing there like two silhouettes in the doorframe. If anyone
had seen us…*

He'd had his instrument in his hand and what felt like a sheepish expression on his face.

Hallvard…?

Yes?

She stepped closer to him, lifted herself onto her tiptoes, wrapped her arms around his neck, and it was her who had kissed him, not vice versa, not at first anyway, not until he was caught in her embrace, then he put down his case and…

After he left, his body still throbbing, he looked up at the neighbouring house. All the windows were dark. One of them was open, but that was the only sign of life.

Up on the main road the taxi they had ordered was waiting for him. Her kiss was like a film over his lips, a taste of ash in his mouth, an aroma of smoke in his nostrils. He could still have turned round and gone back down. But he didn't. He got into the taxi, nodded to the driver and gave him the address in Rosegrenden.

'And that was all?'

'That was all.'

I held my cup of coffee, which I had finished a long time ago. 'What about Berit?'

His eyes flashed with irritation. 'Yes? What about Berit?'

'When did you see her last?'

'When did I last…?'

'Were you by any chance with her last night?'

He scraped his chair away from the table. 'Honestly, Veum. I understand less and less of this. What is it you're actually after? You tell me that Bodil and her husband have gone missing. Then you come here and grill me about what happened to my uncle and these girls' mother in 1957… What are you after?'

He rose to his feet. I peered up at him. He was right, of course. He had every reason to be angry. What was I after?

I shrugged. 'Sorry, Hagenes, but I don't know. There's just

something about this case that has me perplexed. A disappearance that mustn't be reported to the police, conflicts from the
past that keep surfacing, like gas bubbles from the bottom of a
pond, a ship that's due to...'

'A ship that's ... Have you gone completely nuts?'

He was within his rights to ask. I couldn't give him a good
answer.

After he had left, I waited for thirty seconds. Then I went too,
to my car to drive back home. I had nothing better to do.

23

The flat was quiet and dark. From the floor below came the drone of a television, the ageing widower's sole comfort. I never saw his grandchildren; I saw his children once every six months. Sometimes I thought we should get together. We could have a game of chess, if nothing else.

I switched on a few lights and looked around. My own TV stood silent in the corner. The shelves were heaving and chaotic, some books were vertical, some horizontal, and in no particular order. When I went looking for a title it was like doing your tax return and searching for your code. The pictures on the wall were cheap graphics from the early seventies, the ones Beate left when she flew the coop, just in time for International Women's Year in 1975. She merrily flew away; I stayed like the cuckoo I was. On a dresser in my bedroom stood a few framed photographs, one of my mother taken around 1950, one of my parents just before the war and one of Thomas at his confirmation in 1986.

I couldn't escape the truth. It was and would remain a bachelor's pad. After Beate, women had come and gone, most for ever, with the exception of Karen, who had her own base in Fløienbakken, one which she was unlikely to leave willingly and certainly not in exchange for what I could offer her in Telthussmuget.

I flicked through my pile of CDs and found the one I wanted on a night like this: Ben Webster at the Renaissance in Hollywood, 14th October, 1960, when I was in my last year at Bergen Katedralskole and hopelessly in love with Rebecca, my first *grand amour*. Webster played 'Gone with the Wind' before asking the most opportune of questions in most people's lives: '*What Is This Thing Called Love*'?

I went into the kitchen, took a bottle of Simers from the cupboard above the sink and poured myself half a glass of aquavit. The time had come for a resumé of what I knew.

The big question, of course, was: where were Bodil Breheim and Fernando Garrido? And as a follow-up: what had happened to them? Could it have anything to do with this TWO ship docked in Hamburg, waiting for better times? What had led to the racket in the cabin during the Palm Sunday weekend? Was it because Bernt Halvorsen and Bodil had something going on? Was that why Garrido suddenly left his job? Or was it because of Hallvard Hagenes and his loquacious saxophone? *Yesterday all my troubles seemed so far away*.

The name running through both cases was Trans World Ocean, and alongside it: Bernt Halvorsen. I put him at the top of my to-do list for the following day.

After Webster had played another set, this time accompanied by the Oscar Petersen trio on a 1959 recording, I screwed the lid back on the bottle and went to bed, accompanied by a novel I had spent far too much time trying to finish, like so much else in my life.

The following morning came much too soon. Rain showers were queueing up over Askøy, and I walked under an umbrella to my office to check the post and answerphone before venturing on another foray against Bernt Halvorsen and Trans World Ocean.

The intersection between Vetrlidsalmenningen, Bryggen and the central square is one of the most dangerous in Bergen. You never quite know which direction cars will come from next. The best option is to wait for the green man, as the law-abiding citizen you are.

I arrived just too late to cross. The last pedestrians were reaching safe ground on the opposite side. By the market square two packed lanes of traffic were waiting for the lights to change. I was surrounded by people already. The most impatient were literally at my heels to cross as fast as possible once the lights had changed. That was when it happened. As the vehicles by the square revved their engines and accelerated in closed ranks, I felt someone push me from behind. The shove was both powerful and intentional. I stumbled into the street, lost my umbrella, and a woman standing next to me screamed: 'Watch out.' But it was too late, and it wasn't my fault either.

This was one of those moments in life when everything happened at once. Brakes squealed, cars hooted, there was a huge bang as two vehicles collided and carried on in the same direction while I made a desperate leap into the air as if to launch myself heavenward, above all the danger. I landed on a car bonnet and slid off sideways, frantically trying to roll into a tight ball. Hit the kerb, back first, felt a whack in my side and was dragged along the road as a film of everything I had done in my life raced through my brain so fast I could barely catch a single image. For a second, Harry Hopsland hung in the air in front of me, but this time he didn't only dive to his death, this time he locked his eyes on mine and together we plummeted downward, into a bottomless pit. Then the film faded, the images disappeared, everything exploded in white inside my head, as if I had been blinded by a camera flash, and then everything went dark, a pervasive, smouldering darkness, where only the very last remnant of light glowed, like a tiny flicker of fire before it finally surrendered and died. I thought: *So that's that then*, and somewhere in the remote distance I heard a voice gurgle as it swirled down a drain: *Call an ambulance! Medics…*

24

Harry Hopsland and I continued to plummet, twinned in pain, through the darkness. Then, all of a sudden, he was gone and I was alone. Tiggers don't push. Trans World Ocean. I repeat: Trans World Ocean. Who are you? Bodil? No, it must be Berit. I've never seen Bodil. I've landed, in pitch-black. Dazed, I look around. Light is coming in from up above. Knees bent and aching, I begin to walk. A long, heavy staircase in thin air. If I can only get up there, I'll see ... what? The truth? I am the light of life, but who's bloody switched it off?! Was it you, Beate? Beate?

Darkness encloses the staircase. As I climb. Step by step.

I can still see it up there, the light.

Slowly I open my eyes. There are two faces bent over me. Mamma? Pappa? No, they're wearing green ... The woman smiles tentatively. Her face, velvety soft, unfolds in front of my eyes. I gently raise a hand. Wanting to touch her. She takes my hand in hers. It is cool and reassuring. She smiles. I smile back. The man examines me minutely. Places dry, warm fingers around one of my eyes. Helps me to keep it open. Stares. I close the other. He lets go of the first, opens the other. I close the first.

Nausea.

I feel sick.

I move. The woman holds me tight. 'There, there. Take it easy.'

The man nods to the woman. Her fingers rub my forearm. Something wet and cold. A jab in my arm and I close my eyes. I am at the top of the stairs now. I look across. It is beautiful. A mountain landscape, deep green valleys. Hazy mist and sunshine. I sit down. Breathe out. Have to rest now ... rest.

❄

When I opened my eyes again, it was evening. Bright lights. They hurt my eyes. I turned my head. The windows were like dark surfaces, reflections of the room.

A young man was sitting beside my bed. He had short, rather untidy hair that stood up, and the look he gave me was friendly and attentive. 'Veum?' he said.

'Yes.' I carefully raised my head. 'Where am I?'

'Haukeland hospital.'

'What am I doing here?'

'You've had an accident.'

'Oh?'

He placed a notebook on my bed, shifted the biro into his other hand, reached over to shake hands and introduced himself. 'Bjarne Solheim. Police.'

I lay back on the pillow. The movement had been enough to make me feel sick. 'What day is it?'

'Wednesday. Evening. You've only been unconscious since this morning. Do you remember anything about what happened?'

'No. Something to do with a staircase.'

He appeared surprised. 'A staircase?'

I felt exhausted. 'Yes. No. I don't remember.'

'You were knocked down at the intersection by the Kjøttbasar at five to nine this morning.'

My mind was blank.

'Oh?'

The door behind him sighed open. A woman dressed in green entered. Her hair was dark and gathered in a bun by her neck. Her dialect rang a bell. Was it Lindås?

'Don't forget. No pestering patients with questions,' she said sternly to the young police officer.

He looked up at her and flashed her a charming smile. 'I'm just jotting down anything he says.' He held up his notepad. 'He's said quite a bit.'

'He's awake,' I said. I didn't know if I liked what I was hearing.

Miss Dark-Hair shot me a warm smile. It was beautiful. 'Sorry. I didn't mean to talk over your head.'

'OK. He says hello and thank you.'

She came closer. 'How are you?'

'I'm tired. Dead beat.'

'That's concussion. Apart from that, though, the doctor says you've got off unusually lightly.'

'Oh, yes?'

'But he'll tell you himself in the morning. Now I think you should have some rest.' She glared at Solheim. 'Sleep now. That's what you need most.'

'Thank you.'

The policeman rose to his feet. He was slim, well-built and seemed loose-limbed. To me he said: 'Helleve sends his regards. He'd like to talk to you as soon as you're out of hospital.'

'Is he going to charge me with jay-walking or what?'

'I think he has something else in mind. But I won't bother you with that now. Not today.'

'In that case, bye for now,' I said, raising a weak hand.

The angel from Lindås gave me a glass of water and a couple of tablets. Not long afterwards I fell into a deep, dreamless sleep.

When I awoke the following morning, I had a thundering headache. Whenever I moved, I felt battered and bruised. Warily, as if my limbs were made of glass, I tried each one. Raised my right leg. Ditto my left. Right arm up and down. Left arm out to the side, stretch to the bedpost and back.

The door opened, and an ebullient blonde nurse came in, followed by a red-haired colleague. 'Good morning,' they sang cheerily. The blonde put down a breakfast tray while the redhead asked if I wanted to get up. It would be best if I tried on my own, she said, and I saw no reason to disagree.

I sat up in bed, moved the duvet to one side, pulled the night gown over my bare thighs, swung my legs out and down, and jumped while she cautiously supported one arm. I was unsteady on my pins, but I was fine. With one exception. I had a pounding headache, I mumbled.

'That's absolutely natural,' she said. Afterwards she accompanied me to the small bathroom and left me to do whatever I had to do.

I examined my face in the mirror. I had dark shadows beneath my eyes. The stubble on my face varied between shades of dark blond, grey and silver. My body felt as if I had run ten consecutive marathons into a gale and uphill. I was stiff, sore and aching. The slightest movement sent a shock of resistance through my muscles. And in the background my head was pounding. I felt like yesterday's man. Tomorrow was a utopia I would never experience.

Slowly I did my ablutions. When I returned to the room, she had changed the sheets and aired the bed. After I had sat back against a pillow, she asked if I wanted tea or coffee with breakfast.

'Tea. But something for my headache first, please.'

She nodded and left the room. Soon after she was back with some painkillers, which I took with a glass of water before breakfast. Then I was given some tea. I wondered if there was anything else I could ask for while she was at it. 'You wouldn't have a newspaper, would you?'

'Do you think you're able to read?'

'I sincerely hope I haven't forgotten how to do that.'

'I'll see if I can find one in the office. But eat first. It'll do you good.'

I ate, and she was right. It did do me good.

I leaned back in bed and closed my eyes. Yes, I remembered leaving home. Walking down Nikolaikirkealmenningen and Øvregaten. Into the tobacconist's in Vetrlidsalmenningen to buy a newspaper and then…

I wasn't sure if I remembered standing and waiting for the lights to go green by the Kjøttbasar or if that was another day. After all, I did generally walk the same route every single morning.

The next thing I remembered was – Tigger? Tiggers don't push or was that exactly what they did do?

Trans World Ocean. Berit and Bodil Breheim. My investigations. I hadn't forgotten them, anyway. I could recall most of what I had been thinking the evening before. I remembered the conversation with Hallvard Hagenes and all the other people I had met over the last few days: Kristoffersen and Bernt Halvorsen at TWO, the neighbour in Morvik, Harald Larsen in Ustaoset, Sara Breheim, Truls Bredenbekk and frail, old Hans Jacob Neumann.

The only thing I couldn't remember was – Tigger?

My redheaded friend came back with a creased and dog-eared newspaper, which I flicked through aimlessly. One headline told me it was the 'End of Sebrenica'. Serbian forces were besieging the town and its Muslim defenders. Now there was a ceasefire, an evacuation was under way, and there was speculation that Western bombers might attack. The Hardanger plateau was still closed for winter, and FC Brann coach Hallvard Thoresen was cautiously optimistic about the evening's home game against Lillestrøm.

I may have dozed off at some point. At any rate I was startled when the door suddenly opened and six or seven people waltzed in, stood in a semi-circle around my bed and stared at me as if I was something the sea had washed up and they had never seen before.

One man I vaguely recognised leafed through the medical notes hanging at the end of my bed, paused in some places, frowned in others, until, with a disapproving expression, he finally cast a distanced look in my direction. 'You've emerged amazingly unscathed, Veum.'

'What do you mean?'

'You have concussion. You've cracked a couple of ribs ... here.' He indicated where on his body. 'Painful, but with no complications. Your back's badly bruised and will be every colour of the rainbow for a few days, but as far as we can see, there's no damage to your spine. And, even better, your pelvis is undamaged. You must've landed in a ball and rolled around. Physically, you're in good shape and your core musculature is strong. That's what saved you.'

'So, how long were you thinking of keeping me here?'

He looked at me in surprise. 'How long? Aren't you on your way out now?'

A couple of the young men behind him laughed. One of the women rolled her eyes.

He smiled himself. 'Everything's fine, Veum. If you promise to take it easy for at least a week, we can discharge you now. Naturally, we'll give you a prescription for some painkillers, which you can get from the pharmacist here before you leave, and then we'll have you back for a check-up ... Wednesday next week. Will you make a note of that?' The latter was addressed to one of the accompanying nurses, who nodded and jotted it down.

'Well, thank you for all your help,' I said with a strained smile.

'We don't want to see you again for a while, Veum. And don't forget to...'

'To what?'

'Look left the next time you cross the road.'

25

I took a taxi down to my office. I couldn't bear the thought of being jolted around on a bus. 'Take it easy for a week?' Easy for him to say, with a generous pension to look forward to.

I checked the answerphone. No one had tried to contact me. Just as well.

I rang Berit Breheim. She was out, at a meeting, but I explained to her secretary what had happened to me, and said that in the unlikely event that she didn't hear from me for a few days, this was the reason. She should contact me if there were any new developments in the case I had taken on for her, I added. The secretary was kindness itself and promised to pass on the message.

'Thank you.'

I had barely put down the telephone when it rang again. 'Veum? Guess who this is?'

He didn't fool me. True enough he had put on a kind of standard Norwegian, but his Voss accent shone through, thicker than the cigarette smoke over the Pentagon nightclub during the Voss International Jazz Festival. Atle Helleve was the latest scion in the detective family at Bergen Police, a likeable Hordalander with a far more thoughtful temperament than the recently retired Dankert Muus had manifested. With luck, I would never see Muus again. On the other hand, I wasn't blessed with great reserves of good fortune. And as Hallvard Hagenes had told me two days ago: this town was too small to steer clear of someone for too long.

'How can I help you, Helleve?' I said, hoping I didn't sound too wry.

'We were wondering if you could drop by. There's something we'd like to discuss.'

'Oh, yes? Actually, I'm on a sickie.'

'That's precisely the point.'

'I see. Well, are you serving coffee?'

'If you can manage without a chaser.'

'The chaser you generally offer is not much to get excited about. But OK. I'm on my way.'

'And Veum…'

'Yes?'

'Look both ways before you cross the road.'

'I was given the same advice at Haukeland.'

'There you are then. You have lots of well-wishers.'

'Strange I haven't noticed that before.'

We rang off. Afterwards I sat thinking. I just had to admit it. I was in unusually bad shape. The threshing mill in my skull was going for broke, but it was badly maintained and making an infernal racket. The reverberations of it were giving me a headache of immense proportions. There was no choice but to drag myself to the medicine cabinet above the sink and treat myself to two more of the large painkillers I had been given at Haukeland. Then I slowly dipped my face into cold water in an attempt to soothe the feverish feeling on my skin. I was dizzy, I felt sick and as if I were a hundred years old. 'Up and at 'em, ole buddy,' I told my reflection in the mirror, but the only response I got was a pale grimace from a face I barely recognised.

When I stepped outside, the light was odd. It was bright and irritating, and felt like a caustic liquid on my pupils. The traffic thundered past, and waiting at the lights on the corner by Lido café, I experienced stabs of fear in my abdomen. Suddenly a realisation came to me. I hadn't crossed on red. Someone had pushed me.

I waited until people were on the zebra crossing, either side of me, before venturing out. I crossed Vågsallmenningen below the old, dirty-red stock-exchange building, long taken over by a bank, and I was happy to have managed a few more intersections until there was only Domkirkegaten left. Once again, I followed the advice given by the doctor and the police. I looked both ways, and not least over my shoulder, before crossing, entered the police station, reported to the reception desk and took the lift up to the third floor of the new building, where Atle Helleve came out to greet me. They had become stricter about who they allowed upstairs now. I hoped it wouldn't be as difficult to get out again.

Atle Helleve was sporting a trimmed beard and a recent haircut, but his stout body still threatened to pop the top buttons of his shirt. He smiled warmly, shook hands as if we were old chums, and invited me in. 'There's coffee on the go.'

'How long has it been on the go, though?'

He wasn't alone in the office. A dark-haired woman rose from one of the chairs, holding a piece of paper in her hand and with a pensive expression on her face. The big glasses she was wearing lent her an intellectual cast, and she was discreetly dressed in a grey suit with a respectable skirt and a cream roll-neck sweater, a small, gold, oval brooch above her left breast, also oval. We stood looking at each other. She smiled sweetly when she saw that I recognised her.

'Inspector Bergesen has just joined us from Kripos,' Helleve said as he passed. 'I gather you've met before.'

Her lips turned downward. 'Herr Veum and I were on the same boat last December. Or in it, so to speak. The Hurtigruten express to Trondheim. On the same case, would you believe?'

'But that was all we shared,' I said. 'What on earth has brought you to Bergen?'

'Your irresistible charm, perhaps?' She let the suggestion linger in the air for a couple of seconds, then raised her palms defensively. 'No. In a way I'd become sick of all the travelling, and besides, I'm getting married.'

I angled a glance at Helleve. 'Not to you?'

He grinned. 'No, no, I should be so l—. No, Annemette's found herself a biotechnologist based at Bergen University.'

'I don't suppose you've invited me here because you need a toastmaster at the wedding? I'm afraid I'm not very witty at the moment.'

'No, we can hear,' Helleve said, almost shyly. He and Annemette Bergesen exchanged looks, and he took a deep breath. 'Take a seat, Veum. Just a second and I'll pour you a coffee.'

'Now that's service.'

I did as he said, and the coffee was surprisingly good, from the very first mouthful. A clean coffee machine perhaps? I glanced from one to the other. For a moment it was as if we were three good friends planning a wedding. 'What's on the agenda?'

Helleve looked at Bergesen, who gestured that she would kick things off. 'As you know, we had an officer posted by your bed at Haukeland hospital.'

'Yes, afterwards I was struck by your prioritisation.'

'Solheim's job was primarily to note down anything you might come out with while you were still more or less unconscious.'

'That can be quite smutty things, an anaesthetist once told me.' I glanced at Bergesen and winked.

'You're far too old for such thoughts,' Helleve said.

'That's sad to hear.'

'We have the print-out here.' He indicated the piece of paper Bergesen was holding, and she passed it over to me.

I looked down at it. It might not have been very smutty, but it still made me blush. Thank God I wasn't carrying state secrets in my head.

(Sobbing, incoherent rambling)
Harry! We're falling! Harry? Harry … (Crying)

Incomprehensible.
Tiggers don't push.
TVO (???) (Tee … Vee … Oh?)
Bodil? No, Berit? No…
Tigger?
(Incomprehensible)
The light … Who was it who…?
Beate?
(Wakes up, looks up at me and asks: Where am I?)

'Lots of women in this, Veum,' Helleve said.

'Whose names all start with B,' Bergesen added.

'I have a predilection for women whose names start with B,' I said. 'But I can't always distinguish between first and last names.' When I saw her cheeks begin to redden, I added: 'Surely you must've noticed last December?' With an embarrassed smile, she blushed.

'But only Harry made you cry,' Helleve interrupted.

'Yes, but he's dead,' I said, somewhat disorientated.

'Not…? Is this the Birger Bjelland case?'

'Exactly. February this year. Harry Hopsland. As I'm sure you remember, he lunged at me with a knife on a construction site in Sandviken. In the heat of battle, he plunged to his death. I reported myself to the police, and not even Muus suggested a charge. It was self-defence, Helleve. He'd been after me for years.'

'He was after you?'

'Yes, ever since I worked in child welfare.'

'Right. And he worked with Bjelland?'

'He was in cahoots with him, on this occasion at least.'

'Would it be correct to say Bjelland used him against you?'

'You can certainly say that. But where are you going with this, Helleve?'

He raised a sheet of paper from his desk, as far as I could see a photocopy of what I was holding. 'These other names. Bodil, Berit, Beate. Can you explain them?'

'Bodil and Berit are part of a case I'm working on. Nothing criminal as yet.'

'What kind of case is it then?'

'Missing persons.'

He eyed me expectantly. 'And?'

'We can – perhaps – come back to that. Beate…' I cleared my throat. 'That must be my ex-wife.'

'Ex?'

I smiled helplessly. 'We got divorced in 1974. Why on earth would I mention her…?'

'Young love never dies?' Bergesen commented from the side-lines. 'Don't forget that theoretically you could be a dead man now.'

'I'll give that some thought.'

'The bit that Solheim wasn't sure about,' Helleve said, 'TVO, is that correct?'

'Yes, good guess. Except that it should be a W in the middle. TWO, Trans World Ocean, a shipping firm. There may be a connection with the job I'm working on.'

'Dutiful to the last, I see. The present case and your ex. Your last thoughts, theoretically speaking.'

For some reason I found what he said depressing. 'Well…' I looked to Bergesen for help. She just grinned and pushed her large glasses up her nose again.

'Have you anything to add?' Helleve asked.

'Regarding the case?'

'Yes.'

I shook my head, but stopped at once. It had brought on my headache again. 'My client has insisted I keep the police out of it. However … if you promise not to say a word and in return give me a helping hand with a bit of genuine information, I can give you the bare bones.'

They exchanged looks, and Helleve nodded. 'Fine.'

In brief outline, I told them about the disappearance of Bodil Breheim and Fernando Garrido. I mentioned nothing about the events of 1957 and nothing about the *Seagull* and its delayed departure from Hamburg. 'There may well be a natural explanation for it all. I suppose that's why the family hasn't contacted the police.'

Helleve nodded. 'And what was it you wanted in return, Veum?'

'The weekend before he went missing Fernando Garrido was arrested for breach of the peace and spent the night in a cell. I'd really like to see the report of his arrest and, if possible, even better, talk to the officers involved.'

'Have you got a date?'

'The night before Palm Sunday – the fourth of April.'

He rang the duty officer and started the wheels moving. 'They'll call you back, Veum.'

'Great. But did you invite me over just to explain this?' I nodded towards Solheim's report. 'What has suddenly made little old me so important?'

Once again, they exchanged looks, as though I hadn't realised long ago that there had to be more to this. Helleve fixed his eyes on me again. He leaned forward with a serious face. 'There's something else here, Veum. Something about Tigger.'

'Tiggers don't push,' Bergesen filled in.

'Yes, I can see.' I grinned.

'Do you remember?'

'Remember what?'

'If you were pushed?'

'To be honest, Helleve … no. I don't even remember standing at the crossroads as everyone has said I did, but I do know … that I've crossed there so many times, and I was standing quite still. I wasn't moving and I didn't set off too early. There was no reason to. I wasn't in any hurry.'

'So, in other words…?'

I nodded – gingerly, so as not to provoke the headache. 'Yes. That's what I assume. Someone must've pushed me.'

'Exactly. We do too. That makes it attempted murder; in which case we're obliged to investigate further.'

'But what about—?'

He raised a pre-emptive hand. 'This is not all we have, Veum. There's something else. And that's why we've asked you here.'

'Uhuh.' I felt a burning pain, like an impending stomach upset. 'What else?'

'The following,' Helleve said, in business-like fashion. 'One of our undercover officers has sent in a report about a meeting with one of his informants, in which he says…' He picked up a sheet of paper from his desk and read aloud: '"My contact passed on a persistent rumour among the villains that for several months there'd been a contract out on Varg Veum, a private de-tective – business address, Strandkaien 2 – and the man behind the contract was a previously mentioned B. Bjelland, currently in Bergen Prison."'

'Business address?' I mumbled. 'Impressive.'

'Nonetheless a serious matter, Veum, to those whom it may concern.'

'The *whom* is me, I take it?'

'Yes.'

26

Annemette Bergesen and Atle Helleve regarded me sombrely, as though they themselves had delivered this apparent death sentence.

'This is the sort of crime we take very seriously, Veum,' Helleve said. 'We'll do everything in our power to put an end to this contract.'

'Hence … your man at Haukeland?'

Helleve nodded. 'Hence that too.'

I opened my palms. 'Actually, I've been living with this since September last year, when I was in Oslo working on a case that became a great nuisance to one of Birger Bjelland's – what shall I call him? – business associates there.'

'So, you've known, in other words?'

'I overheard a conversation while I was there, but … as nothing happened, I dismissed it as an empty threat. A downside of the profession, one might say. It wasn't by any means the first.'

'Look at it from another angle, Veum. I doubt his desire to finish the job has diminished in the meantime. After all, you more or less single-handedly uncovered the racket that put him behind bars, hopefully for a good many years to come.'

'And it could be many more,' Bergesen added, 'if we can verify this so-called contract – and find the perpetrator.'

'They'll already have had him on the carpet,' I said. 'For failing. You'd better hoover that carpet and see if you can find any remains.'

'Let's be serious now, Veum.' Helleve leaned forward. 'Would you like us to provide some police protection?'

I had to laugh. 'Sorry, Helleve, that's the first time I've been offered that service. It wouldn't have happened in Muus's time.'

'I mean it.'

Bergesen broke in again. 'The police can't sit and watch this

unfold, Veum. Whether you like it or not, we'll have to have sur-
veillance on you for a while yet.'

'Well, if you take the night shift…'

'You may think this is a laughing matter,' she replied coolly.
'*We* do not.'

'So long as you don't encroach on my territory.'

'That reminds me.' Helleve picked up the telephone and got
the duty officer on the line. 'How's it going with the report we
asked for?'

While he was listening, I turned to Bergesen again. 'When's
the wedding, if I may ask.'

She smiled. 'By all means. Mid-June.'

'Have you got anywhere to live?'

'We're keeping an eye open. Any suggestions?'

'We'd have to put out a contract on the pensioner on the ground
floor. On the other hand, I've had him for such a long time…'

'We'll find something.'

Helleve put down the receiver. 'Off you go, Veum. One of the
officers who brought Garrido in is on duty. You could chat to
him, if need be.'

'Thank you. Right then, I'll…' I made a move to leave.

'Fine. Don't forget what we said. And don't hesitate to
contact us if anything occurs.'

'Thank you for your attention, as the bride said on her
wedding night.' I winked at Annemette Bergesen. 'No reference
to you. On this occasion.'

'So kind.'

I went to the door. 'See you again, I'm afraid. Bergen's a very
small town, as you'll soon come to realise.'

When I was downstairs again, I found Ristesund, the duty
officer, waiting for me. He was well-built with a reddish-brown
moustache, fair hair and a sunny disposition. 'I heard you were
asking after me, Veum.'

'Well, not you personally, but if it was you who brought in Fernando Garrido for breach of the peace over the Palm Sunday weekend, I would like a few words with you, yes.'

He looked askance at me. 'Has the sister-in-law engaged your services – the lawyer? There are no problems, I trust.'

'An ever-so-small compensation case? No, no. If you're nervous about possible legal moves, I can put your mind at rest. But … is there somewhere private we can talk?'

'Yes, in there.' He pointed to an office at the back. 'I'll just…' He leaned over his grey-haired colleague at the reception desk and picked up the log. 'Now let me see. Here it is. Sunday, fourth of April, 00.40. "Man, forty years of age, brought in for breach of peace. Night patrol called after neighbour's complaint. Man resisted with such force he had to be cuffed and then put in drunk cell. File number" … Well.' He peered up at me. 'I've already copied the report. We can have a look at it in there. Cup of coffee?'

I didn't want to risk it. It might ruin my good impression. 'No, thanks. I've just…'

We entered the tiny, sparely furnished office. Ristesund sat down at the narrow desk along one wall, cast a glance at the screensaver on the computer, swivelled round on the chair and indicated the visitor's chair by the door. He passed me the typed report, signed by himself and a colleague called Bolstad. 'You can't take this with you, but you can skim through it, so you've seen it.'

The report was about as minimalist as the office we were sitting in. All it could add to what I already knew was that Fernando Garrido – identified here by his full name, date of birth and address – had been 'roaring drunk', that his wife – identified here as Bodil Breheim – had seemed 'indignant and agitated', that the police patrol unit summoned had done 'every-thing in its power' to calm tempers but Garrido had 'resisted our

intervention with such force that ultimately we found ourselves
forced to handcuff him and take him to a drunk cell'. It also said
a 'charge of assaulting a police officer' might be pending and that
Fernando Garrido had 'on his own initiative' called a solicitor,
Berit Breheim, 'his sister-in-law incidentally', and he had been
released.

'Any further developments in this case?' I asked.

Ristesund stroked his moustache for a while and shrugged.
'Not as far as I know. It's up to our solicitor to consider the
charge, of course. But it was nothing serious, and as the individual concerned had a clean record and no previous involvement
with the police, I assume the case will be shelved. I mean ...
Bolstad and I are not exactly wimps, so he didn't represent a real
threat.'

'In other words, he didn't injure either of you?'

'Does it look like it?' Ristesund grinned.

'Did you get an inkling of what might've caused the row?'

'No, but we know who we're dealing with. He was pretty
drunk and out of it. She seemed quite stressed. I think I wrote
"indignant" in the report. Either he was jealous, or vice versa.
That's what often—'

'Vice versa? Was there anything to suggest she'd started the
whole business?'

'No, no. I didn't mean it like that. These cases are often about
jealousy. Or her spending too much money on clothes and stuff.
Or generally that they shouldn't have moved in together. The
usual. Then Pops gets plastered, Mumsy gets a sock in the kisser,
and the following day they're all lovey-dovey again.'

'Are you telling me there were signs she'd been punched?'

He mulled that one over. 'No, not that I can recall. However,
she wasn't strip-searched. If you saw some of the photos we have
in the archives, pictures of wife-beating victims, your spine
would run cold, Veum. The face might be fine, forearms too,

everything outwardly visible, but when they're in casualty and they have to strip … Bruising everywhere. Cigarette burns. Cuts from knives or razor blades.' He grimaced. 'What some people have to put up with. You'd think there was no limit.'

'But in this case you had no suspicions?'

'No, but what I'm saying…'

'Yes?'

'…is that everything's possible. Why don't you ask her yourself? Or ask her sister to talk to her?'

'That's exactly the point. We can't talk to them.'

'To who?'

'Bodil Breheim and her husband. They've simply gone missing.'

He gazed at me in astonishment. 'What do you mean? Has this been reported to the police?'

I shook my head. 'This is where I come into the picture. There could be a rational explanation. They may've reasoned that they should go on holiday together to make amends. Garrido's just thrown in his job and must've had some holiday owed to him.'

'Well, that's probably what's happened then.'

'It wouldn't be the first time, would it.'

Ristesund mumbled into his moustache: 'I could tell you stories, Veum. A few months ago, we hauled in a fella for more or less the same thing. Him and his old lady were fighting like cat and dog, and the last thing she shouted before we led him into the police van was: "Lock him up for good. I don't want to see him again." And who came to the cell early next morning, dolled up like I don't know what with a packed suitcase in tow? What about the charter trip to the Canaries then? Surely he hadn't forgotten? She had the tickets with her and they were like a couple of turtle doves on their way to the waiting taxi. So' – he opened his palms – 'they're probably down on the Med having a good time, this Fernando and his señora.'

'Let's hope so, Ristesund.'

He felt a dull throb at the back of his head. The headache was coming back.

As I left the police station, there was just one thing that bothered me: why was it that whenever someone was certain there was a rational explanation for everything, I was even more convinced of the opposite?

27

I needed some fresh air.

What about a trip to Morvik? I wondered. For all I knew, they could even have returned home.

I fetched my car from Øvre Blekevei. Before leaving, I tried once again to contact Berit Breheim, but the secretary said, with regret in her voice, that she still wasn't back.

'But is she getting my messages?' I insisted.

'I'll make a note that you've called again,' she replied, with a weariness in her voice now.

It was a mild April day with variable cloud, a pleasant southerly breeze and only a gentle hint of rain in the air. When I reached the top end of Hesthaugvegen, the fjord lay below me, motionless, squeezed between the mainland and the island of Askøy. A sole freighter was cutting a narrow channel through the warp and weft, heading north along the coast.

I drove down to the sign warning visitors this was a *PRIVATE ROAD*. The garage door was locked this time too. There was no car outside and no one reacted when I rang the bell. But I didn't go in. Instead, I followed the gravel path around the house. Unless I was much mistaken, I had seen a boathouse roof the last time I was here.

I was right. From the terrace in front of the cabin some steep stairs led down to the sea. The boathouse faced the bay to the north. To the west a concrete pontoon protruded from the land. On the edge stood a man in a green angler's hat, holding a fishing rod and staring out to sea. It was only when I had descended so far down the stairs that he could hear the sound of my shoes on the uneven concrete that he turned his head. It was Sjøstrøm, the nosy neighbour.

I strolled over to him. 'Any bites?'

He nodded toward the yellow plastic bucket next to him. 'Few.'

I looked inside. There were two adult cod and one that had barely reached confirmation age.

He glanced at me with curiosity. 'Any news?'

'I'd hoped *you* had some.'

'Me?'

'Yes. That you'd tell me they were back, I mean.'

'Oh?'

'You haven't seen anything of them?'

'No, I—' There was a sudden tug on the line. He pulled up the rod, pleased to see it straining, and started reeling in the line. 'This one feels good ... Veum, wasn't it?'

'Yes.'

'Hang around and I'll give you one for dinner, free.'

'Can you eat them then?'

'I'll say you can. There's such a strong current here that they're top class. I can guarantee you that. They contain just enough phosphorus for you to find your todger in the night to have a pee.'

'Mhm…'

I stood watching as he skilfully landed the greyish-brown cod, which, as far as I could judge, weighed about a kilo. With seasoned hands, he broke its neck, then chucked it into the bucket with the others. 'Watch out, you lot. Your uncle's here.'

I nodded toward the boathouse. 'I assume that belongs to Breheim and Garrido, does it?'

'Yes, but they haven't put their boat in the sea yet.'

'You don't have one yourself?'

'No, I…' He elegantly cast his line into the sea again. 'I used to have one, but when I got divorced, I couldn't afford it anymore.'

'Hm, I know the problem.'

'I'll get myself a little rowing boat or something. I can moor it over there.' He pointed to a mooring line on the rock south of the pontoon. 'You almost have to have a boat when you live somewhere like this.' With a sweep of his head he indicated the coast and smiled with pleasure. 'Lots of free lunches out there, Veum. Makes a big difference to your monthly budget.'

'You don't know where they keep the boathouse key, do you?'

'Feel under the cladding. I may be wrong, but I think there's a spare key on a nail by one of the concrete supports. I seem to remember watching Garrido look there.'

'I'll take a peek.'

'Do that.'

'Hope the fish bite.'

'Woo-hoo!' This time the rod bent in an arc and he concentrated on it again. 'Drop by for your dinner, after.'

'Thanks.'

I went back to the boathouse. The door on the side was secured with a standard Yale lock. I followed Sjøstrøm's advice and felt under the cladding behind the concrete posts. My fingers found a small plastic bag attached to a nail. I coaxed it off, opened the bag and took out the key. Then I opened the side door. Before going in, I saw Sjøstrøm land a big, fat cod.

The boathouse was empty. At any rate, there wasn't a boat inside. The carriage it had been on was at one end and rusty rails led under the front gate to the sea. There was a ladder against the back wall. On another wall there was a variety of fishing equipment: nets, traps and buoys – in good condition, but barely used, from what I could establish. Several cans of boat varnish and paint, some empty boxes and a quantity of plastic bags containing all sorts of things made up the rest of the inventory in the freezing cold shed, where the water lapped in and out under the gate.

I looked around. There was nothing special to take note of beyond what I had already seen. In a corner there were a few empty bottles, beer and Coke. One Coke bottle contained a transparent liquid. I unscrewed the cap and sniffed warily. Turpentine. I screwed the cap back on.

My head was pounding. There was a crowbar at the back of my skull. Was someone trying to break in? Or out? I had to sit down and grab the nearest box. I felt dizzy and unwell. The boat was gone. The car was gone. The house was empty. In a way, it seemed as though Bodil Breheim and Fernando Garrido had never existed.

With a heavy head, I stood up and went back out into daylight. I left the door open behind me and ambled over to the pontoon. Sjøstrøm glanced in my direction, stared straight ahead, only to turn back to me as if he had read something terrible on my face.

'No boat.'

He looked at me in surprise. 'Really? There wasn't a boat inside?'

'If you don't believe me, go look for yourself.'

'Hold this for a mo…' He passed me his rod and did as instructed.

I took his rod and slowly reeled in while he walked to the boathouse and stepped inside. The empty lure came back just before he returned. I cast the line out again. I had never had much luck fishing.

He came up beside me. 'You were right,' he said, and I refrained from making a comment. Then he took the rod and cast the line again, further, with a ruminative expression on his face. 'The only explanation I can imagine is that they must've sold it last autumn, when I was away for a fortnight down south.'

'Or you would've seen, you mean?'

He nodded. 'Definitely.'

'What if they've taken it out? Or they went away in it over Easter?'

He scanned the sea, and I followed his gaze, as though the

answer lay somewhere out there. He slowly shook his head. 'It was a beautiful Easter, I'll give you that, but … No. It's too early in the year. A day trip, OK, but not for any longer, not for weeks like this…'

I sighed. 'Well, anyway, I don't really know where to look next. How long did you say you'd lived here, Sjøstrøm?'

He was slowly reeling in. 'Since seventy-eight, seventy-nine. We'd just got married. Ten years later it was finito. The marriage, I mean.'

'So you've been alone for almost four years?'

'A small anniversary next year, Veum. Can you imagine?'

'I've celebrated quite a few of them, Sjøstrøm. You're definitely not alone in that boat.'

'No, you may well be right.'

'My understanding from the last time we spoke is that contact between you and your neighbours had never been the warmest.'

'Well, as I said before, they took our view away when they built up there.' He nodded toward the cliff behind the boathouse. 'But it wasn't all bad of course. We shared expenses on the road down to our properties. There were things that had to be done once in a while. Gravel, drainage etc. You know, neighbourly things.'

'What about your wife?'

'My ex?'

'Yes? Two women living next door to each other like her and Bodil Breheim…'

He arched his eyebrows and snorted. 'Women living next door to each other? Nice one. My problem was that my wife was never at home. She was working all hours. No wonder we never had any children. We barely had enough time to produce them. That's your new woman, Veum. Ask an expert. Career is everything, family nothing. A bloody feminist, that's what she was.'

'I'm sure…'

'And Bodil wasn't much better.'

'In what respect?'

'Well, with all her gentlemen visitors.'

'Surely it wasn't that bad?'

'Oh, no? I told you last time. There was the saxophonist. And then there was…'

'I was talking to Hallvard Hagenes. He'd only been here once, he said.'

'Possibly, but I saw the other guy several times.'

'And you're sure he was coming to see her?'

'No one else lives down here.'

'I was thinking he might have been visiting Garrido.'

'Bloody funny then that he never came when Garrido was at home, eh?'

'Ye-es…'

Again, he faced the sea. And, once again, he cast out the line.

'Well, I'd better be off.'

'But…' He nodded toward the bucket. 'I promised you a dinner.'

I peered down at the fish. One was still gasping for air, like a heavyweight boxer hanging over the ropes after the final, definitive count. 'I'll pass on this, Sjøstrøm. Next time maybe.'

'There may never be a next time, Veum. The future is a pig in a poke.'

He was proved to be right. The future was a pig in a poke.

28

Returning to the cabin, I discovered I was no longer the only person wishing Bodil Breheim and Fernando Garrido were back home. Someone had parked a black Audi Quattro right behind my car, and standing by the entrance was Kristoffersen from TWO, looking as though he could tear down the door with his bare hands.

Catching sight of me didn't exactly sweeten his mood. 'Veum!' he barked. 'What the hell are you doing here?'

I approached him with caution. 'I could ask you the same question.'

He turned to me, puffing his chest out to its full breadth, took a cigarette and lit it. Full of disdain, he blew the smoke in my direction. 'I need to speak to Garrido.'

'You're not the only one.'

'No? Well, this is important.'

'How so, if I might ask?'

'We have unfinished business.'

'Indeed? Concerning what?'

He gesticulated. 'You can't just walk out of a company like Trans World Ocean and expect to have no further obligations. There are piles of unfinished jobs on his desk. And who got bloody landed with them, do you think?'

'So now you want to him to do short-term casual work?'

'He quit his job without giving us any notice, Veum. As if the very devil were after him.'

'That devil wasn't you, was it?'

He swelled out his chest again. 'And what do you mean by that?'

'I mean … You don't strike me as one of the kindest men in the world.'

'And what the fuck's that got to do with you?'

I formed a circle with my right thumb and first finger and

held it up. 'This much, Kristoffersen. So long as this isn't the cause of his disappearance.'

He narrowed his eyes. 'Have you found out where he's staying?'

I pretended to give the matter some thought. 'Right now there are signs he may've gone to sea.'

'To sea?'

I nodded towards the open water. 'Their boat isn't here anyway.'

'Oh, yes?'

'They've probably anchored in Utvik.'

'Utvik?' His face darkened. 'What the hell are you saying, Veum?'

'I don't know if you remember. When we had our cosy little chat before the weekend, I asked you if Garrido's disappearance could have anything to do with the *Seagull*.'

A certain nervousness seemed to have him in its grip. The cigarette protruded from between his lips like a diving board, and his jaw muscles were churning. 'The *Seagull*?'

'It's due in Utvik, isn't it?'

He hesitated. 'Err...'

'Well, that was why Garrido quit, wasn't it?'

He came closer. I could see him clenching his fists, and they were on the large side. I noticed that the first time we met. Nevertheless, I held his gaze. I reasoned that he would be giving himself away if he opted for fisticuffs.

'Tell me, Veum, who is paying for your services, actually?'

'Didn't I mention that last time we met? The family.'

'Garrido's?'

'No, Bodil's. Her sister.'

'You mean Berit?'

'Yes, I mean Berit. Do you know her?'

He snorted with irritation. 'And what's she after? The moon and the stars?'

'What?'

'She's a lawyer, isn't she? They never move a centimetre unless there's profit in it.'

'Unlike your kind, you mean?'

'Unlike bollocks, Veum.'

'I'd like to return to—'

'Me too. When you meet Garrido, Veum. If you meet him…'

'You aren't sure either, I can hear.'

'Do me a favour and pass on the following message: his old colleague Kristoffersen would like to see him, in private. And tell him not to do anything hasty because if he does…'

'If he does…?'

He swivelled on his heel. Strode to the front door, raised his foot and kicked it. Then he turned back to me. 'If he does, I'll come out here and tear his house down over his head. Tell him that. And I'll do it single-handed. I won't need any help.'

'Clarity itself. I'll give you that.'

'Will you pass that on?'

'I'll consider it. On the other hand … You're not actually my employer, Kristoffersen. How much are you willing to pay?'

'Tell me the price, Veum.'

'More than you can offer, I'm afraid.'

'Oh, yes?' His eyes were full of contempt.

'An honest face and a good heart.'

'You're a cheapskate, I can hear.'

'So cheap you can't afford me,' I replied.

For a second or two we stood glaring at each other. Then he gave Garrido's door a last kick, turned and marched straight to his car. For an instant I feared he was going to give my Toyota the same treatment, but he did the opposite. He ignored it completely, got behind the wheel of his Audi, started the engine and reversed out of the drive and up to the main road without so much as a farewell nod. I was deeply offended. I had tears in my eyes all the way back to Bergen.

29

At the third attempt I got Berit Breheim on the line. I was back in my office, and there wasn't a single message on the answerphone.

'I was just about to ring you,' she said, after I had been put through to her.

'Then I've saved the firm a couple of kroner.'

'In fact, I've been out all day. Lots of meetings and on top of that….'

'Yes?'

'My half-brother, Randolf, rang. He was in town and wanted to have lunch with me.'

'Right. Your mother mentioned she was expecting him home when I spoke to her. Is he staying up there?'

'With Sara? Yes.'

'So you had lunch together?'

'Yes, we … He was worried about Bodil too. Sara had told him of course – as you'd told her. He and Bodil had kept in touch for years, he said, but it had been more sporadic recently, and he hadn't heard anything from her since Christmas.'

'Since Christmas?'

'Yes, he'd received a Christmas card, but that was it.'

'Hm.'

'But…' She shifted tone. 'How are things with you? I heard you'd had an accident?'

'Yes. I was hit by a car down by the Kjøttbasar. I'm afraid I'm not completely over it yet.'

'How awful for you. It was an accident, I assume?'

'I really hope so. If not, they failed.'

She hesitated. 'So, what are you intending to do now?'

'To be frank, I don't know. I've just come back from Morvik. It transpires their boat has gone as well. But the neighbour thinks it might have been sold. Last autumn.'

'I see.'

'There's something I still have to check out. Fernando's family in Spain.'

'Yes, I'd been thinking about that, so I've already done it.'

'I thought you said…'

'I did, but they've been missing so long, I rang his brother. I skirted round the subject though. I pretended Bodil and Fernando were on holiday somewhere in the sun, but hadn't left their address with anyone. And asked if they'd dropped by. But no luck. They definitely hadn't been to Barcelona.'

'What's his brother's name?'

'Don't you trust me?' she snapped.

'Yes, I do, I certainly do … but just to be on the safe side.'

'Eduardo Garrido.' She gave me his telephone number too. 'If you do ring, please be careful what you say. The relationship between the two families is sensitive enough as it is.'

'What do you mean?'

'Well, the usual stuff. Mostly a gigantic cultural difference. As I'm sure you appreciate.'

'Yes, perhaps. Well, I think we've played most of our cards for the moment. The only one I have left is the link between Trans World Ocean and Garrido's sudden departure. A colleague of his up there, a certain herr Kristoffersen, is keen to get in touch as well. And I'd like to have a few more words with Bernt Halvorsen. I may try an old strategy and visit him at home. People of his inclinations are more vulnerable there.'

'That was why you surprised me at home the other evening, was it?' It was a casual comment, but I could hear the testy undertone.

'Sorry. You've seen through me.'

'Report back to me as soon as you have something new.'

'You're not easy to get hold of.'

'Try anyway.'

After ringing off, I made a note of a new name on my pad: Randolf Breheim. Bernt Halvorsen's name was already there. I put an exclamation by the former and underlined the latter, not that that signified anything except that both were worth some kind of attention.

Once again, it struck me how restricted my options were in cases like this. If I had been the police, I could have requisitioned passenger lists from Flesland Airport, the ferries and even the railways. In this way I could have confirmed whether Bodil Breheim and Fernando Garrido had been on any of them. I could have contacted Telenor and would have been given print-outs of calls: who they had rung and who had called them. As a private investigator I had little else but myself and my extremely limited imagination. What was more, my head was in a sorry state at the moment after hitting the cobblestones on Wednesday morning.

The way I felt, though, it was an advantage to work by telephone. I dialled Sara Breheim's number. A youthful man's voice answered: 'Breheim here.'

'Ah, hello. Varg Veum here. Am I talking to Randolf Breheim?'

'You are.'

'I'm investigating the disappearance of your half-sister, Bodil.'

'So I've heard.'

'Would it be possible to have a chat with you?'

'Regarding what?'

'Bodil first and foremost.'

'We-ell, I don't see how I could contribute anything.'

'Leave that to me. When could we meet?'

'I'm busy today, but … early tomorrow maybe? There are a few things I have to do in town.'

'A cup of coffee at the Ervingen, half past nine – would that suit you?'

'Mm ... fine. But don't get your hopes up. I haven't had much contact with Bodil for years.'

'Every little helps. See you tomorrow.'

'Ervingen. Nine-thirty. OK. Bye.'

'Bye.'

I sat staring at the telephone. Then I stared at the clock. Bernt Halvorsen was undoubtedly one of those people who worked long hours. But around children's TV time even the most obsessive top manager was back home to check their little sweethearts still had eyes to see with, so long as they were focused on the TV screen and not demanding too much from him. Afterwards he could go back to the office or lock himself in his study, if it wasn't one of the days when his wife dragged him to the theatre, a wine club, the cinema or whatever other activity he couldn't stand. Long ago, in my child-welfare days, I had seen the saddest outcomes from this form of family life, and I didn't exactly have the impression the climate at the top of industry had improved since.

As it was Thursday, it was potato dumplings and salt-cured meat two floors below me. I had my dinner there in the company of a retired pastor, who told me about his special interest in the composition of psalms, then we both immersed ourselves in a newspaper, his naturally enough the Christian *Dagen*, mine a far more dubious organ. Afterwards the pastor went his own way, apparently to an evening concert in the Holy Cross Church. As for me, I fetched my car and drove to Hopsneset, where I arrived more or less in the middle of children's TV.

When Edvard Grieg settled in Trondhaugen in the mid-1880s, it was, by the standards of the day, way out in the sticks. Now the property was encircled by motorways and modern construction sites, and the once-so-peaceful Lake Nordås was only a partially restored sewage pool, surrounded by an increasing quantity of densely built housing estates and criss-crossed by speedboats in the summer. So much for Grieg's lyrical *To Spring*.

In Hopsneset people lived in secluded majesty, a few of them descendants of the original population, by far the majority of them new arrivals with bank accounts awash with money, the kind that won't dry up before the Apocalypse.

I found Bernt Halvorsen in a house with a concrete-and-glass façade and gable walls of natural stone, behind a picket fence and up a drive laid with crushed marble, appropriately enough, as Marble Island wasn't far away. It was his wife who opened the door; a reserved, kindly woman with blonde hair, slim glasses and a surprised expression on her face. It struck me instantly: I had seen her before, last week somewhere.

'Fru Halvorsen?'

'Yes?'

'My name's Veum. Is Bernt Halvorsen in?'

'What's it about?'

'Business, I'm afraid.'

'He's reading to the children at the moment.'

I was wrong about one thing. He was, perhaps, a better father than I had initially anticipated.

I looked past her, into the large hallway. 'It's not possible to interrupt?'

'How important is it?'

'It's about a ship. If you could slip a message through to him. Tell him Veum is back, as arranged, to talk about the *Seagull*.'

'I see. Can't it wait until tomorrow?'

'What's he reading that's so difficult to interrupt?'

'*The Brothers Lionheart* by Astrid Lindgren.'

'Ahh…' I looked at my watch. 'I can wait then, until today's bedtime story is over. What do you do for a living?'

'I'm a lawyer,' she said in a chill tone.

'Right, so you probably know Berit Breheim, do you?'

She rolled her eyes. 'I was up against her in court a few days ago.'

'Ah, that's where it was. I knew I'd seen you before. You were the opposing counsel.'

She studied me. 'Exactly. You were speaking to Berit, I remember that now.'

'Are you on first-name terms?'

'Of course. It's only in court we're on opposing sides, sometimes. We're both defence counsels.'

'But in this case she was on the wrong side, in your view?'

'Absolutely. He didn't exactly make a likeable impression, her client, did he.'

'He did not. I agree. I was on your side too.'

From inside the house someone called her. She sent me an apologetic glance. 'They may've finished now. I'll go and see.'

To be on the safe side, she closed the door behind her and left me standing on the doorstep. I turned my back to the house. A tidy lawn, not mown yet this season. Spring flowers in full bloom, daffodils and crocuses, tulips and rhododendrons in bud, rose bushes with green shoots. A few fruit trees and some berry bushes. A swing and a climbing frame. The perfect idyll. A beautiful place to grow up.

The door behind me opened. Bernt Halvorsen stood in the doorway like a bouncer. 'Veum?' he said, with a face that said I wasn't getting in, even with some fake proof of age; he had already seen through me.

'Yes, hello. Nice that we can have a chat.'

'I do not intend to have a chat, as you put it. What the hell do you mean by coming here and disturbing me at home?'

'You yourself told me, via your kind watchdog in Kokstad, that I should drop by another day. So here I am.'

'Listen, Veum—'

'Out of consideration for your wife, I didn't say a word about Bodil Breheim.'

'Bodil Bre—' He stepped out of the house, pulled the door to behind him and said in a low, intense voice: 'And what the fuck's that supposed to mean? What are you trying to insinuate?'

I hesitated. My headache was back. I was having difficulty gathering my thoughts. 'Listen, Halvorsen,' I said wearily, 'the following facts are indisputable: Fernando Garrido chucked in his job. All of a sudden. The night before Palm Sunday he ended up in a drunk tank after some disturbance at home, after you visited them on the Saturday morning.'

'What?!'

'Now he's disappeared. Both him and Bodil. And I have a reliable witness who saw you, not just that Saturday, but several times before, at their house. While Garrido himself was away. Does that give me a reason to ask you questions?'

'A reliable witness?'

'Yes.'

For a moment I could see he was hesitating. Then he said: 'OK. I'll admit the following: one – yes, Fernando Garrido did quit at TWO, very suddenly, but that wasn't my choice. Quite the opposite.'

'Aha?'

'Two – yes, I was at their place on the Saturday you mention. Not to visit Bodil, as you suggest, but to get Fernando to change his mind. We needed him. He does a good job.'

'But he declined?'

'Yes.'

'Why was that, do you think?'

'He didn't give a reason, but he seemed very determined, almost a bit...'

'Yes?'

'Well, he seemed nervous somehow, and he reacted very emotionally when I tried to press him.'

'Sure it wasn't the fact that you visited his wife while he was away that he reacted to?'

He raised his voice a notch. '*Three* – I was never at Bodil and Fernando's when he wasn't there.'

'My witness claims the opposite.'

'Your witness is lying.'

'Garrido came back unexpectedly that Saturday, didn't he.'

'Unexpectedly? I arrived there a little before he did. That's all there was to it.'

'Oh, yes?'

'Yes!'

'My word against theirs, it's called in court.'

'We aren't in court now.'

'No.'

He glowered at me. 'My wife said … you mentioned one of our ships.'

'Yes, the *Seagull*. She's docked in Hamburg, hasn't she?'

'Maybe. What's so interesting about the *Seagull*?'

'I'd guess you know that better than I do, Halvorsen.'

He met my eyes with a flinty stare. 'I have no idea what you're referring to.'

'It'll come out at some point.'

'Tell me, Veum, who do you work for?'

'That's the question Kristoffersen asked me.'

'Kristoffersen?'

'He's looking for Garrido too.'

'Not without reason, if he is. Garrido's left a lot of unfinished jobs. If he stands by his decision to leave, we'll need to check him thoroughly before he walks out the door. You can't just leave.'

'Bodil's family is also wondering what's become of them. So you can't help?'

'All I can imagine is that they've gone on a long, undeserved holiday.'

'Oddly enough, that's what everyone says. But no one's received a postcard, and they didn't tell anyone where they were going. Strange, don't you think?'

'Very. Was there anything else you wanted?'

'No, unless you have any more to say.'

'Goodnight, Veum. If I ever see you again, it'll be too soon,' he said, opening the door and stepping inside.

Before he managed to close it completely, I shot: 'Don't count your chickens.'

But he had already locked the door on me. He wasn't interested in what I had to say either. Another wasted trip. All I had gained from it was a headache.

30

Before meeting Randolf Breheim the following day, I went up to my office to check the answerphone and riffle through whatever post there was.

On the answerphone there was a hasty message from Torunn Tafjord: '*The* Seagull *has left Hamburg. I'm in pursuit. Contact you on arrival in Bergen.*' I imagined her following the ship, like a seagull, over the North Sea. If she wasn't athletically paddling a canoe, that is.

The post didn't contain much more than bills, which I put on the pile, neatly organised according to due date. The top ones were well overdue, but I assumed it would be a week or two before the first debt collectors came knocking at my door. What I really needed was a nice, meaty job with regular payments. Perhaps I ought to send Berit Breheim my first invoice before she changed her mind.

I took the first newspaper of the day down with me to the Ervingen, paid for a cup of coffee and five waffle hearts and found a seat by a window. On page two I found an article written by the Bergen Police. They were searching for 'witnesses to a traffic accident on the Kjøttbasar/market square intersection at 8.55 am on Wednesday, 21st April.' It said further that 'a man in his fifties was hit by a car coming from the market square towards Bryggen.' To my relief, I was able to confirm that 'the man was discharged from hospital with minor injuries the following day', but the police were still interested in talking to 'any eye-witnesses of the incident'.

A man with a trim, red beard, dark hair and a fresh complexion approached my table. At once I saw there was something familiar about him. 'Veum?'

I nodded and we shook hands.

'Randolf. I recognised you from the courthouse.'

I quickly identified him in my mind's eye. He was one of the friends in the crowd that had gathered around the accused in the break. It struck me that here again was someone linked to the legal case his half-sister had been involved in last week, not that I could see any possible connection with the investigation I myself was carrying out.

While he went to the counter, I watched him discreetly from a distance. I thought I could see in him some of his mother's facial features, but the chin and mouth had to be the father's, a taut smile that bore hints of arrogance. He came back with a Coke and a prawn salad baguette. 'I hope he'll be fine.'

'He?'

'Terje, of course. They pass sentence today, at three. But he'll be acquitted.'

'Are you sure?'

He took a bite from the baguette and swallowed before answering. 'If every woman you end up in bed with dragged you off to court, where would we be, eh? The only winners would be the lawyers.'

'And among them your half-sister.'

'Well, I'm sure she can manage perfectly well without my help.'

'But it was you who got her this case, was it?'

'I recommended Terje contact her, yes.' He grinned. 'You know … A female defence counsel in rape cases … is probably not a stupid idea, is it.'

'Probably not. How did you know Terje though? What's the rest of his name?'

'Terje? Terje Nielsen. I've known him since we were boys. His uncle, Kåre Brodahl, worked in my father's shop. And then we found ourselves in the same school. Upper secondary. Tank upper secondary.'

'So he already knew Berit too?'

'He knew about her, of course. But, you know, Berit's – what is it? – thirteen years older than us. When we were school pals, she'd long flown the nest.'

'What's the relationship like between you and your brother and your two half-sisters?'

He shrugged. 'Very, very good. We arrived in two batches, as you know, but my mother was very keen not to make any distinctions, so she didn't favour Bodil and Berit over Rune and me.'

'Favour?'

'Yes, pay more attention to. Give permission to go on holiday alone, that kind of thing. If we so much as grumbled, she would always say: "We should feel sorry for them. Don't forget that, boys. They lost their mother under such tragic circumstances."' He gently imitated his mother's way of speaking.

'But they were quite a bit older than you, as you point out yourself.'

'Yeah, yeah. I'm not complaining. Don't get me wrong.'

'And later? As adults. Are you still in contact?'

'Yes and no. I've been in Svalbard the last few years, and before that I was in Trondheim. There are family reunions and so on, of course. Even Rune I don't see that much anymore, except at the reunions. He's got a wife and kids. I'm single and fancy-free.'

'I've sort of gathered that.'

'You were mostly interested in Bodil, I gather.' He eyed me sceptically. 'She and Ferdinand are supposed to have gone missing?'

'Fernando, I think he's called.'

'I know. But we thought Ferdinand was much funnier.'

'Ah, I see. Well, I don't know if they've disappeared or they've gone travelling without telling anyone.'

'They must know at Fernando's workplace, surely?'

'He quit.'

'What? From TWO?'

'Yes, has that come as a surprise?'

'Inasmuch as … What else can he do? Or has he been head-hunted?'

'Maybe. I have no idea. How well did you know him?'

'Not very. We were at their wedding, of course. Grand affair. He has a dead classy sister, by the way. But I'm not much good at Spanish, and her English was pretty bad, so we … well.' He smiled in a way that perhaps was supposed to seem secretive. To me it seemed more sheepish. 'There was a whole delegation up from Spain, but they kept a careful eye on each other. I don't think they were interested in any further alliances.'

'So nothing for you?'

'Not of any duration, no.'

'How's your contact been with Bodil lately?'

'Not so good. In fact, I don't think I've seen her – or Fernando – since Christmas eighteen months ago.'

'But Berit said you and Bodil were in contact a lot earlier?'

'Earlier, yes. She was closer in age, of course, so she lived at home for longer than Berit. And consequently had a kind of big-sister feeling for both Rune and me. At any rate, she was very good at writing to me during my Trondheim years. When I was in Svalbard at first, too. But then her communication petered out, bit by bit. It wasn't a sudden end. The intervals between letters became longer and longer. And I have to confess that I wasn't very good at replying either. So, it was my fault as much as hers.'

'This Fernando Garrido. What impression did you have of him?'

He put the last piece of the baguette in his mouth, washed it down with a mouthful of Coke and took his time. 'Well, I'm not sure I had any impression. He was a bit stiff. When we discussed

things, he sometimes seemed quite obstinate. He was a foreigner, Veum. You just have to say it as it is. My opinion has
always been that birds of a feather works best.'

'In other words, you weren't hugely in favour of this marriage?'

'Does it make any difference? My sisters – half-sisters – live
their own lives. They can marry whoever they like as far as I'm
concerned, as long as it's not another woman.'

'Oh, you wouldn't like that?'

'No, because ... Would you?'

'I don't have any sisters.'

'No, but in theory.'

'Well...' I took another sip of coffee instead of answering and
examined my little notepad. 'Kåre Brodahl, you said. Is he still
alive?'

He frowned. 'Kåre Brodahl. Of course he is. Why do you
ask?'

'Mm, I made a note when you mentioned it. And he was employed by your father?'

'He's still working in the same line of business, I think.'

'Where?'

He gave me the name of a gentlemen's outfitter in
Strandgaten. 'You could buy a suit there. You look as if you could
do with one.'

I ignored the comment and thumbed back through my notes.
'Just one last thing ... You have an aunt – Solveig, is that right?'

He appeared even more taken aback. 'Yes?' Then he grinned.
'Tell me, do you suspect Kåre Brodahl and Aunty Solveig are in
cahoots and have kidnapped Bodil and Ferdi ... sorry,
Fernando?' He gave a patronising laugh. 'If so, I'm afraid Berit
has employed the wrong person.'

'Possibly. Solveig Breheim?'

'Solveig Sletta. She's married.'

'But she's your father's sister?'

'Correct. Was there anything else you required?'

'Where does she live?'

'In Nye Sandviksvei, where she's lived for as long as I can remember.'

I made a note. 'Right, well … If you should remember anything else…' I gave him my business card.

He looked at it with an evident lack of interest. 'I'll consider whether to pass it on. Even if I don't have a clue what you're after.'

'No? You don't seem particularly concerned about what might've happened to your half-sister and her husband.'

'Why should I be? They've always followed their hearts. I don't imagine for a second that anything has happened to them.' He looked at his watch and stood up. 'I have to go now. I've arranged to meet Terje.'

'Are you going out to celebrate already?'

He glared at me. 'Why delay? The result is a foregone conclusion, believe you me.'

We sent each other a measured nod. I had a strong sense that the lack of enthusiasm was mutual.

I gazed out of the window. On the Bryggen side, cars droned past, without hitting anyone today, not yet anyway. The spring light rose over the town, white, remorseless. On the mountainsides the blue shimmer told us it wouldn't be long before there would be an explosion of green. It was time for a spring clean, inside and out.

After Randolf Breheim had gone, I sat over another cup of coffee, sifting through my notes. Afterwards I walked up Strandgaten to have a look at suits.

31

A gentlemen's outfitters of the decorous variety, early in the morning, at a time of the year when there are no sales, is like a hiatus in life. There is no hurry. The lighting is harsh. The men who work there are friendly, experienced and can tell your waist measurement at a glance. They address you in low, considerate voices, as though you have come into the shop to arrange a funeral. The muzak issuing from the speaker system is not calculated to annoy anyone except keen music-lovers and other sensitive souls. Here even Herb Alpert & the Tijuana Brass would be a provocation.

The undertaker who received me showed me down to the department on the basement floor, where Kåre Brodahl presided over a none-too shocking selection of suits in grey, brown and black. Most men below retirement age would have fled at once. I put on a good face and pretended I was interested.

Kåre Brodahl was a slim, grey-haired man in his early sixties, well dressed, his hair arranged into neat, kempt curls. He smelt of fresh after-shave and gave the impression that he had the situation totally under control. 'A suit? For everyday use?' His sceptical eyes ran down my current outfit – black leather jacket and black jeans – and clearly considered a change might be advisable.

'Mm,' I said, not to give him too much encouragement. 'Randolf Breheim recommended I come here.'

'Randolf?' He brightened up. 'That was nice of him. Is he at home?'

'He's following the trial.'

His smile faded. 'Ah, that.' His eyes narrowed. 'That's not why you're here, I hope.'

'No, no. I need a suit. But as chance would have it I've been making enquiries about some events in the distant past.'

'Oh, yes?' He unhooked a grey suit with a discreet stripe from a clothes stand. 'This one maybe?'

I sighed. 'I think I'd better try it on, hadn't I?'

'Naturally. Behind here.'

While I slipped behind the dark-blue curtain, removed my shoes, hung up my trousers and jacket and put on the grey suit, we kept our conversation going through the curtain. 'Concerning your boss, Ansgar Breheim.'

'Ansgar?'

'When his first wife died.'

There was a silence outside.

I poked my head through the gap. 'Did you hear what I said?'

He cast a disapproving glance at my bare legs. 'I did hear what you said, yes. Tell me, does it fit?'

'Yes, yes. Just a moment.' I poked my head back in, pulled on the trousers, tucked my shirt in, shrugged on the jacket, flipped on my shoes and stepped back into the room.

He didn't look convinced. 'How does it feel on?'

'Bit wide at the waist, isn't it?'

'Yes, actually it is. But we can take it in. That's no problem. The length looks good.'

'You worked in Breheim's shop, didn't you?'

'That's correct.'

'Around that time?'

'When fru Breheim died? Yes, I suppose I did.'

'That must've been a shock?'

'Was it a shock? You have to remember, herr…'

'Veum.'

'This is all quite a long time ago. The end of the fifties, wasn't it?'

'1957.'

'Exactly. A lot of water has passed under the bridge since then.'

'And you knew his second wife too?'

'Sara, yes. I knew her better than his first wife. Sara and I were work colleagues.'

'And you stayed in contact, later?'

'Contact, mm. We weren't exactly close friends. My nephew, Terje, and Randolf were pals. But I was an employee there until the shop was sold in 1983. Then I found this job here.'

'I'd like to go back to what happened when fru Breheim died.'

'Tell me – are you interested in this suit or not?'

I viewed myself in the mirror. 'I'm not sure. It's a bit formal, isn't it?'

He arched his eyebrows ironically. 'Depends on what occasions you're thinking of wearing it. As an everyday suit, it might well be a little too formal, yes. Yes, indeed. What is your work actually?'

'I'm a private investigator.'

He looked as if some food had gone down the wrong way. 'A private detective. Do they really exist?'

'One does anyway.'

He sniffed. 'And all you have to investigate is cases from thirty-five, thirty-six years ago?'

'Mm. Is there anything you can tell me about it?'

'About what happened then? No...'

His eyes. They were what he remembered best.

The gaze that seemed to return from far, far away. Ansgar Breheim sitting with his back to the wall beside the stage, a bloody serviette in front of his nose and mouth, mumbling deliriously: He just knocked me down. Flat...

And then Sara: What shall we do, Kåre?

A jab of pain in the lower back, as Ansgar sat up.

We'll have to get him to casualty. We'd better take him, we...

And, afterwards – all the rest.

But it was the eyes he remembered. That was what he would never forget.

'Well, what can I tell you? I remember Breheim coming to work on the Monday morning, his face pale, struck dumb. On Tuesday afternoon we heard the rest of the story. It came as a shock to us all, I can tell you. Fru Breheim, who was so beautiful and alive, and now she was … Like in Welhaven, you know.'

'Welhaven?'

'"Quietly swims a wild duck". Johan Sebastian Welhaven's poem about a duck. The beautiful creature, or whatever he calls it, that is fatally wounded, swims to the bottom of the sea, clamps hold of the seaweed and dies, alone.'

'Well, Tordis Breheim didn't die alone. She took someone down with her.'

'Nevertheless…'

'Were you a little smitten by fru Breheim as well, perhaps, Brodahl?'

'Smitten? Well. She was a beautiful woman. No one who met her remained unaffected. That's how she was.' His face wore a transported expression, as though it wasn't five minutes since she was last here.

I went into the fitting room to take off the suit. Where had *I* been in 1957? Could I have crossed her path, by chance, in the town centre, where the threads of lives and destinies were interwoven over decades and centuries?

When I came out, I said: 'Of course you remember her two daughters from then?'

He eyed me from a distance, still lost in his dreams. 'Yes, yes. Berit's even become a lawyer.'

'She's defending your nephew.'

'Yes.'

'You haven't been following the case?'

Again, his eyes narrowed in a way peculiar to him. 'No, why would I? It's not exactly a topic of conversation in the family. This is basically my sister's problem. And Terje's of course.'

'You mean…'

His frustration boiled over. 'For Christ's sake, it must be possible to have a woman without forcing yourself on her?'

I nodded. 'I agree with you. But Berit's clearly driven a hard line with the prosecution. By the way, they pass sentence at three today.'

'I see.'

'But what interests me most is the two sisters. Berit and Bodil. Have you had any contact with them over the years? Since their mother died, I mean.'

'Yes and no. They popped by the shop now and then, of course, and I obviously knew their stepmother. But I've already explained that.'

'Bodil, the younger of the two. Have you met her in recent years?'

He slowly shook his head. 'No, not since she was … But why are you asking about all this?'

'She may've gone missing. At least no one knows where she is. That's why I'm digging around.'

He looked at me in disbelief. 'And that's supposed to have something to do with what happened to her mother in 1957?'

'No, no, no. Not necessarily. It's just that the old story keeps rearing its head at unsolicited moments.'

'Let the dead rest in peace, Veum. That's my view of the matter.'

'Even though their spirits are abroad?'

'Their spirits are abroad?'

He looked mystified as I left, and I made no attempt to enlighten him.

32

Where was I in 1957? I asked myself again, as I left to see Solveig Sletta. I had rung her in advance. When she heard what my visit was about, she instantly invited me to her home in Nye Sandviksvei. Immediately before the Rothaug bend, she explained. 'I can put some coffee on if you like?'

'I'm already on my way.'

In 1957 I had been fifteen years old. In September, when Tordis Breheim and Johan Hagenes plunged to their deaths, I was in my second year at Bergen Katedralskole and in love with a girl called Gro, with whom I went on a bike tour to Askøy in the pouring rain. Every day I walked to school through Strandgaten, where my office is now. Every day I passed the shop where Ansgar Breheim, Kåre Brodahl and Sara Taraldsen worked. Perhaps I had even passed Tordis Breheim on the pavement a few times, so close that I could have touched her – inconceivable of course; after all she had been an adult woman and I a gauche teenager. If it were possible to run a film of our lives backward and pause it at such places, I would stop the film there, let the frame flicker, get up from my seat behind the projector, go over to the screen and study it carefully. There was still traffic going through this part of Strandgaten back then. It was only in the seventies that it was pedestrianised. Sundt & Co still had their 1889 building. People from fjord regions still walked from Nykirke quay to the Fish Market to do the shopping that could only be done in the centre of Bergen. Strandgaten was still the town's number one shopping street where every business was represented and not a single premises was empty. And there, on the pavement in front of Breheim & Co, a beautiful redhead stopped, glanced at her reflection in the shop window and straightened her hat, then pushed the door open and made her entrance, stunningly attractive as always. On the pavement behind her, I strolled in, my schoolbag under my arm, my mind everywhere else but here – on Gro or Svanhild, or whichever girl I had on a pedestal that particular week – blind to everything else, blind to the images I would so love to recall now, thirty-five or thirty-six years later.

But 1957 was a long time ago. Everyone I met who had been involved in the events of that year was in their sixties or older. Solveig Sletta was no exception. The woman who opened the door when I arrived had grey hair with a streak of gold, which suggested she could have been a Goldilocks in her younger days. She was quite small, pale, with a smooth complexion but a fine mesh of wrinkles that revealed her age. She was wearing a blue, factory-knitted dress with a little string of pearls around her neck; the only other jewellery was a wedding ring.

'Fru Sletta? My name's Veum.'

'Your call gave me such a shock. Have they really gone missing, Bodil and Fernando?'

'That's what I'm trying to ascertain.'

'OK … Come in.'

She lived in the last row of houses before Rothaugen School. On the opposite side of the street there was a building that would definitely have won a medal for the ugliest construction in Bergen. The emergency hospital run by the addiction organisation, the Blue Cross, had been erected in 1977 and would frighten off the most hard-bitten alcoholic, and perhaps that was the intention. Unlike the timber houses down in Skuteviken, by the bay, the building was as hideous as the Fylkesbygget, county hall, in Nordnes. These were memorials of an architecture over which only one sentence could be passed: the sooner they were demolished, the better. And once the demolition job was complete, Solveig Sletta would have her old panorama back.

She poured us both a coffee and sat down with her back to the window, for understandable reasons. Not even a sober person could bear to look at the emergency hospital for more than a couple of minutes at a time.

She passed me a small dish of pastries. 'Help yourself. And then tell me what's happened.'

Very briefly I put her in the picture, and finished by asking the usual question: 'When was the last time you spoke to Bodil, fru Sletta?'

Her eyes were bright blue and distant. 'Mm ... the last time was probably February. She used to drop by occasionally on her way to town. But otherwise I see little of her. I have my own children and grandchildren, you see, and my husband's mother is still alive, so I have a lot to do.'

'Your husband?'

'Yes. His name's Hans. He's at work. He works for the railway, in case you're interested.'

'As a train driver?' I said, mostly out of politeness.

'No, no. He's an office worker. In the planning department,' she said with emphasis, as though that was something to be proud of.

'How did she seem, Bodil, the last time you met her?'

'How did she seem? There was a sort of despair hanging over the two lasses, if you ask me.'

'Lasses? Are you referring to Bodil and Berit?'

'Yes. I still call them that.' She smiled sadly. 'I don't know if you're acquainted with what happened to their mother?'

I played possum, shook my head and said: 'No. What did happen?'

Aunty Solveig didn't need to be asked twice. 'Tordis, their mother, was – I think I can say this – a very liberal woman. One autumn day in 1957 she drove her car into the sea with a lover, up at Hjellestad, and both of them died.'

'Really?'

'Yes, and he probably wasn't the first man she'd frolicked

with. In full sail, so to speak, she could mesmerise a room. Men's eyes were glued to her, like flies to fly paper.' She raised her eyebrows archly. 'She was very attractive, there were no two ways about that, but you know what they say, Veum: beauty is only skin deep.'

'You didn't like her, I infer?'

'We shouldn't speak ill of the dead ... I felt sorry for the lasses, but nevertheless ... If you ask me, they were better off when Ansgar married again, Sara this time.'

'She was an employee in his business, wasn't she?'

'She was.'

'Could there have been something between her and your brother before the business with fru Breheim?'

'Not at all. She had a boyfriend at that time. They were as good as engaged.'

'Oh, yes?'

'Not only that, he was in the firm too.'

'Really? And who was it?'

'Kåre Brodahl, if I've remembered correctly. God knows what's happened to him. But that ended after Ansgar and Sara ... that is to say, before Ansgar and Sara ... Well, you know what I mean.'

I nodded. I did know what she meant. And I could have told her what happened to Kåre Brodahl. But I refrained.

'Let me tell you something,' she continued. 'Hans bought all his clothes at Ansgar's shop. He got a family discount, of course. He waited until the day before the big sales started and so on. I always had to go with him because men haven't got a clue about clothes.' She ran a critical eye over my outfit. 'Not Hansi, anyway. But during the first few years after Ansgar and Sara had married ... Kåre Brodahl was still an employee there. I just can't understand why he didn't hand in his cards. But enough of that. It was like stepping into the Cold War, herr Veum. Sometimes the atmosphere was so close to freezing point it must've been agony trying on clothes there.'

'Yes, I'm sure. It must've been rather a strange situation.'

'A balance of terror, I called it. And Brodahl stuck it out. He didn't quit until he had to, when Ansgar died and Sara decided to sell up. Where he is now, as I said, I have no idea.'

'But can this have anything to do with the first fru Breheim's death?'

'Nothing at all. I was looking after the children myself the weekend it happened. Sunday morning, Ansgar rang and asked if the girls could stay until the evening, and when I asked if there was anything the matter, he just said: "It's Tordis. She hasn't come home." In the evening, when he came to pick up the girls, he seemed out of it and what was more…' She put her hand to her mouth. 'His face was swollen, and black and blue, after that brute Tordis was involved with knocked him down. Can you imagine? The lover punches him, and then his wife goes off with the lover. They got what they deserved if you ask me.'

'How did the two girls take it?'

'Bodil was so small, I doubt she can even remember her mother. Berit got a little hysterical when she saw the state of her father. But they went home with him, and two days later we were told, all of us. It was as though a shock wave went through the whole family. It took us a long time to recover, some of us.'

'But your brother married quite quickly afterwards, didn't he?'

'Not until the year of mourning was up. But that was probably because of the lasses. I mean, they had to have a mother. And Ansgar wasn't cut out to be on his own.'

'You're not the first person to say that.'

'Then it must be right.'

'Earlier, you said there was still a kind of despair hanging over both Berit and Bodil.'

'Yes.' She stared into space. 'You know, neither of them has had children. Sometimes I almost feel that's what they've chosen. That they're carrying a fear inside them that they might act as selfishly towards their children as their mother did to them.'

'Such experiences can have physiological consequences too, I've heard.'

'Physio—? What do you mean?'

'That even if they wanted children with the whole of their hearts, they wouldn't be able to conceive because of the physical resistance inside them.'

'Really?' She looked at me dubiously, and I wasn't a hundred per cent convinced myself.

With that, the conversation was as good as over. Before leaving, I couldn't help but ask: 'Who did Berit marry, actually?'

Deep in her own thoughts, she said: 'Rolf. A nobody, Veum. Believe me, an absolute nobody.'

She didn't say any more, and I didn't pursue the point. It wouldn't be difficult to find out more. One telephone call to Karin Bjørge would do the trick. But when I got back to my office, I had a visitor.

33

She had sat down at the table in my waiting room, cleared away the seventies magazines, despite their collector's value, and plugged in her laptop. When I put my head round the door, she barely troubled herself to look up. At any rate she seemed to be taking her time to round off the sentence she was writing before she closed the lid, jumped up and came towards me, a small bundle of feminine energy with dark hair, oval glasses, laughter lines and an outstretched hand.

'Mr Veum, I presume?'

'And you are?'

'Torunn Tafjord. We've spoken on the phone.' The Ålesund intonation was clearer now that we were in the same room.

'Of course. Welcome to Bergen.'

She smiled as she waited for me to open the office door. Two locks. After opening the door, I said: 'Do come in. There are not many people who can be bothered to wait. They don't have the time. But I've had it for years. It's difficult to part with.' When she didn't understand, I added: 'The waiting room.'

All she had with her was the laptop and a little rucksack, the kind you carry on day-hikes. Her attire consisted of a green windcheater over a black jumper and dark-blue jeans. There was something windblown and fresh about her that reminded me of a hikers' cabin on Hardanger plateau, late in September when most other walkers have returned to the lowlands.

'Have you been waiting long?'

'About half an hour. I came on the lunchtime flight from Copenhagen. Under normal sailing conditions, the *Seagull* should be in Utvik by early tomorrow morning.'

'And what will she be carrying?'

'There's a container on deck that was hoisted on board one night in Casablanca. But perhaps just as important is this: what has she come to pick up?'

'Right. Please sit down. Shall I put on some coffee for you?'

'Do you have any tea?'

'Just teabags, I'm afraid.'

'Fine.' She grinned. 'It's better than coffee anyway.'

While I filled the kettle and found some teabags, she looked around. 'This is the first time I've been to a private detective's office. Is it a profitable business?'

'Not when you run it like I do. On principle I don't do marital affairs of any kind, and I'm sad to say I don't have the capacity to embrace industrial espionage.'

'So what do you live off?'

'I help to locate missing persons. Young people running away from home for example. Right now, there's a married couple who haven't informed their family where they are.'

'And have you discovered their whereabouts?'

'No. So now you can begin to understand why this won't make me rich.'

'Mm.'

'But I take on a number of jobs for an insurance company, with whom I have a kind of fixed arrangement. That's what keeps my head above water.'

'It's much the same for me. As a freelancer, I'm also dependent on employers who are willing to pay for what I do, and they aren't always.'

The kettle boiled, switched itself off and I poured hot water into two mugs, each with a teabag. I glanced over at her. She was standing in profile against the window, and the light from outside reflected on her photochromic lenses. She had classical facial features: straight nose, resolute chin and a slightly wry smile. Age-wise, I would have placed her in her mid-forties, but her clothes, quick movements and concentrated energy made her seem younger.

'Your geographical range is obviously greater than mine,' I said. 'At least judging by where you've rung me from.'

She smiled. 'This time at any rate. From Conakry to Bergen.'

I carried the mugs of tea to the desk, and we sat down on either side of the worn surface. 'Can you tell me what this is all about?'

She nodded, leaned forward, opened her rucksack and took out an envelope that, it transpired, held a wad of colour photographs. She pushed one of them over to me and said: 'Look at this. Dawn in Conakry.'

I studied the photograph. It showed a small harbour with palm trees in the background. A smiling African wearing a long, colourful shirt over his bright shorts was waving to the photographer. 'Was it you who took the photo?'

'Yes, that's Pierre. My local contact.'

'Pierre?'

'French is still the official language there. Lots of people still have French names.'

She pushed over the next few pictures. 'Here you can see the *Seagull* being loaded about a hundred kilometres south of Conakry.'

The photographs had been taken from quite a distance, and a couple of blurred vertical lines in the foreground revealed that she had been hiding behind reeds. A specially designed black tanker lay alongside a primitive quay. A huge loading pipe was turned towards some uneven terrain, which bore most resemblance to a colossal rubbish heap.

The *Seagull* was a self-loading tanker of 2,800 tonnes unladen weight, from the 1980s, and during recent years it had specialised in transporting chemical waste, she explained with surprising expertise. 'The shipping company has an agreement with an international disposal consortium to offload waste here, in the part of the world we have good reason to call the cradle of civilisation,' she concluded, before adding with indignant emphasis: 'It was on the African continent we climbed down from trees and spread across the plains. The first humans. Now we're returning the compliment, in the form of toxic waste, sparing our own continents.'

'Is it legal or not?'

'At an official level, there's no problem,' she said with emotion. 'Local authorities are compensated with money and expertise. Morally, of course, this is reprehensible. We all know it is, and that's why this trafficking is never spoken about. In the annual accounts it's camouflaged under a variety of headings. Ships' papers are filled out with such discretion that you would think this was about international contraband. At a government level, no one knows about it, and when the UN occasionally raises the matter, the silence from wealthy nations is eloquence itself.'

'And Norwegian companies are involved?'

'We're a seafaring nation, aren't we. Money doesn't stink. Isn't that the slogan of our times?'

'Is this what you're going to write about?'

'Yes. A commission from one of the big national newspapers. I was given the job because I'd written several reports on international environmental politics before.'

'But when you first rang me, you weren't in Conakry. You were in Casablanca.'

She gave a faint smile. 'Could you imagine a better place to be to ring a descendant of Humphrey Bogart?'

I held her eyes. 'No, not really.'

'But there was another reason.' She picked another photograph from the pile. 'Here.'

It was the same ship, but now at a different harbour, much bigger and far more modern than in the first pictures. The photograph had been taken from land, from a terrace or the top of a flat roof, and behind the ship the horizon was razor sharp.

'Look here,' she said, pointing to another photograph, taken against the light with a golden overtone. 'This is an evening shot.

The deck's empty.' She held up another photograph. 'This is from the following morning. Spot the difference.'

'I can see.' The light was whiter, the contours were sharper and there was a blue container on the deck.

'It was craned on board during the night.' She pointed to the container. 'Not long afterwards the *Seagull* was under way again.' In the next photograph we saw the ship after it had set sail. 'Next stop, Hamburg.'

'*Jawohl*. And what happened there?'

'Exactly. What did happen there? Nothing.'

'Really?'

'There was a conspicuous lack of activity. As though everyone were waiting for a sign from above. I tried to get on board, said I was a journalist and wanted to write a report about the crew's stance on the Seamen's Mission. But it was no use. The crew was from the Philippines, I was informed. They never went to the seamen's mission. And the officers? No, they're from Poland. All of them? The others don't have any time.' She threw her arms in the air. 'I had no option but to give up. But then I managed to engage a couple of the officers in conversation at a local bar ...'

'Oh, yes? How did you approach them this time? As a belly dancer?'

She sent me a phlegmatic stare. 'No, I oozed charm.'

'And what did you get out of it?'

'About the same as I told you when we spoke on Monday. They were waiting to be contacted by someone called Birger Bjelland before setting a course for Utvik.'

'Did they say that to your face? The bit about Birger Bjelland, I mean.'

'No, that was something I overheard. They were discussing how late the ship was going to be, and then one said to another, and I quote: "Fuck this Birger Bjelland. He's never been reliable." End of quote.'

'He was right.'

'Yes, you told me the last time we chatted that he was a shady character.'

'What's more, he's in clink, as I told you. They can't have contacted him, yet they set off a few days later?'

'Yes.' She splayed her hands. 'They must've spoken with the shipping line instead. Tell me. Did you go down to Sveio?'

'Yes, in fact I did. But there's nothing there apart from an old quay and a disused factory, which is regularly visited by what looks like tankers. Now that you mention it…'

'The perfect place to take on board toxic waste. Brilliant, herr Veum.'

'You can call me Varg.'

'Varg.' She toasted me with her mug of tea. 'Torunn.'

'Torunn.'

She took a swig of the tea. 'How do you get there?'

'I can drive you. It's two ferry rides. About three hours from here.'

She nodded pensively.

'Have you got anywhere to stay?'

She pointed upstairs. 'Fifth floor. They haven't got the room ready yet.'

'Practical. But then…' I looked at my watch. 'I should've been in court five minutes ago. When do you want to travel down?'

'As soon as possible – tomorrow.'

'Tomorrow's Saturday. The first ferry leaves Halhjem at seven.'

'Could we make it?'

'If I can pick you up here at six.'

'Is that too early?'

'Not for me.'

'Then I'll be here at six.'

I accompanied her out and we parted company on the stairs, Torunn to take the lift up to the hotel reception desk on the fifth floor, me to dash to the courthouse in the hope that I would be in time to hear the sentence passed in the case Berit Breheim had taken on to defend Terje Nielsen.

34

But I was too late; at least for the judge's summing-up. However, there was no doubt about the result of the court case. Arriving on the third floor of the courthouse, the first thing I noticed was the plaintiff, facing the large hall and crying against a pillar, with her lawyer, Halvorsen, and the same young woman as last time. They were both doing their best to comfort her.

I nodded to Halvorsen; she sent me a measured nod back. Around the corner I found the victors. Terje Nielsen was being loudly congratulated by Randolf Breheim and his other pals, while Berit Breheim and the police lawyer were being interviewed by a couple of journalists, one of them holding a microphone displaying the Norwegian Broadcasting Company's initials.

The outcome was a fact. Terje Nielsen and his friends were already on their way out to celebrate, but Nielsen himself studiously avoided looking in the direction of the plaintiff as he left.

When Berit Breheim had finished speaking and had exchanged a few words with the police lawyer, she tore herself away and came over to me, leaning against the railing overlooking the hall.

'What's next?' I asked. 'Sue the plaintiff for compensation costs?'

'Save your cracks for a more suitable occasion, Veum. Anything new in the case you should be concentrating on?'

'I'm following the Trans World Ocean thread at the moment. A ship calling itself the *Seagull* is due in Utvik in Sveio early tomorrow. Does that ring a bell with you?'

'Not at all.'

'This Terje Nielsen…'

'Yes, what about him?'

'He's Kåre Brodahl's nephew, I understand.'

'That's correct, but—'

'And Kåre Brodahl was employed in your father's shop when…'

'That's correct too,' she said, impatiently looking over at the hall.

'Do you remember him?'

'Of course I do. He was a shop assistant there for years, right until the business was sold.'

'Yes. Actually I meant do you know him?'

'Well, not really. They were never close friends, Pappa and him, not before and not after…'

'My information is that he was going out with your step-mother before she and your father found each other.'

For a moment she was speechless. Then she reacted. 'Do you know what, Veum? This conversation is becoming more and more absurd. For an investigator, I must say you're finding out the most incredible things no one asked you to investigate. If you'd been *half* as efficient with regard to the job you were commissioned to do, I really wouldn't object.'

'It's just that this story from 1957 keeps bobbing up from the bottom of the sea, like a mine.'

'Well, neither the case against Terje Nielsen, nor his uncle's possible relationship with my stepmother, have anything to do at all with Bodil and Fernando's disappearance. I'm one-hundred-per-cent sure of that. If you don't come up with something new soon…'

'I've told you before. You should put the police on the case.'

She rolled her eyes. 'Yes, and we all know how efficient they are.' She fixed her eyes on me again. 'Do I understand that you'd like to be relieved of your assignment?'

I instantly saw the pile of unpaid bills in front of my eyes. 'No, no. Not unless you insist.'

'No. Not yet. But we're approaching a deadline, Veum. If you can't come up with something new by Monday, I'll be tempted to dismiss you. Understood?'

'Deadline is the operative word. Will you take up my case if I fail?'

'I'll take the case, yes. Off you,' she said, nodded and made for the lift.

Personally, I preferred the stairs. Usually that is the place to fire the best parting shots. But this time I couldn't come up with a single cutting remark. I must have been off form or else I had too much on my mind.

35

A ferry terminal in Vestland, with the rain lashing against the windscreen, is not a place to be. Raindrops formed circles in the black sea off the harbour, the hot-dog stall on the quay was closed, and the crew on the ferry considered it too early to raise the boom and let us on board. In the car behind me the driver was drumming his fingers on the wheel and staring angrily at me as though it were my fault, everything. If it hadn't been for Torunn Tafjord, this would have been almost unbearable.

She was a talkative woman. During the course of the thirty minutes it had taken us to drive from Strand quay to Halhjem, I had been given a quick resumé of her career starting from when she graduated from Ålesund School 'or the Latin school as we call it' in 1968, went to Oslo to study language and literature 'English, German and literary science', ended up at journalism college and, after two years, got a job in her hometown, at *Sunnmørsposten*, in the summer of 1974. From Sunnmøre she made the traditional career move up to the Norwegian Broadcasting Corporation, with whom for a period, some years later, she was the voice from London. In 1984 she was back in Norway. During which time she had married, given birth to a child, divorced and in recent years started freelancing, with no fixed base and large parts of the world as her operational area, for as long as the right employers were still interested in what she could deliver. 'At the moment I live in Dublin.' 'Why?' 'Why not? It's a good place to live. Some friends of mine have gone to Berkeley, California, for two years and I'm looking after their flat, just south of Dublin Castle, in the meantime. I'm planning to write a book.' 'What about?' 'The exploitation of the third world, the scourge of our times. A problematic issue that's only going to grow until at some point it will overwhelm us whether we like it or not...'

I had nodded. I was in total agreement. The thing was that the cases I worked on usually had quite different and far more personal causes than the exploitation of the world's poor. However, before we were finally waved on board, I had told her what I had found out about Fernando Garrido, his relationship with TWO and the as-yet unexplained disappearance. She had listened, attentively, impatiently, as though constantly on the point of asking counter-questions, especially when I referred to the skirmishes I'd had with Kristoffersen and Bernt Halvorsen. *Unfinished jobs,* was that what he called them? Yes, something like that anyway. She had looked at me, deep in thought, and actually for more than a minute she had been silent, before starting to speak again.

As the ferry was manoeuvring its way through the narrow sounds at the mouth of Halhjem, we took seats in the cafeteria on the top deck. During the fifty-minute journey to Sandvikvåg in Stord she briefed me on the case she had been researching for several months.

I ventured a conclusion. 'In other words, toxic waste no wealthy country wants within its borders is dumped in one of the world's poorest countries in exchange for state support. Does that mean…? Are we talking here about a form of official policy?'

She gave a restrained smile. 'This is one thread we haven't quite unravelled yet. There's another journalist, with good connections in government circles, who's working on that part. But to me it seems obvious there's some understanding between the government department and the companies that transport the waste.'

'I assume your publication is planning a series of articles?'
She nodded.
'When?'
'That depends on when we get the final breakthrough. What

I'm hoping is that today we'll get pictures of the *Seagull* filling its tanks again, and preferably such good ones that the tankers delivering the waste can be identified. On Monday I intend to confront the managers at the shipping company responsible with what we've slowly managed to piece together. If this leads to a breakthrough, we'll be good to go at the beginning of May.'

'Ask for Bernt Halvorsen. And if you need a bodyguard, I'm…'

She laughed. 'I'll give it some thought.'

'What about this container?'

'Well, for the time being it's a mystery. It's also one of the reasons I'd very much like to be around when the *Seagull* docks.'

As we drove across the island of Stord, the weather lifted. The intervals between showers were longer. At Skjersholmane we were able to drive straight onto M/F *Hordaland*, which would take us across the fjord to Valevåg. We stayed in the car during the crossing. From there we could see the first rays of sun sweep across the blue-and-white mountain formations in Kvinnherad and Etne. I was suddenly reminded of the summers of my childhood in Hjelmeland in Ryfylke, with my grandfather, the vet: the fishing trips on the fjord, the girls on the neighbouring farm. When I told Torunn, she smiled gently. 'Yes, I have memories like that too, of Godøy and Giske.'

'Why is the sun always shining in such memories, do you think?'

She shrugged. 'The Vestlander's innate talent for repression, if you ask me. It must've been raining most of the time.'

'Yes, it must.'

South of Valevåg we passed the terrain blackened by the great forest fire from Whitsun the previous year. The charred tree trunks left standing reminded me of ruins from the war, of a petrified forest where nature had been brought to its knees by its own forces.

Torunn was following our progress on the map. We turned off by the municipal centre in Sveio and drove west. We passed the general store where I had been on the previous foray. There were no cars outside this time either. When we reached the gate with the *NO ADMITTANCE* sign, I quickly confirmed that the solid padlock was still in place and there were no visible signs of activity behind the high fence. We parked some distance away and walked back. A nervous vigilance came over my companion, which hadn't been there before. Her blue eyes darted here, there and everywhere, as though searching for indications, signs in the countryside others would have missed. Back at the gate, she stood with her fingers around the wire netting and her face pressed against the fence.

I pointed to the rock I had climbed up the previous time. 'We'll have a perfect view from there, Torunn.'

She chewed her lower lip. 'You think that's where we should take up a position?'

'We can't stay here anyway. If anyone comes, they'll see us. And from up there we can get over the fence more easily.' I patted the rucksack I had brought along. 'I've got some bolt-cutters.'

She flashed a smile. 'A man of action. I like that.' Then she turned to the bushes at the side of the road. 'Well, what are we waiting for?'

I walked past her and took the same route up as on the previous occasion. A couple of times I turned and held back some branches for her. We didn't say a lot. I was saving my energy for the final ascent. I could still feel the effects of the traffic accident like a virus in my body. Several times I had to stop and take a deep breath while pretending I was getting my bearings. As we approached the summit, I motioned for her to keep her head down. 'If the ship's docked, it's maybe a good idea not to stand out against the sky,' I said.

She nodded.

Slowly, we moved up the last part. 'Where's the quay from up here?' she asked.

I gestured with my hand.

'Then I suggest we stay on this side,' she said, pointing to the east of the rock.

I agreed, and nodded. Nevertheless, I felt like a cross between Running Bear and Master Detective Kalle Blomquist when we finally poked our noses out – Torunn first, I noticed – only to find the quay was uninhabited.

We looked out to sea. The inshore waters revealed no signs of life; only by the skerries known as Bloksene could we see the white foam of breakers hitting the rocks. In the distance, though, like a black shadow on the horizon, a ship was on its way in.

Torunn took a small pair of binoculars from her rucksack and held them to her eyes. She quickly adjusted the lenses. Then she lowered them and turned to me with a contented expression on her face. 'It's the *Seagull*. I'm pretty sure anyway.'

She passed me the binoculars. I focused on the ship at sea, but from this distance I was unable to see a name or a shipping logo. 'I recognise it,' she said, opening the main section of her rucksack and taking out a Thermos flask and two mugs. 'Cup of tea while we wait?'

I nodded. 'You've had more foresight than me, I see.'

'Be prepared,' she said, making the scout salute.

She was an easy person to spend time with, even on a weather-beaten rock in Sunnhordland. Over the next few hours, she told me that her career as a girl guide had been relatively brief, her marriage a little longer, what music she liked, what books she read and on what terrain she had slept travelling around the world on all manner of causes. And they were not so few. My cases were bagatelles by comparison.

It took the *Seagull* about two hours to approach land. Then she lay to, as though waiting for a signal to allow her to dock. There was no sign of life on the quay.

'What's the significance of that, do you think?'

She shrugged. 'We'll have to wait and see.'

Through the binoculars we observed hectic activity on deck.

Torunn commented: 'They're obviously trying to contact someone. They keep looking over here.'

'Could they have spotted us, do you reckon?'

She didn't answer, but from then on I decided to keep an eye on the land behind us as well, down the path we had made through the bushes.

'There's the container,' she said, passing me the binoculars again.

I examined the large blue container on the deck of the *Seagull*, and was none the wiser. A member of the crew checked to make sure everything was in order a couple of times. That was all.

Another hour passed. Now we were no longer exchanging personal experiences. All our attention was focused on the ship at sea, the quay below and the land behind us. We couldn't see the road from where we were lying, but we regularly heard the distant drone of passing traffic.

Suddenly she touched my arm. 'Something's happening now.' She grabbed her camera and found a position to take photographs.

I looked down at the harbour. A dark sports car had driven down onto the quay. A door opened and a big man stepped out, wearing a long, dark jacket with the lapels turned up and a scarf fluttering in the wind. He was speaking on a mobile phone and making signs to the ship. Immediately afterwards, a launch was lowered and a ladder dropped. Two men clambered into the launch, started the outboard motor and set a course for the harbour. The man on the quay stood waiting for them.

'Can I…?' I pointed to the binoculars.

She passed them to me, and I raised them to my eyes.

'Exactly what I thought.'

I felt her gaze on my face. 'Do you know him?'

'It's one of the men I was telling you about. Kristoffersen from TWO.'

'It's not so surprising that one of them has turned up.'

'No, it isn't. All that's missing now is Garrido on board the launch.'

But he wasn't.

The two men in the launch wore officer's uniforms. As they climbed up to the quay, I was able to say with some certainty that I had never seen either of them before. I passed the binoculars back to Torunn, who quickly identified them. 'The captain and first mate. I wish we had professional listening equipment at our disposal.'

'Unfortunately I'm not so up-to-date on the tech front,' I said. 'They don't look very friendly anyway.'

I could see that too, even without the binoculars. Fragments of what they were saying reached us whenever they raised their voices. Kristoffersen made a gesture with his arm and walked away from the two officers, as though what he really wanted to do was throw them in the sea. Then he returned, pointing to the horizon. One officer gesticulated back. The other threw his arms in the air.

'He's telling them to sling their hooks, it seems,' I said.

Her expression was tense. 'If they do, I absolutely have to have a photo of toxic waste being taken on board.'

'They may've been warned off ... by my enquiries.'

She sent me a concerned look. 'Perhaps. In which case it's my fault too. For putting you on their trail.'

Down on the quay, the discussion was continuing as loudly as before. Finally, Kristoffersen punched a fist into the palm of one hand and karate-chopped the air, as if to emphasise his message: *That's it*. Afterwards he spun on his heel, strode to his car, got in, reversed out of the harbour area and accelerated with such venom that we could smell rubber up from where we were. He drove in the same direction he had come. 'Exit messenger, stage left,' I mumbled.

The two officers stood calmly watching as though this had all been playing to the gallery and that he would reappear any moment. When he didn't, they conferred. Torunn didn't lower her binoculars for a second; she followed with intense interest as if she could lip-read what they were saying. Finally, it appeared they had come to a decision. One climbed down to the launch and started the motor. The other stayed on the quay.

'What now?' I asked.

'No idea.'

The man below us lit a cigarette, paced up and down the quay, spat into the water and had a pee from the edge without checking to see if he was alone or not. 'Avert your eyes,' I said.

Torunn rolled them demonstratively, to emphasise that she had probably seen more exciting things than an officer having a pee from a quay in Sunnhordland. I believed her.

The other officer was back on board the *Seagull*. We could see him pointing and giving orders. Not long afterwards the black ship slowly manoeuvred its way in. The officer below walked to the far end of the quay. When the ship had come in close enough, a hawser was thrown ashore, which he tied to a mooring bollard, and the *Seagull* elegantly glided alongside. Up on deck they swung the crane into position and Torunn readied her camera again. 'It's the container. They're going to unload it.'

'Possibly.'

She was right. A few minutes later the blue container was hanging in the air over the deck. Then it was skilfully angled over the quay and lowered. The officer below directed it to its final resting position and released the cables so that it could swing back just as elegantly.

For a moment he stood examining the container. Then he turned his gaze landward and we involuntarily ducked. When we carefully raised our heads again, the hawser had been removed, the man in the officer's uniform was already climbing the ladder and the *Seagull* was reversing away from the quay.

We watched her turn. Then she steamed full ahead for the channel south of the skerries and the open sea beyond. Later we saw her, on a course for the horizon, as if drawn by an invisible magnet, smaller and smaller every time we looked up. The container stood on the quay like a memorial to drowned seamen, left in Sunnhordland for someone to come and collect.

Again, Torunn lowered her binoculars. She looked at me. 'What do you think?'

I shrugged. 'Contraband?'

'But the TWO man didn't seem to want to have anything to do with it.'

'Or he didn't know anything about it?'

She sent me a sceptical look.

'Imagine the following situation,' I said. 'There's no doubt you're on the trail of an extremely dubious export, especially from a global perspective. We reveal to the exporters that we're onto them. I daren't hazard a guess as to how TWO and the *Seagull* communicate, but it almost seemed as if the *Seagull* had sailed to Utvik against the will of their employer.'

'I'm with you so far.'

'When TWO was informed of this, by radio from the ship maybe, they sent Kristoffersen down to sort matters out, which he did in his usual diplomatic fashion.'

'I can see you have personal knowledge of him.'

'And he wasn't particularly charming then either. However, the reason the *Seagull* has completed its journey to Utvik may be that they have another cargo on board. You said yourself you'd overheard the name Birger Bjelland mentioned when the ship was docked in Hamburg. And Birger Bjelland has done so much on the fringes of what's legal. The problem is that Bjelland's been in prison since the end of February.'

'And the last time the *Seagull* was in Norway was in early February. In other words, the ship's bosses may not know what's happened to this Bjelland.'

'At any rate, they won't have had any contact with him.'

She shifted her pensive gaze back down to the quay. 'But why did they leave the container here?'

'In the hope that Bjelland or someone else would come and take it away maybe? Or just to wash their hands of it. Dump it and forget the whole business, somehow. Perhaps they felt what they'd done was dangerous enough – transporting it through the customs territory without declaring it.'

'What do we do now then?'

'Hm, wait and watch? Or go down and have a look?'

She nodded slowly. 'Yes to the former. Let's wait and watch. If nothing happens before this evening, we can consider the next step.'

'And in the meantime? Have you got a storm kitchen with you as well?'

'No, but I'm used to living off basic rations when needs must.'

'There's a general store down on the road. We could go down there and get some provisions.'

'You go. I'll stay here in case something happens.'

'Sure?'

'Absolutely.'

With that, I headed back down through the shrub, found the car where we had left it and drove the few kilometres back to the store. Less than half an hour later I was back with an assorted selection of food: a packet of crispbread, a couple of tubes of cheese, a can of stew that could be eaten cold at a pinch, some apples and oranges, a bar of chocolate, a carton of juice and some bottles of mineral water.

She eyed my choice of purchases sceptically. 'Were you thinking of eating that?' she asked, pointing to the stew.

I shrugged. 'You never know how hungry you can get.'

'Then I think I'll stick to this part of the menu,' she answered, sinking her teeth into an apple.

I nodded in the direction of the harbour. 'Nothing new?'

She shook her head. 'Dead as a dodo.'

It was a long day, and the longer we sat, the clearer it became that it was still a long time to midsummer. At regular intervals, we stood up and flapped our arms to keep warm.

As an example of how much worse it could be, she told me about a trip to Svalbard she had once done for a report, with the temperature well below minus thirty. Their snow scooter had seized up, and she and a local photographer had been forced to spend the night in a snow cave until they were found the following morning by a search-and-rescue team. 'We were packed together so tightly that we were on the point of getting engaged.'

'I'm up for that. I can take a hint.'

'It won't get that cold here,' she said sternly, but with a little smile playing on her lips.

By eight it was getting dark and still nothing had happened. I took out the bolt-cutters. 'Shouldn't we begin to think about how to get through the fence?'

She admired the equipment with a savvy nod. 'Let's wait until midnight. If they've struck some deal for the container, the pick-up will very likely take place after dark.'

We did as she suggested. We waited until midnight. My legs were stiff, my body was cold and there was a hollow in the pit of my stomach that not even the thought of tinned stew could fill. I could have probably come up with more enjoyable ways of spending a Saturday evening. She, on the other hand, appeared to be conspicuously cheerful. She kept checking the time.

At long last it was midnight, and she said: 'Right, I think we can risk it now. If you can cut a way through the fence, let's go down.'

I already had the bolt-cutters in my hand. 'Hope it isn't alarmed.'

'Does it look like it is?'

'No.'

I went to work. It took surprisingly little effort to cut open the wire-netting and make a hole big enough for both of us to clamber through. We packed our things and took everything with us. On the other side of the fence, the cliff sloped down to an old warehouse, partly cut into the rockface. In some places it was so steep I had to hold her hand on the way down. At one point we had only willow bushes to hang on to. We emerged at the back of the old building, where there was a stench of mould and decay. Only when we rounded the corner did the refreshing salty sea air hit us.

The blue container grew in size with every step we took. Now it was so close we could read the writing on it. On the side there was an identification code: *UA-5143-CB*. In a plastic envelope there was a typed sheet of paper in French, a customs declaration stamped by the authorities in Casablanca, Morocco, saying the contents were *'matériel agricole'*.

I looked at Torunn. 'Agricultural material?'

'Could be anything.'

'Judging by the smell you would think it was rotting meat inside.'

She nodded pensively. 'There's a market for the illegal import of African meat.'

At that moment I heard a sound. I felt my body stiffen. 'Alive though?'

She stared at me. 'What do you mean?'

'Didn't you hear?'

'Hear what?'

I placed my ear against the container. 'There's something moving inside.'

'What?!'

I banged my fist against the hard metal surface. 'Hello! Anyone there?'

A weak sound of banging came from inside the container. And an even weaker voice in a language we could barely recognise as French: *'Ohé! Au secours … allons mourir … Au secours…'*

37

'Help ... we're dying,' Torunn Tafjord exclaimed. 'They must've been in there since ... for over a week.'

'Then it's time they came out. How the hell do we open the bugger?'

The container was locked externally with one bolt at the end. When we flipped the latch and shoved the metal bolt holding it in place to one side, we were able to open the door. The stench hit us and we involuntarily turned our backs.

Torunn's voice trembled: 'That's ... disgusting.'

I leaned forward and looked in. It was pitch-black inside. The stink of urine, excrement and acrid sweat was overwhelming. 'Hello?' I searched for some remnants of my school French and whatever I had picked up during a couple of short leaves in Marseilles thirty years ago. '*Vous êtes libres.* You're free.'

On the floor of the container, I saw something move. An emaciated, human-like creature was crawling toward me. A cadaverous face looked up. His eyes were rolling. His black moustache was spattered with vomit. His tongue looked blue as he ran it over his dry lips. '*Nous allons mourir...*'

'*Non, non,*' I protested, then I had to switch over to English. 'We're going to help you.'

Torunn joined me. 'Let me ... I can speak French. You try ... ringing for help. These poor people have to go to hospital, and the sooner the better. And if I were you, I'd ring the police too.'

'Absolutely.'

I rang 112 and reported the situation. The duty officer took note of where we were and said he would call the ambulances himself. 'Stay where you are,' he concluded.

'We have no immediate travel plans,' I mumbled, but he had already rung off.

Inside the container the thin legs of someone who hadn't sur-
vived the journey stuck out from under a blanket. A group of
bewildered people began to assemble on the quay. Wide-eyed
and open-mouthed, they surveyed the scene around them.
There had been between twenty and thirty people in the container. The majority of them men, mostly between twenty and
forty. The women clung to their men. One of them was clearly
pregnant and supported by an elderly man and a boy of fifteen
or sixteen. There were several young boys and two mature
women. They looked like North Africans. The men were skinny
and sinewy; even the pregnant woman looked strangely hol-
lowed out. Several of them had broken nails and hands bleeding
from cuts, as though they had been trying to claw their way out
of the container. About half of them spoke French, the rest a language I assumed was a form of Arabic.

'It's the kind they speak in parts of Algeria. Sounds like
Berber,' Torunn explained.

'You don't speak that too?'

'I'm afraid not, but I know a few common expressions.'

The poor souls looked at us as if we were Martians. Torunn
found out that they thought they were in Germany.

'No, you're in Norway,' she explained in a slow voice.

'*Norvège?*'

'*Oui, oui,*' she nodded, and when the news spread to the
others, they looked, if possible, even more terrified.

Torunn had taken out her camera and was photographing the
scene. 'What were you promised when you arrived?' she asked.

'Work,' said the exhausted spokesperson.

'Freedom from terror,' added another, a man in his thirties.
'Islamists! Murderers! They kill anyone who thinks differently.
Our women are whores, they say. They destroyed our village,
and killed our women and children. Slashed at them as they lay
sleeping! If we'd stayed, we would be dead too.' The outburst

made him go dizzy, and he slid down the side of the container
until he was sitting on the ground.

Torunn turned to the first man again. 'And how much did
you pay for this?'

The man named a sum, and she shook her head with indig-
nation.

'This is the standard fee. It was cheap,' he said.

'Cheap? My God,' Torunn muttered, casting her eyes around,
as if looking for support. In the distance we heard the first heli-
copter. Not long afterwards, it was hovering above the harbour
area. It had hardly landed before the first rescuers were running
towards us, crouched, as the downwash from the rotor blades
blew their hair forward.

We welcomed the first arrivals and explained the situation to
them as succinctly as we could. While paramedics saw to the
preliminary, superficial examinations of these unexpected
guests, we heard, from up at the main entrance, a roar of engines
and metal being cut, then gates being pushed open. Not long
afterwards two civilian cars, a police car and two ambulances
raced down to the quay.

One of the civvies-clad policemen was a tall, broadly built
fellow with blond, almost white, hair, light-blue eyes and a ruddy
complexion. He shook hands with Torunn and then me. 'Arve
Sætre, police chief in Sveio.' Then he introduced two officers
from the other car. 'I understood from the gravity of the call to
us that we would require assistance from Haugesund. So, these
men are Detectives Holgersen and Liland.'

We greeted each other politely, and everyone was briefed on
the situation again, as far as we understood it. Holgersen, a well-
built man with cropped hair and rubicund cheeks, asked: 'This
man from the shipping company had left the area before the
container was craned ashore then?'

'Yes,' I said.

Liland came in a smaller format and had only a thin outcrop of hair around his ears. He looked at me with a ruminative air. 'Does that mean he may not have known about it?'

'It might do, yes.'

'But it doesn't clear them of suspicion with respect to whatever else is shipped from Utvik,' Torunn said.

Sætre raised his eyebrows. 'Whatever else?'

'Toxic waste, chemicals. That sort of thing.'

Holgersen cast a glance at Sætre. 'Do you know about this?'

Sætre shook his head. 'I can't remember seeing any complaints.'

'You wouldn't,' Torunn clarified, with feeling. 'It's other countries that have reason to complain.'

'All they probably notice here is the traffic,' I added. 'And that's mainly at night, from what I've heard.'

'Well…' Holgersen looked toward the gate, where a white estate car was just coming in. Now it was heading towards us. It was a Toyota Carina with *HA* in big letters on the side. 'Oh, Christ. The vultures have landed. Brace yourself, Liland. Smile for the camera.'

'The press?' I asked.

'The local paper, for now,' Holgersen mumbled.

'Then you've got competition,' I whispered to Torunn.

'Perhaps it's time to … You don't need us any longer, do you?' she asked.

'No, that's fine. We've got your names and mobile numbers, haven't we?'

Sætre nodded.

Before Torunn's colleagues from *Haugesunds Avis* had taken up position, we had discreetly withdrawn up to the gate.

'I've never enjoyed seeing my picture in the newspaper,' I said.

'Nor me,' she said. 'Believe you me.'

With steely eyes and firm strides, we made our way out, as though on an important mission. No one stopped us from going back to my car. No one shouted and told us to stop where we were.

*

When we parted company in Bergen, three and a half hours later, it was Sunday morning. 'What are you going to do now?' I asked.

'Sleep, primarily. Then I'll type up my impressions. And you?'

'The same as you. Sleep, that is. Afterwards I've still got this other case I'm busy with. Maybe I'll be able to unravel that too.'

She sent me a sidelong glance from the passenger seat. 'Thank you for your company,' she said, with a searching glance, then leaned forward and hugged me.

'Don't forget my offer,' I said. 'If you should find yourself visiting TWO.'

'As a bodyguard, did you say? I can usually manage on my own.'

'I can drive you to Flesland Airport, if you want.'

'Both maybe?'

Another probing look. Then she smiled, opened the door, took her rucksack from the back seat and, entering the hotel, sent me a final wave, went inside and was gone.

I drove home, crawled into bed and slept until seven in the evening. But on the way to my bedroom, I consulted the telephone directory and found Kåre Brodahl's home address.

38

He lived on the east side of Fosswinckels gate, walking distance from an august charitable institute for single women known as the Frøkenstiftelse, where women of a mature age still resided. If he came to be short of a companion, he wouldn't have far to go. They could usually talk, these so-called 'spinsters', and when they played bridge in the evening, you could hear the fruitiest language.

With a feeling of mildew over my eyes, the result of a long day's sleep after the events of the night, I had chosen to walk into town. By Grieg Hall I crossed up Strømgaten and into Fosswinckels gate. I found the building where Brodahl lived. According to the nameplates by the doorbells, he was on the ground floor. The lights were on, but the curtains were drawn. Only a mysterious glow, as if from an opium den, penetrated through the sombre, heavy material.

I rang the bell. After a short wait, Brodahl's voice sounded in the intercom by the bells. 'Yes?'

'Veum here. I don't know if you remember me?'

'I do.'

'Have you got a moment?'

There was a silence. He was hesitating.

'It won't take long.'

'Well…'

The lock buzzed. I pressed down the handle and opened the door. Brodahl was standing in the doorway to the left, a few steps up. He was wearing a dark-burgundy, old-fashioned smoking jacket with a decorative pattern on the lapels, white shirt and tie, dark trousers with a sharp crease, black stockings and reddish-brown leather slippers. In one hand he was holding a CD cover; the other beckoned me in. The light inside made his trim curls shimmer a silver colour, but his face was in shadow.

'What's this about?' he asked as he took my worn leather jacket with a disapproving look and hung it up, after first creating a seemly distance on the stand between it and his outdoor clothes.

'A rendezvous with forgotten years, as someone suggested the other day,' I said. 'If you can tolerate a literaturisation of the whole business.'

'A literaturisation?'

'Yes.'

The flat was west-facing; a bachelor's pad of the tasteful variety, with landscapes on the walls, leather-bound books on handsome shelves and small sculptures on escritoires and display cases. The CD collection was impressive, spread across three polished, dark-brown wooden stands. Over the sound system Mozart was making elegant use of bassoons the way Ellington would use woodwind around two hundred years later. Brodahl went to the amplifier, lowered the volume and indicated a couple of comfortable leather chairs around a small table, perfectly placed with respect to the loudspeakers. In front of one chair there was a tumbler with something fizzy in, and before taking a seat he asked me if I would like to join him. 'A little whisky soda, Veum?'

'Why not?'

He filled a glass, placed it on a tray, carried it over and passed it to me like a professional waiter. Finally, he sat down across from me and raised his glass in a silent toast.

I toasted back. I put down the tumbler and looked around. 'You live alone, do you?'

He nodded gently. 'Turns out I do.' Before I could follow this up, he continued: 'What did you mean by "forgotten years", Veum?'

'Are you sure you can't imagine?'

'Forgotten is forgotten. In which case you may have to remind me.'

'Oblivion is an odd phenomenon,' I said philosophically. 'I mean ... we've all completely forgotten certain events in our lives, while the people closest to us still remember them. Who knows for what reason. It might be because we consider them unpleasant, of course. Incidents that took place when we were young, for example, that a schoolfriend remembers but we've repressed. Then there are things we choose to forget, to the extent that we can, or experiences that are so peripheral we hardly bother to remember them. Oblivion is an arbitrary phenomenon, but I can assure you, Brodahl, it's quite astonishing what the brain can repress once it puts its mind to it.'

He arched his eyebrows in wry amusement. 'You don't say. And where's this lecture taking you, herr Veum?'

'I need some help to fill in a few gaps, Brodahl.'

'Gaps?'

'The last time we spoke, I don't think you told me everything. I think you forgot something.'

He ran a bony hand through his hair while weighing me up. 'Such as?'

'Sara Taraldsen, later to become fru Breheim – number two, as it were. You forgot to tell me that frøken Taraldsen and you were as good as engaged.'

'Who told you that?'

'A reliable source. And when I spoke to Sara Breheim last Monday, she didn't want to tell me the name of her escort that September night in 1957 at Norge Hotel, just before Tordis Breheim and her lover died. The man who'd helped her take Breheim home afterwards. Why not?' When he didn't answer, I added: 'It was you, Brodahl, of course.'

'Oh, yes? I'd almost forgotten.'

'You'd wanted to forget, I think we'll say.'

His eyes met mine, with neither defiance nor hostility. But rather with sorrow.

'The reason you still live alone perhaps?'
He sighed. 'Maybe.'

Sara ... sweet, little, dark-haired Sara, whom he had fallen in love with the first moment she set foot in the shop, when the owner showed her round and introduced her as a newly employed assistant in the department for shirts, ties, underwear and stockings. The ever-cheerful Sara with the bright, rippling laugh and the mischievous glances, perhaps not always as meaningful as they were perceived. She was twenty-one when she started; he was one year older. They were the youngest members of staff and were treated as such, with well-mannered condescension, by those who had been there longer. Was that why they had sought each other's company, for mutual moral support? It took him two years to find the courage to ask her out. First to the cinema. He could still remember ... Doris Day and James Stewart ... 'Que Sera Sera'. Afterwards an open sandwich and a glass of wine each at the Norge. It was this they were going to celebrate the year afterwards, that September night. It was a year since he had first invited her out.

But then...

He had known without knowing. It was only afterwards he saw it with the utmost clarity. When, in 1958, she married Ansgar Breheim, who had been a widower for barely a year, it dawned on him, in a prophetic vision, that she had always had her eyes on Breheim, but she had held herself back, of course, because he was married – and not to just any woman.

Sara...

Was that perhaps why he...?

I waited.

He looked at me. 'I ... It's true that I, that we ... that it was Sara and I who went with Ansgar Breheim that night, first to the hospital and then home.'

*Afterwards he had accompanied Sara home. She lived close to
Rothaugen School in Hilbrandt Meyers gate, but when he went to
kiss her goodnight, her mind seemed to be anywhere but on him …
He could understand why. Events had taken a dramatic turn. What
should have been an intimate evening…*

Brodahl stood up. He went over to one of the escritoires,
pulled out a drawer and took a small box from inside. Then he
came back, sat down, opened the box and held it out for me.
Inside, there was a beautiful ring with a light-blue, almost white,
stone inset.

In a choked voice, he said: 'I was carrying this in my pocket
that night, Veum. I'd planned to…'

I admired the ring and nodded gently.

'Afterwards an opportunity never presented itself.'

*She slipped away from me. Her eyes became more and more
distant day by day. Ansgar Breheim demanded more and more of
her time, and when he asked, she made an excuse: But you have to
understand, Kåre. The man's in despair, as you can imagine.*

Despair? He certainly knows how to make the most of it, Sara.

*Make the most of it? Watch your tongue now, Kåre. Think twice
before you say any more.*

Alright, alright.

I could see it now. The outline of a terrible sorrow. One that
would never quite leave his eyes.

'But … back to that night.'

'Mm.'

'You walked back to Sudmanns vei, didn't you?'

He didn't answer.

'It's thirty-six years ago, Brodahl. You're not risking anything
by telling me now. You won't lose anything either.'

'I won't?'

'You might salve your conscience?'

He tried to hold my gaze, but failed. He kept looking away. 'Alright then. I walked back. But it was him who … He told me to.'

'Really?'

Suddenly he looked incredibly young, despite the silver curls. 'After all, he was my boss, wasn't he.'

'Well…'

'Before Sara and I left, while I was helping him into bed, he said: "Take Sara home, Kåre, and come back here."'

Back here? I said.

Yes, you've hardly had anything to drink, have you?

No.

Then you drive me…

Drive? I said.

I know where they are, Kåre.

He paused. I urged him to carry on. 'Right. And did you?'

'Yes. It was a nightmare, of course. After what had happened. Some things are so vivid, so unreal, that it's precisely because of *that* you don't forget, Veum. The unreal nature of it.'

The drive there. Ansgar Breheim sitting beside him, getting angrier and angrier the further they left the town behind them. As if he was working himself up:

I'll give them what for, I'll show them what for.

He had tried to calm him down: Shouldn't we just go back, herr Breheim?

Back home? To what?

There's nothing we can do now anyway.

Oh, yes, there is. There certainly is!

The roads at night, dark, deserted. He didn't remember meeting a single car. At any rate, no witnesses came forward.

'Another drink, Veum?'

'Yes, please.' I pushed my glass over to him.

He took it with his own, filled them and came back. He didn't use the tray this time, and I could clearly see his hand trembling.

'When we got to Hjellestad, we saw their car, where they'd parked it.'

'Did you two recognise it?'

'No, but it was on their parking spot. It must've been the musician's car.'

'What happened next?'

He took a large swig from the glass. 'I wanted to stay in the car, but he insisted…'

You're coming with me, Kåre.
But, herr Breheim.
You know what'll happen if you don't.

I looked at him. 'OK, he was your boss, as you said, but there's a limit. He couldn't demand so much from you.'

'There was something else.'

'Mhm?'

'He had a hold over me.'

'What kind of hold?'

'I'd been hard up. There'd been a price reduction the year before. I'd made a few minor changes to the price tags.'

'Embezzlement, in other words.'

He looked down. And without looking up, he said: 'He found out, naturally, but agreed not to report me to the police so long as there was no repeat and so long as I never objected again to anything he suggested.' He looked up. 'He was probably thinking of pay negotiations and so on, but, well, that was how we ended it.'

'So tell me, how did the whole story end?'

'We caught them in the act. Fru Breheim and this Hagenes.'

They had made their way through the forest. The night had been at its darkest, but the light from the cabin windows was enough for them to approach without any difficulty. Besides, Breheim was leading the way, and he knew the area like the back of his hand.

They went to the window and peered in.

At first, he couldn't see anything. Only the flames from the fire, the lamp hanging from the ceiling, a bottle of wine, two glasses ... Something moving on the floor, a back arching, dull thumping noises...

Breheim had been beside him, paralysed with shock. Then he abruptly turned away. Kåre stayed where he was while Breheim strode around the corner, up the stairs and into the cabin. From outside he watched the scene, as if in slow motion, as Breheim tore open the door and was suddenly standing in the middle of the room. The two of them got up from the floor, and he saw her – Tordis Breheim – as he had never seen any woman before. For a moment she was completely naked, white skin, red hair. Then she grabbed the blanket they had been lying on and held it in front of her, as if this was a stranger she had to hide from. The naked man beside her seemed so helpless that it almost made Kåre want to laugh. He had been trying to cover his privates with his hands, but he found it difficult to stand up straight at the same time.

In a furious rage Ansgar Breheim strode to the wall, pulled down the shotgun hanging there, pointed it at the other two, and without taking his eyes off them, opened a drawer, took out a box, emptied it on the dresser, broke the gun and inserted two cartridges.

Ansgar! he heard Tordis scream, through the window pane. Don't do it.

Herr Breheim, Hagenes begged, then fell to his knees in front of him.

He didn't hear what Breheim said.

Motionless, he stood watching as Tordis Breheim and her lover were ordered to get dressed, to put on everything from their underwear to their outdoor clothes and shoes. Then Breheim forced them out of the cabin, holding the loaded shotgun like an unassailable argument. He had never seen a shotgun before.

When they stepped outside and Tordis Breheim spotted him, an expression of relief spread across her face:

Oh, herr Brodahl, thank God. For a moment I thought he was alone.

But Johan Hagenes didn't know what to make of him. He was having trouble stopping his legs from buckling beneath him.

Down to the car, Breheim barked. And don't you try anything. One hasty move and I'll shoot. To him he said: Kåre, there's a saxophone inside. Go in and get it.

But...

Just do it.

It was no use protesting. He went into the cabin, found the instrument and took it back out.

'Just a moment,' I said.

He looked at me in surprise. 'What?'

'Do you remember if the mouthpiece was on the saxophone?'

'The mouthpiece? I haven't a clue. I have about as much idea about saxophones as I do shotguns.'

'Mm ... then he must've taken it off himself, and neither Breheim nor you noticed.'

'Shall I go on?'

Before leaving the cabin, he had cast a final glance around. The

wine bottle, the two glasses, the blanket that was left on the floor –
as if the two who had spent the evening there had just gone to bed
for the night…

Breheim had stared at him impatiently when he finally came out
of the cabin. In a silent procession they walked through the dark
forest: Tordis Breheim first, then Hagenes, then Breheim with the gun
pointing at them, and finally himself, with the saxophone. When they
were down by the cars Breheim ordered his wife and Hagenes into
the Opel, with Tordis at the wheel. He opened the rear door and held
out a hand:

Saxophone, Kåre.

When Breheim had the instrument in his hand, he threw it onto
the back seat.

Reverse my car so that we're free to move.

As if in a trance, he followed Breheim's instructions.

Breheim got into the black Opel, at the back, shotgun in hand.
He pulled the door to, but didn't lock it. Kåre reversed Breheim's
Volvo out, as he had been bidden.

He looked at me, mouth agape, like a fish on land.

'That was the last I saw of them, Veum. I swear it.'

I stared back. 'But not of Breheim. You saw him again.'

'Yes, I did.'

'That same night, I would guess.'

He nodded. 'I pulled into the side of the road and waited. Not
that anyone else was going to come past, but … After a while he
came strolling around the bend. Alone. I didn't dare ask him what
had happened. I was frightened he would shoot me too.'

'He didn't shoot them either though.'

'I couldn't know that.'

'What did he do with gun?'

'He took it back to the cabin. For all I know, it's still hanging
there.'

I cast my mind back. 'Yes, in fact, I think it is.'

'Afterwards…'

'Yes?'

'Afterwards we drove home,' he said drily, as though with that he had finished telling the story about a very normal Sunday outing with the family.

'But later, when what happened to Tordis Breheim and Johan Hagenes came out, why on earth didn't you report this to the police?'

'And be hauled in as an accomplice? Because that's what I was, Veum. He had a hold over me, an even stronger one than before.'

'Yes, but you had one over him too.'

'I suppose so.'

'Now I think I understand fru Sletta when she called what she experienced inside the shop a "balance of terror".'

'Fru Sletta? So that's who…' He nodded bitterly to himself.

'He had something on you. You had something on him. But in the heat of battle, you lost Sara.'

'Yes.' Again, the sorrow rose in his eyes – it was clearer now, now that I knew what had caused it.

He had never seen a naked woman before. He would never see one later either, except in the cinema and on television. He had lost Sara for ever. There were no others. Going to a prostitute would be unthinkable. All he had done had been to wait. And wait. And wait. But when 1983 came and Ansgar Breheim died, there was nothing left. Not for him anyway.

I let him pursue his thoughts before continuing. 'Do you have any contact with Sara today?'

He shook his head. 'No, I … I occasionally hear things, through my nephew, but that's all.'

'And you don't have any contact with Bodil or Berit either?'

'None at all.'

'Well…' I drank down the last mouthful in the tumbler and stood up. 'Then I won't disturb you any longer. Now at least I know what happened in 1957. Not that it helps me much in 1993; but thank you for being so honest with me under very little pressure.'

He didn't answer. He looked desiccated, squeezed dry. There was nothing more there, for anyone. He had lived for much too long in the shadow of what had apparently been his *grand amour*.

Love is blind, they say, but that is a bare-faced lie. When love is not mutual, it is a blight. Strolling home, I felt a little wiser and hummed an old Alf Prøysen song. But I was no Solomon and no one would have been proud to see the fruits of my labours, not even the song's lowly hatmaker.

39

Early the next morning I walked down to my office.

The events in Utvik were splashed all over the newspapers, but neither Torunn Tafjord's nor my role in the drama was mentioned. Newspapers, radio and TV had followed up with a mass of background material about legal and illegal immigration, human trafficking and the consequences this might have for Norwegian asylum policies, as if they could be any stricter than they already were.

Trans World Ocean had called an impromptu press conference on Sunday evening. I had watched it myself on the evening news. Bernt Halvorsen had appeared pale and pinched as he made it clear that the company had nothing whatsoever to do with the alleged trafficking. He pointed a finger of guilt at the captain of the *Seagull* and a 'disloyal servant' inside TWO. It was announced that the police had sent a warrant via Interpol for the captain's arrest as soon as his ship docked. For the time being, it was in international waters and the company was unable to say 'offhand' where it was headed. 'We're awaiting developments,' was all Halvorsen was in a position to say regarding a new destination. *Not bloody surprising,* I said to myself, *after Kristoffersen had told them to sling their hook.* And what about the 'disloyal servant'? people at the conference asked. Could Halvorsen reveal the name of the individual? Not at this moment, came the answer. What was the ship transporting? It varied from commission to commission, he answered. In which market? On this occasion they were returning from the west coast of Africa, he said. What were they doing in Utvik? Utvik wasn't a scheduled stop on this trip, Halvorsen averred. *Oh, no?* There must have been quite a lot at stake for them to lie so publicly.

I rang Breheim, Lygre, Pedersen & Waagenes, the firm of solicitors. I had got used to her voice now, the woman who usually took my calls. Not that she was of much help. 'I'm afraid fru Breheim isn't in today,' she told me. 'She's got time off in lieu.' 'Can she afford the time?' I asked. 'She finished a difficult case on Friday and needed a couple of days off.' 'I'll try her at home then.' 'You do that, herr Veum. Have a good day.' 'Thank you and the same to you.'

Then I dialled Berit Breheim's private number. But no one picked up. Before I had a chance to call Karin Bjørge, as I had planned, the outer door went. Immediately afterwards, there was a firm knock on the waiting-room door.

'Come in.'

'Thank you,' said Torunn Tafjord, already on her way in, wearing the same sporty outfit as before, a rucksack hanging casually over one shoulder. She flashed me a friendly smile. 'Could you by any chance drive me to Flesland?'

'With pleasure.'

'I have an appointment with Bernt Halvorsen himself at ten-thirty and when I discovered it was on the way to the airport, I…'

'My car's ten minutes away,' I said.

'What's that compared with the climbing we did recently?' she winked. The laughter lines by her eyes were like Chinese fans, light and airy. She must have slept well. At any rate, she was brim-full of energy again, from what I could see.

On the way to Skansen I asked her whether she had seen the conference headlines. She had.

'Yet still you got an appointment, unscheduled?'

'I made them an offer they couldn't refuse.'

I glanced at her clean-cut, determined profile. 'Oh, yes? Did you threaten to take me along if you didn't get one?'

'No need. I gave them the choice. Either they use the opportunity to "correct" my information in advance or wait until it was in print.'

'And they went for it?'

'With the skeletons in their closet, it wasn't exactly a surprise.'

'Let's hope we don't join the skeletons.'

'You're game then, are you?'

On the way to Kokstad I told her that I had got to the bottom of the thirty-six-year-old case, at least.

'Right to the bottom?'

'I think so.'

'Let's hope you're right. But my experience is that down at the bottom, where it's so dark, you can never be sure.'

'It doesn't matter too much how accurate that part of the story is. Right now, I'm wondering more about how much Fernando Garrido could've known of the to-ings and fro-ings in Utvik. Because I doubt this was the first time they'd docked there.'

'I don't think so either.'

This time we didn't need to negotiate our passage through the security channel at TWO. We were expected. That is to say, Torunn was expected. And the guard I knew wasn't there. The new one wasn't quite the same format, but there were similarities. They were cut from the same cloth, it seemed. He eyed me suspiciously, but Torunn swept all uncertainty aside by announcing in a confident voice: 'He's with me.' Nobody would have dared to challenge her.

They didn't appear very pleased, Halvorsen and Kristoffersen, when we bumped into them in the corridor outside Halvorsen's office. Kristoffersen came out of the office first, crimson-faced, the blood vessels in his temple pumping. Catching sight of me, he clenched his fists and barked: 'I should've reconfigured your face the first time I saw you.'

'Thank you. I have my own plastic surgeon.'

'You stank of trouble from the very first minute.'

'A compliment I'm happy to return.'

'A big-mouth too.'

'Contagious, I'm afraid.'

He threw an upper cut, not to hit me in the face, but to demonstrate his strength. Nevertheless, I stepped back.

'Kristoffersen,' Halvorsen said reprovingly, 'haven't you got us enough bad publicity in the last few days?'

'Me? But for Garrido, none of this would've happened. It's because of him this guy's come out of the woodwork.'

Torunn was following with interest, and Halvorsen turned anxiously to her. 'Torunn Tafjord?'

'That's me.'

'Don't take his behaviour seriously. The man's off-kilter. He's just resigned.'

'Him too?' I muttered.

For a moment I lost concentration. Kristoffersen used the opportunity to grab my shoulder, swing me round and force me up against the wall. His face was close to mine, so close I could smell nicotine on his breath. 'Veum,' he said, in a low, menacing voice. 'Next time you cross a road, make sure you look all the way around you. It might be me standing behind you this time.'

I met his eyes. 'So it was you who—'

He slammed me against the wall, then let go and turned away. With a final unfriendly glare at Halvorsen he left.

I straightened my clothes and grinned at the other two. Halvorsen turned to Torunn with a displeased expression. 'I thought we had an arrangement with you, fru Tafjord. What made you bring … him?' He made a sudden gesture in my direction.

'You and I can be less formal,' she said. 'Herr Veum has been helping me with the case. I thought you were already aware of that. Wasn't that why Kristoffersen was sent to Utvik in such haste?'

'In such haste? Kristoffersen acted on his own initiative. The company had absolutely nothing to do with that business.'

'No?'

'No, but…' With a resigned sigh and a quick glance around him he motioned for us to join him in the office. To his secretary, who had been sitting with the world's blankest expression on her face, absorbing everything that was being said and done, he said: 'We don't want to be disturbed. Is that understood? No telephone calls. No enquiries. Nothing.'

'Of course, herr Halvorsen,' she replied, not without a touch of irony. But that was probably down to the somewhat out-of-place 'herr Halvorsen'. I was fairly sure they were on first-name terms, as was the norm in modern companies. She was dark-haired, wore glasses in a thick frame and a fashionable suit in grey and black. I wouldn't have minded a secretary like her myself.

Bernt Halvorsen closed the door behind us. He ushered us to a sitting area around a coffee table on which there was a bowl overflowing with fruit, but he didn't offer us anything, not even so much as a cup of coffee. The face he put on wasn't especially inviting either.

The office was grandiose. Admittedly, the shiny dark-brown desk was only just big enough to play table tennis on, at a pinch. However, the oriental carpet led to a little cup with a golf ball in, and the bag of clubs handily placed in a corner revealed what he did in any breaks he might have: practise his putting.

Panoramic windows opened out onto Flesland and Kobbeleia. In front of the distinctive profile of the Liatårnet mountain on the island of Sotra, silver planes took off and landed at regular intervals. But his windows were so well insulated and the air-conditioning was so finely adjusted that barely a sound reached us.

Bernt Halvorsen leaned back in his leather chair, stroked his neatly trimmed beard and said with measured composure, addressing Torunn: 'What was it you wanted? Beyond what we said at the press conference last night, we have no more comments to make.'

'The fact of the matter is that I've been keeping a close eye on the traffic for several months.'

'What traffic? I've already made it clear that this must be something Kristoffersen has been doing off his own bat. And I can assure you, fru Tafjord, of one thing: this man's time at the company is up. For good. He resigned less than ten minutes ago.' He steadfastly refused to drop the formal term of address with her. If I had been her, I would have taken that as a compliment.

'I wasn't—'

'Furthermore, I urged him to report himself to the police before anyone else did. I didn't want to reveal his name until I'd spoken to him personally, but sooner or later it will come out, that's obvious.'

'I wasn't thinking about the alleged human trafficking.'

'No? What were you thinking about?'

'The other traffic between Utvik and Conakry.'

He didn't drop his mask, but I could see his jaw muscles churning. 'Conakry?' When she didn't respond, he added: 'What traffic are you referring to?'

'You know as well as I do. And when this gets into the press, it will be documented.'

'Oh, yes?' He sent her a condescending look. 'But you still haven't told me—'

She interrupted him. 'The dumping of toxic waste in the third world.'

'The dumping … Goodness me. Is that what you said, fru Tafjord? Dumping?' She wisely kept quiet and let him run out the line. 'If that's the case, there are a lot of accessories.'

For a second, she held her breath and let the words sink in. Then she focused on him again. 'So you admit it, do you?'

He didn't answer, but his cheeks were slowly going red.

'Even though you're trying to share the guilt with others,' she continued remorselessly. 'But I can assure you, the heads of the Ministry of Foreign Affairs are going to be hauled over the coals too. Nevertheless, you're the exporters. It's you who earn the money. I doubt the freight gets the best prices on the market.'

'You'll have to ask our suppliers.'

She eyed him suspiciously. 'Suppliers?'

'Yes, what else would I call them?' His eyes wavered. He was on the point of exploding.

'I don't suppose you have some names you can give me?'

He looked at her sullenly. 'That's confidential business information.'

'You don't want to tell me?'

He shook his head firmly. 'Not one.'

While they glared at each other, I seized the opportunity to break into the conversation. 'Then I'd like to go back to Garrido for a moment.'

Halvorsen looked in my direction and shouted: 'Garrido?'

'Let's assume the following: according to you, Kristoffersen has been operating on his own in his dealings with Bjelland.'

'Bjelland? Who's he?'

'The man behind the human trafficking, I'd say. That's what he does. Anything that's illegal enough to earn him big bucks.'

He blew out his cheeks. 'Right. I've never heard of him.'

'I'm not so sure I believe you. But, as I said, if we assume Garrido somehow discovered what Kristoffersen was up to, disguised – at least on the surface – by the legal traffic at Utvik, it could then be fear of Kristoffersen that made him throw his hand in so suddenly and go underground.'

'Fear of Kristoffersen?'

'Kristoffersen could've threatened him the way he just did me. He had good connections on the wrong side of the law, don't forget that.'

'Isn't your imagination running away with you now, Veum?' Torunn interrupted. 'Tell me—'

'Yes, I'll tell you,' Bernt Halvorsen yelled, rising from his chair. Then he slumped back, waving his arms at me. 'This man here, whom you seem to have full confidence in ... Do you know what he dared to claim, fru Tafjord? That I was having a relationship with Garrido's – my employee's – wife. That I was visiting her at home when her husband wasn't there. And that I, that we' – he made two-finger quotes in the air – 'were "caught in the act" in their house and ended up having a huge row with Garrido, whereas in reality I was there to persuade Garrido to return to his job.'

'But you don't know what made him quit?' she said.

'I have no idea. I've already told you.'

'The other freight, he didn't object to that? The one he knew about.'

'Which one?'

'Toxic waste,' she replied unambiguously.

'Yeah, yeah. He never said a negative word about it. Why would he? We have the authorities behind us, fru Tafjord. Whether you like it or not, this is official Norwegian policy.'

'Official?'

'Yes – but discreetly hidden behind a veil.'

'A very robust veil, if you ask me.'

'As robust as the one Kristoffersen pulled over his Bjelland connection?' I interjected.

'Can we forget Kristoffersen?' Halvorsen erupted. 'He's a dead man.' Then he caught himself. 'I mean, as far as this company goes.'

I fixed my gaze on him. 'Not the only one maybe. We still haven't found Garrido.'

'You're exaggerating, Veum. What I said to him didn't help matters. Garrido wouldn't be persuaded. It was his own decision to quit.'

'And what happened then?'

'He quit. I've just told you. On Monday morning he came in to clear his desk. No one's seen him since. No one regrets that more than me.'

Torunn scrutinised him closely. 'Alright then, but this is at best a side-track. I want to get back to the main discussion. So you confirm that you've been transporting toxic waste from chemical concerns in Norway to the third world? In full knowledge of the facts and with full consent?'

'Down there, they're happy to get it.'

'Happy?'

'They get paid.'

'With what some would call blood money.'

He glared at her. 'Call it what you like, fru Tafjord. We're not the only company in Norway doing ... this.'

'I'm sure you aren't. But you are in fact the first to admit it. Could that be because...?' She paused.

'Because of what?'

'Well, what I'm thinking ... Compared to what Veum and I discovered this weekend, you probably don't think what you're doing is particularly serious?'

He looked at her with visible distaste. 'I think you should go now. I've said all I'm going to say about this business. You can come back when you can document the rest of your claims, fru Tafjord. Until then I refuse to make any further comment.'

'No comment is also a kind of comment,' I mumbled.

He had stood up, but Torunn hadn't moved. 'Herr Halvorsen, don't be at all sure we won't produce the documentation you're so confidently demanding.'

'You do that, fru Tafjord,' he said with vehemence, still using the formal term of address. 'Your time is up for today.' He turned to me. 'Not to mention yours.' He used the informal form. I had become used to being spoken to with a lack of respect while

Torunn wasn't. Nonetheless, I was impressed by his ability to manipulate the grammatical forms at will and with such consistency.

He didn't bother to accompany us out. As we left, I heard him say to his secretary: 'No more phone calls for me. I'm going to make some of my own.'

Who to? I wondered as we got into the lift to leave the building.

On the way down, I asked: 'Where are you going?'

'Home first of all. Dublin. But I won't stay long. As soon as I've found out where the *Seagull* is heading, I intend to be standing on the quay with the rest of the welcoming committee.'

'I don't know how much help I was to you, actually.'

'More than you imagine, Varg.'

I drove her to the airport and accompanied her right to the security control. As always in such places I could hear *Casablanca* in my head. Of all the private-investigator joints in all the towns in the world, she walks into mine.

Before she went towards the waiting guards, she stretched up onto her toes and gave me a quick hug. With one hand on my shoulder, she leaned back slightly and examined my face with her keen eyes. Then she smiled, tossed her head and was on her way.

She got through security without a problem. On the other side, she turned quickly and sent me a last wave. Then she was gone, like a backpacker's dream of a travel buddy. I missed her already.

Slowly I walked back down to the car. While I was here anyway, I decided to visit the cabin in Hjellestad again. For some reason, I felt there was something unfinished left for me there.

40

In Hjellestad there was remarkably little activity on the sea and even less on the roads. The weather had definitely changed. The clouds were drifting away, carried on a good-natured breeze, and the thermometer had risen to just below twenty degrees, sensationally high for the end of April.

I parked my car where I had on the previous occasion, got out and followed the path up to the cabin. Among the trees the heat was almost oppressive. The scent of forest and heath was as intense as perfume, and the birdsong even livelier than before. It was as though they, these small bundles of feathers bursting with hormones, had never been more up for the challenges of life than this year.

On the hill the cabin emerged between the trees, red with blue window frames. The pile of logs was untouched, the flower beds as overgrown as before. It was though time had stood still up there, as though the whole place was at rest, in one of life's backwaters.

Outside the cabin I stood observing my surroundings. I felt a sense of unease pulsing through my veins, a kind of premonition of something indefinable but menacing, as if the shade cast by the tall trees around the cabin were shadows of past misdeeds, acts that could never be erased from the atmosphere of the place. Even the bright, clear daylight filled me with a sense of dread. If it had been night, I could have hidden in the darkness. Here I stood naked and exposed to whatever might happen.

Knowing what I did about the events of 1957, I asked myself: was this a kind of echo I could see, a reflection I could hear? Behind the trees over there – could I still glimpse their silhouettes in the September gloom? Ansgar Breheim and Kåre Brodahl slowly approaching the cabin, their eyes fixed on the lit window, silent, not talking? The couple inside – were they still making love? Or were they lying back, resting in each other's arms, exhausted, happy and yet slightly ashamed? Could they sense, at all, the dark shadows making their way to the cabin: the black spies in the night, the harbingers of death? Could they feel in their hearts that this was the last time, that they would never make love with each other again? How much do we know before the messenger of death is suddenly at our door, holding a loaded shotgun in his hands, the flames of hell burning in his eyes? Did they pray? Did they fall to their knees? Did they hope to talk their way out of it? Surely at least they could have talked to Kåre Brodahl?

Shadows of echoes; echoes of shadows.

Then all at once … like a shimmering in the air, like a kind of earth radiation … I could see other images, newer ones, I could hear the echo of words that had been said, of lies that had been told, the impromptu art of veiling the truth, of deceiving much cleverer people than me. I began to see a pattern, the contours of a plan, the semi-legible imprint on a forgotten writing pad. Once again, a chill ran through my body, which made no sense on a day like today.

The peace was broken. I looked at the cabin between the trees. The setting was idyllic. Sunshine gilded the grey roof and was reflected in the light wood of the chopped logs. Below the tree trunks grew clusters of cream primulas; the spring's earliest and most resolute flowers. But this idyll was a falsehood. There was something awry.

Was there anything visible, which might reveal what was wrong?

I listened. The birds were still singing, but it was no longer the song of courtship. It was chorales about a lost love, an elegy lamenting Tordis and Johan, who met their fate among these trees in September 1957. Today, so many years later, the birds were still singing for them. Weren't they? Or were they singing for someone else? The very idea made my head spin. Past and present merged into one, and I was whirled around in the undertow.

To tear myself out of this unpleasant feeling, I seized the keyring I still had in my jacket pocket. I pulled it out and rattled the keys as if to warn the ghosts inside that a guest from reality, a man of flesh and blood, was standing outside and about to enter.

I searched for the right key. I inserted it into the lock and twisted it. When I pushed the door in, there was no longer any doubt that a terrible drama had taken place. There was such a lot of blood inside.

41

For a moment I just gawped. A broad band of blood extended from the door I had unlocked towards the sitting-room door, which was also wide open.

I leaned forward and peered into the cabin. I couldn't see anything.

'Hello, is anyone there?'

Not a sound.

I suppressed my eagerness to enter. Instead, I stepped back, onto the grassy slope around the cabin. I took out my phone, but had to move away from the trees to find coverage. I called the police and told them what I had found.

'Blood?' the man at the other end said, as if he wasn't sure his ears had heard right.

'Yes.'

'But no one's hurt?'

'I called out, but no one answered.'

'So you don't know what might've happened, in other words?'

'No smoke without fire, isn't that how—?'

He interrupted me. 'In other words, you haven't been inside yet?'

'It could be a crime scene. Have I your permission to go inside?' When he hesitated, I added: 'Is Helleve there? He knows about this investigation.'

'Just a moment.' He came back to me quickly. 'He's out. Anyone else?'

'Bergesen maybe.'

'Just a moment.'

Success. I had her voice in my ear. 'This is Inspector Bergesen.'

'Veum here.'

'Oh, you've already been told, I can hear.'

'Told? I don't follow you.'

'Helleve and Solheim are there now.'

'Where now?'

'Bergen Prison. The man who pushed you into the traffic that morning has confessed.'

'Really?'

'He was picked out from mug shots by a number of witnesses. Turns out it's an old acquaintance of ours, possibly yours too.'

'I'm waiting.'

'A certain Fredrik Hansen. Popularly known as…'

'Fred. So Bjelland was behind it?'

'That's the conclusion we drew, too. That's why Helleve and Solheim are with him now.'

'With Bjelland? He'll never admit anything.'

'Time will tell, but—'

'Besides, I suspect I know who ordered the job.'

'Oh, yes?'

'Someone called Kristoffersen. That's not why I'm ringing though.'

'No?' She sounded surprised.

'No.'

'So, what's this about?'

'I'm afraid I've reached a point in my investigations where I will have to call you in.'

'What was your case again? A missing couple?'

'Yes, I'm up at their cabin now, in Hjellestad. And this time there's an awful lot of blood here.'

After I had briefed her on the situation, her response was clear. 'Stay where you are, Veum. By which I mean, go down to the road and meet us there. We'll be right up.'

Before following her instructions, I paced slowly around the cabin. I was very careful where I put my feet so as not to destroy any possible evidence, and when I leaned over to one of the windows, I made sure I didn't touch anything.

I couldn't see a body. The furniture was as before. The landscape paintings and the old photographs were where they had hung, the TV was in the corner, the radio and the record-player beside it. But there was half a bottle of red wine on the table. Along with two glasses, and only one of them had been drunk from. When I raised my eyes to the wall, I saw it. The shotgun was missing.

I leaned forward. On the floor, in the middle of the room, someone had bled, a lot. A line of blood led to the door, as though someone had been dragged in that direction.

That was as far as I got. In the distance I heard sirens and went down to the road to meet the police. I stood waiting by my car as though I were a host welcoming people to a nice day out in the country. But they didn't seem very happy, neither Jakob E. Hamre nor Annemette Bergesen. And they had quite a contingent with them, as if they were expecting a massacre.

'How many dead are there?' Hamre bellowed as soon as he was out of his car.

'No idea. Lots of blood,' I said.

He viewed me with scepticism. 'Are you saying you haven't been inside yet?'

'Yes. Experience tells me that's not a good idea. But...'

Bergesen came up alongside him and stood listening.

'Yes?'

'I peered in through a window. I couldn't see anyone.'

If anything, he seemed even more sceptical now. 'Let me warn you, Veum. If you've dragged us all up here to examine a nose-bleed after a harmless punch-up, then...'

'Send me an invoice, Hamre. Are you trying to walk in Muus's footsteps now he's retired?'

Bergesen cleared her throat. 'Perhaps we should…?' She nodded towards the path behind us.

'Right,' Hamre growled. 'We won't find an answer chitter-chattering around here. You take the lead, Veum, as you know your way around up here.'

Walking through the trees, Bergesen asked: 'Have you any suspicions as to what might've happened?'

'Let me put it like this: I have a well-grounded fear that the couple I've been searching for over the last week or so have finally turned up.'

'Were they by any chance the people you were looking for in Utvik as well?' Hamre asked sarcastically.

'No, that was initially another case. Have you been involved in that?'

'Oh, we received a call from Haugesund and were asked to check out some of the local details.'

'Trans World Ocean?'

'For example.'

'A connection is not impossible.'

'Really? What kind of connection?'

'Mm, we'll have to wait and see.'

'I don't want to find out you've been holding something back, Veum.'

'No, no. Let's just deal with one thing at a time, Hamre.'

We had reached the cabin. I had left the door open and they went straight there. For a moment they stood eyes agape as well. Then Hamre beckoned one of the forensic officers over. He and Bergesen were given the equipment they needed. They put on disposable overshoes and transparent head coverings and gloves before entering.

I stayed outside. No one had invited me in. I listened attentively for outbursts or reactions inside. But I heard nothing. Not so much as a resigned sigh.

I turned away. I met the gaze of a young police officer with sandy hair who had been left outside, either because they wanted to spare him or keep an eye on me.

I nodded to him. 'I don't believe we've met.' I held out a hand. 'Veum.'

He squeezed my hand perfunctorily. 'Melvær.'

'A Melvær from Sunnfjord?'

'No, but my father was.'

'So you're following in his footsteps?'

He shook his head firmly. 'No, no. He was a college lecturer.'

'Ah,' I said. 'Nothing's the way it used to be. Not Sunnfjorders and not the police force.'

My gaze landed on the square lid over the well with the robust padlock and the new boards. *What the...?*

Involuntarily, I took a few paces in that direction. The young officer looked at me suspiciously.

I pointed. 'Do you see what I see?'

His face broke into an expression of dismay. Then he nodded. 'That's blood. There too.'

The grass was flat. It was obvious something had been dragged across the overgrown lawn. I motioned towards the well. 'Over there, wouldn't you say?'

We followed the trail, on either side of it, and ended up in the same place, by the lid over the well. Melvær leaned over and studied the padlock. 'Don't touch it,' I said.

He looked at me as if I thought he was an idiot. 'It's locked.'

'Blood,' I said, pointing to the edge of the lid.

He nodded. 'The person ... Someone must've been bleeding one hell of a lot.'

'You generally do if you've been hit in the chest at close range by a blast from a shotgun.'

'Let's hear what Hamre has to say,' he said, straightening up.

We stood by the well waiting. Thoughts raced through my

brain. There hadn't been any blood here last Friday. Neither here nor inside the cabin. So who had been bleeding here in the intervening period?

Again, I visualised the tragic love triangle of 1957. Tordis Breheim, Johan Hagenes and Ansgar Breheim, with Kåre Brodahl as a geometric point on the outside. But what if that wasn't how it had been? What if he had been part of the triangle too? Had he been closer to Tordis Breheim than he was willing to admit thirty-six years later? Perhaps Ansgar Breheim hadn't been up here at all? Perhaps it was Brodahl alone who…? Didn't my previous experience tell me that everyone lied? Wasn't it frequently the case that the biggest problem was seeing through the lies to what was hidden behind them, what we in thoughtless exaggeration called the truth?

But the evidence from 1957 had long been washed away. This was fresh.

I found it difficult to visualise Bodil Breheim and Fernando Garrido in my mind. All I had was some old photographs, good enough for me to recognise them if I bumped into them, but not good enough to imagine them as living people.

And now? Would I recognise them if it were them in the well?

Hamre and Bergesen appeared in the doorway, pale and concentrated. They stood outside the door conferring. Pensive, they looked in our direction.

Melvær, beside me, shouted: 'Hamre.' He pointed to the ground by their feet.

They looked down, and their eyes followed the trail from the door sill to the well.

When they reached us, Hamre asked Melvær: 'Have you had a look in?'

'It's locked.'

Hamre looked to me. 'Do you know if there's a key anywhere?'

I took out the bunch I had in my pocket and examined the ones I hadn't used. 'None of these, I reckon. It's probably hanging on the wall in the cabin somewhere.'

'I'll check,' Bergesen said. 'Is there a brand name on the padlock?'

Melvær leaned over. 'Stico, it says.'

She went back in while Hamre stayed.

I asked him: 'Did you find anything inside?'

'No. There was nothing apart from the blood.'

'You've got something to analyse anyway.'

'Let's tackle this one step at a time, Veum. This couple … What ties them to the cabin?'

'It belongs to the family. Hers, I should add.'

'What are their names?'

'Bodil Breheim and Fernando Garrido.'

'Breheim?'

'Berit Breheim's sister, if that means anything to you.'

'The lawyer?'

I nodded.

'I see. And how long have they been missing?'

'To be accurate, they've been gone from their home, according to my information, since the Wednesday of Easter week.'

'Soon be three weeks, in other words.'

'Garrido was last seen at his workplace the Monday of that week. But I've been here since they went missing. On the Friday, the week before last. And there was no blood here then.'

He regarded me with those serious, ever-observant eyes of his. It was quite a while now since our paths had first crossed, time in which I had learned that Jakob E. Hamre was the kind of policeman who neither said nor did anything hurriedly. When he did go in to action, it was always with due consideration.

'Garrido has just quit his job at Trans World Ocean,' I added.

I watched him absorb this information. 'Do you mean to say he could be involved in this business down in Sveio?'

Before I had a chance to answer, Bergesen reappeared in the cabin doorway. 'I found this in the kitchen.' She held up a small key. 'It's the same brand anyway.'

We assembled around the well lid. Still wearing forensic gloves, the detective inspector crouched down. Without touching more than was necessary, she inserted the key into the lock and turned. There was a soft click and the padlock sprang open. She skilfully removed the padlock from the hinge and placed it in a transparent plastic bag, which she then gave to the young officer. 'Give this to Andersen, will you.'

Hamre had crouched down beside her and stuck his fingers in under the edge of the lid. With a jerk, he pushed it up. A chain rattled and tightened, preventing the lid from tipping over fully. A foul stench met us. As a pure reflex, I closed my mouth. I wasn't going to drink any of the water from this well. The two inspectors didn't look desperately thirsty, either.

We all leaned forward and looked into the well. It was almost full. The water reached up to forty centimetres below the cement edge.

'Jesus,' Bergesen exclaimed.

'Hm,' Hamre said.

I said nothing.

For a moment we straightened up and looked sombrely at each other. This was confirmation of what we had feared.

A pale face stared up at us. The eyes were dulled. Most of the upper body was visible. There was a large, open wound in the man's chest, where the gun had discharged its shot. Some of it was lodged in splintered bones, like black boils in the flesh-coloured lacerations. The water was turbid. The hair of the deceased floated on the surface.

Realisation went through me like a shock wave. This was

neither Bodil Breheim nor Fernando Garrido. This was someone I had spoken to myself, only a few days before. But he would never play the saxophone again.

Hamre read the expression on my face. 'Is this Garrido, Veum?'

'No, this is Hallvard Hagenes. His uncle died here thirty-six years ago.'

'Thirty-six?'

'And does that death have any connection with this?' Bergesen asked, with disbelief in her voice.

'Not that I can see,' I answered.

42

Dead men don't play the saxophone. Dead men lie supine, eyes vacant, listening to music we others cannot hear. And they have taken its secrets with them.

I could feel their eyes on my face, as though they were waiting for a more exhaustive explanation. Instead, I thought aloud. 'He and Bodil Breheim, it might appear, were having a relationship.'

Bergesen nodded. 'In other words, what we see here might be the result of a classic love triangle.'

'What was the bit about the uncle, Veum?' Hamre asked.

'His uncle and Bodil Breheim's mother definitely did have a relationship in 1957. They were caught in the act, quite literally, up here by her husband and one other person. I can go into detail later. The way I've had it explained to me, Johan Hagenes and Tordis Breheim were forced to drive their car into the sea from Hjellestad quay. They both died.'

Hamre raised his eyebrows. 'Forced?'

'With the help of a shotgun hanging on the cabin wall as recently as the previous time I was here.'

'The same one?'

'Well, I can't be precise about that, Hamre. But there was definitely a shotgun on the wall, and now there isn't.'

'How do you know?'

'I looked through the window after I rang you.'

'Hm.' He observed me, deep in contemplation. 'And this Breheim was charged, was he?'

'No, the case was never cleared up. In fact, it was never a case. It was pronounced a suicide. A death pact, if you understand what I mean, between two unhappy lovers. It's only now that ... Actually, it was me who got to the bottom of this.'

'Master Detective VV strikes again,' Hamre quipped. 'And

true to form,' he said to his colleague, 'always too late. In this case, a mere thirty-six years.'

Bergesen nodded, her face concentrated. 'But that, as far as I can discern, has nothing at all to do with this.' She indicated the corpse in the well. Then she looked at me.

I shrugged. 'Not unless a tendency to act in this way is hereditary.'

'Perhaps we'd better send someone to check Hjellestad quay, do you think?' Hamre suggested.

I didn't answer.

'Is there any more you can tell us about this Hagenes?' she asked.

I told them all I knew, but I could hear with my own ears that it wasn't much.

In the meantime, more police had arrived. Hamre told one of the officers to call an ambulance so that the dead body could be taken away. Then he turned back to me. 'When did you last see him, Veum?'

I made a quick calculation. 'It must've been on Tuesday.'

'A week tomorrow, in other words.' He shifted his gaze to Bergesen. 'But he obviously hasn't been here that long.'

'No chance,' she said. 'If I had to guess, I'd say this happened quite recently. Probably the weekend just gone.'

Hamre summed up. 'So we have a body in a well, with a fatal shot to the chest. We don't have the assumed murder weapon, probably a shotgun our main witness, herr Veum, saw on the wall in the cabin. We have a named couple who have been missing from home since Easter. There's a lot that's still unclear, but all the evidence suggests we're dealing with a classic crime of passion.'

I felt my forehead tighten. 'Perhaps your suggestion, Hamre, wasn't so stupid after all.'

'Which one?'

'To check Hjellestad quay.'

He eyed me, frowning. 'Are you serious?'

Bergesen was more open to the idea. 'Can you imagine someone simply copying the events of 1957?'

I nodded. 'Not down to the very last detail perhaps, but … yes.'

Hamre stroked his brow. 'If I understand you correctly, Veum, you're saying that if we search the sea near Hjellestad, we may find the Garrido couple?'

'But my understanding,' Bergesen said, 'was that there were no dead bodies up here in 1957.'

'No, there weren't,' I replied, 'and that may be the big difference.'

'So, the scene is different anyway?'

'Yes … It's a kind of mirror image, if you get what I mean.'

'No, I don't think I do, quite.'

I looked at Hamre. 'Well? What's it to be?'

He glanced from me to his colleague with an expression of resignation. 'Can you be bothered to go with him? If you two see any evidence to suggest there's something in what he's saying, then call a crane by all means. This could be a long day – a very long day.'

Annemette Bergesen and I exchanged looks. Her eyes were blue, bottomless, her lips full, the contours of her face angular. Around her neck she wore a turquoise silk scarf, loosely knotted.

'And there was you thinking you'd come to a peaceful town,' I said.

She smiled. 'This is actually my profession, you know.'

'Dead people.'

'Most are alive, luckily.'

'Guilty and innocent.'

'More or less, yes.' She turned back to Hamre. 'Perhaps you should come with us? In case we find something.'

Hamre frowned at her. 'Don't you start.'

'You never know.'

'Oh, alright then.'

It ended up with all three of us walking down to the road and driving to Hjellestad quay, with Bergesen at the wheel. Summer was in full bloom. The sun was beating down from a cloudless sky, and the thermometer outside the shop said twenty-two degrees. I wouldn't have minded jumping into the sea myself.

To the east of the quay, a concrete boat ramp sloped down into the sea. We got out on the quay. From the ramp, we could see the seabed, dotted with seaweed, then it suddenly descended into the depths, where the water was darker.

And just there...

Of course, it could have been a sunken boat that no one had bothered to raise. It could have been junk someone had dumped, the way that some people have a habit of doing. Or it could have been the reflection of the rear window in a car, parked for good – or until someone considered it worthwhile checking whether the parking meter had run out.

I don't know which of us saw it first. But it was Bergesen who made the first tentative observations. 'Goodness...' She pointed. 'Down there ... It really does look like ... Doesn't it?'

Hamre nodded dolefully.

'Anyone feel like a swim?' I asked.

Hamre was already on his way back to the car to ring the central switchboard at the police station. Bergesen shook her head. 'It's too late anyway. Besides, I left my swimming costume at home.'

'Swimming costume?' I said, loosening the buckle on my belt. But I let it go. She was right. It was too late.

It was going to be a long wait. If we had needed to, we could have become close friends during that day; at least got to know each other better. Hamre came back with the message that a frogman unit was on its way. We heard the vehicle long before we saw it; it arrived with the sirens wailing. The two divers greeted Hamre and were given their instructions. While they dived down, we stood on the quay watching. Bubbles told us where they were, forming an arbitrary pattern in the greyish-green water; bubbles rising and bursting, like shattered dreams. If we strained our eyes, we could catch a glimpse of them as they moved around the car below, like carrion-eating fish around their prey.

They didn't re-emerge until ten minutes later. One of them pulled off his mask and beckoned to Hamre. The rest of us followed him. The diver looked up at us.

'It's a taxi.'

'Right,' Hamre said.

'There's a woman behind the wheel. Buckled in. No one else. And one more thing. There's a shotgun on the backseat.'

'No saxophone?' I asked.

Taken aback by the question, he looked up at me. 'No, a shotgun. You know, *bang, bang.*'

Hamre heaved a huge sigh. 'Good. The crane's on the way. Can you check the car again thoroughly to see if you can find anything of significance?'

'And check the rear doors are shut properly,' I said.

The diver looked at Hamre with raised eyebrows. Hamre nodded.

More waiting; more topsy-turvy thoughts. Suddenly everything seemed to explode in front of my eyes. What had initially been just a somewhat suspicious disappearance, a case that had been difficult to get a proper perspective on, had in the course of a few hours developed into a drama of unexpected proportions, not only with the body in the well up by the cabin, but now with an even stronger allusion to the events of 1957: a dead woman in a car that had driven into the sea off Hjellestad quay.

'If, in fact, it is Bodil Breheim sitting in the car,' Hamre said while we were waiting for the crane, 'then we have at least two possibilities. Maybe she killed Hagenes. Afterwards she took the murder weapon with her, got into the car and drove into the sea of her own free will. That's happened before.'

'And the second?' I said.

'If we take what you told us about the events of 1957 as the basis, it would be as follows: Fernando is the guilty party. After shooting Hagenes, he forced his wife at gun point to repeat her mother's actions and he – as you claim Breheim did originally – jumped out of the car at the last moment. In which case, we'll have to find him.'

'And the third?' I insisted.

'Is there a third possibility?'

I looked at Bergesen, expecting her to come up with a suggestion, then continued, addressing Hamre again. 'The problem is that both Bodil Breheim and her husband have been missing for more than two weeks. I've met Hallvard Hagenes in the meantime. Twice. The scenario of him and Bodil Breheim coming up here for a frolic, only then to be surprised by Garrido, simply makes no sense.'

'It doesn't fit with what happened in 1957, you mean?' Hamre grinned.

'It doesn't fit with anything.'

The crane truck arrived, and the last phase of the wait began, the last and the most difficult. We didn't have any more ideas to exchange. All we did was watch the process of the car being hauled ashore.

The truck backed as far down the boat ramp as it could. The two divers carried the hook down into the deep. After a while one came up to the surface and signalled that the car was securely attached. Afterwards the black Mercedes was pulled backward, up from the sea. The truck drove up the ramp and dragged Hallvard Hagenes's car with it. As the water was still gushing and trickling out of it, we went over, leaned forward and peered in at the woman sitting behind the wheel, pale and wet and as dead as you can be.

For the second time today, I suffered a huge shock, and not for a second did I think about who I was going to send the bill for my services. Because it wasn't Bodil Breheim in the car. It was her sister.

43

Another recent acquaintance was being laid in a body bag today and transported to Gades Institute for an autopsy. The shotgun was taken from the back seat and carefully wrapped up as well. I stood on the quay, idly watching. No one came to wrap me up, and I was fine with that. I was still alive.

Annemette Bergesen sauntered over, not exactly to comfort me though. 'How should we interpret this, Veum? Have you got a view on it?'

I shrugged. 'They knew each other. Once, a long time ago.'

'In which way?'

'They'd been close friends when they were very young. In 1972 to '73. But her sister came between them.'

'Oh?'

'They formed a kind of love triangle even then. Berit lost Hallvard to her sister, if you know what I mean.'

'She took him from her?'

'Mmm. I wouldn't like to say who took whom from whom. And it was twenty years ago.'

'They didn't have any contact later?'

'Yes, they probably did. I know for certain he was in Bodil's house as late as February this year.'

She seemed interested. 'Really?'

'According to him, it was perfectly innocent, but … he may've been lying to me, of course. In this profession that's what you learn. People lie all the time. Besides, he half admitted it himself, that he'd met Berit again, at a later date. But from there to…'

'Neither of them was married?'

'He wasn't. She had been.'

'Who to?'

'Don't know. Someone or other. It wasn't her I was investigating. It was her sister.'

'So Bodil Breheim and Hallvard Hagenes had been…?' She gazed across the sea. 'Where do you think they are now?'

'Bodil?' I shrugged and splayed my hands. 'I have no idea. Right now, I feel like a terrible failure. When the bodies that turn up are not those you'd expected, it's like everything's been turned on its head, nothing is as it appears, or as the people I was speaking to made it appear.'

'Do you mean she was lying to you?'

'Berit Breheim?'

'Yes.'

'Looks like it now. But what reasons would she have for wanting to do that?'

'Mm, well, what indeed? To hide another crime maybe?'

'It doesn't make any sense. What's more, we still haven't found anything to indicate a crime with regard to her sister and husband.'

'No – more the opposite perhaps. At this point, however, they have to be our main suspects.'

I stared at her blindly. 'So you don't think…?'

'Think what?'

'Well, the most likely explanation is still that Berit Breheim drove into the sea herself, after shooting Hallvard Hagenes in the cabin.'

'And why would she do that?'

'As I said – they were part of a love triangle twenty years ago. Perhaps later as well. What if this triangle was recreated later, so to speak.'

She pursed her lips. 'Do you think so?'

'I don't think anything anymore. And my client's dead. From that point of view, and from mine, the case is over.'

'Good.' She nodded firmly. 'Then I suggest you go home, Veum. If you get any brainwaves about what might lie behind this, I'd urge you to tell us, straight away. As you yourself say, from your point of view this case is over.'

We nodded to each other, wearily, like after a long joust in court, where neither of us was very pleased with the outcome. I ambled back to my car. She stayed in the quay area.

I hadn't made any promises to her. Which was just as well. I hadn't even reached the road to the airport before I turned off, took out my phone and tapped in the number I had been ringing regularly over the last ten days. Then I got the third shock of the day. For the first time, someone answered.

'Fernando,' a man's sonorous voice said, with hardly any accent. I was so taken aback I lost my ability to speak. 'Hello, is anyone there?' he repeated irritably, with a more obvious accent now. I still didn't know what to say and before I had a chance to articulate a few sensible words, he cursed in his own language, with no accent at all, and rang off.

That didn't matter. Now I knew where I was going. But on the way to Morvik I couldn't stop thinking that this was an odd time to reappear, wherever they had been in the meantime.

44

It was early afternoon when I drove past the sign saying *PRIVATE ROAD*, down the steep hill and into the car park behind the white box-shaped house. The snowdrops had flowered since my last visit and the daffodils had shot up. The garage door was open and I could see the glistening bonnet of a blue car. It was a BMW 520. I automatically glanced up at the neighbour's house. All I could see was a reflection in the large window panes.

I got out of my car, walked over and rang the bell. Shortly afterwards, I heard quickening footsteps inside. The door opened, and for the first time I came face to face with Fernando Garrido. I recognised him from the wedding photograph. He had regular facial features, pronounced eyebrows and a golden-brown tan. His teeth were gleaming white and his eyes brown, but the styled hair, which had been black in the photograph, had a silver patina. He eyed me with suspicion. 'Yes?'

'My name's Veum. Is Bodil Breheim at home?'

'That's my wife. Yes, she is. What's this about?'

'It's about her sister.'

'Berit?'

'Yes, could I come inside?'

He shrugged, opened the door and let me in. The hallway was as big and empty as last time, but melodious guitar music flowed out of the sitting-room sound system and there was a faint aroma of food. All of a sudden, the house was inhabited.

He led the way and I followed him into the sitting room. Candles were lit and someone had placed cut flowers in a vase. 'You've been away?' I asked casually.

'Yes,' he said. Without any further comment he motioned me to one of the elegant chairs. 'Take a seat and I'll fetch my wife.'

I stood by the window. Down in the fjord a hobby yachtsman was running before the wind – a privileged person in this beautiful weather. Over on Askøy a large yellow crane was swinging a jib across a building site. Not everyone was on holiday. Hearing footsteps behind me, I turned in her direction.

Bodil Breheim stood in the doorway, her hair shorter than in the photograph, wearing faded blue jeans and a mottled grey blouse. In her arms she was holding a small, black-haired child, barely a year old, with dark-brown, oriental eyes and golden skin. The child was looking up at her trustingly, and she could barely tear her eyes away to look at me. 'What's happened?'

Her husband appeared behind her. Not one of us sat down. For a moment it struck me that the way we were standing was like a sculpture group, yet another of these strange triangles in this case, but with a brand new and extremely surprising factor in the middle of us.

'I should introduce myself. My name's Veum, Varg Veum. Ten days or so ago your sister employed me to do a job for her.'

She reacted with surprise. 'What job was that?'

'You've been away?'

'Yes, we went to China to pick up little Therese here, or Li, which is her real name.'

'We've been away for two and a half weeks,' Garrido added.

'Yes,' I said. 'We've noticed.'

'Noticed?'

I looked at Bodil. 'You didn't think to inform your sister of your travel plans?'

'Why? Berit and I have barely spoken for the last four years.'

'Oh?'

She shook her head. The little girl in her arms gurgled. Berit looked down and smiled. When she looked up again, her eyes were moist.

'So your sister had no idea you were going to China for a child?'

'As I said, we haven't really been in touch since Pappa died, and even less after she and Rolf split up, in 1989.'

'But your stepmother said … Didn't you go to a Christmas party, at your half-brother Rune's house?'

'For Sara's sake, yes, we did. But we didn't talk. Berit and I, I mean.'

'Strange.'

'If you had any idea…'

'Yes?'

'No, this is private and personal. Sorry.'

I turned to Garrido. 'But you were definitely in touch with Berit three weeks ago.'

He looked down. 'Yes.'

Bodil sent him a look, and for a moment, sparks seemed to be flying between the two spouses. Then she turned back to me. 'What do you know about this?'

'I know that a neighbour complained about the noise…'

'Neighbour,' she snorted, and the little girl opened her eyes wide in fear. Her face began to pucker up. 'No, no, no…' And her little face quickly turned into a smile. 'Don't worry, my darling. Mamma's not angry. Not with you…'

'It was all my fault,' Garrido said. 'I couldn't control my temper, and then all of a sudden the police were at the door. I was furious and, well, they took me along with them. I had to spend the night in a drunk tank!' His temper was clearly beginning to stir again. At any rate his voice was louder. 'The only lawyer I knew, apart from business lawyers, was … Berit.' He glanced shyly at his wife. 'I should've thought about Bodil, but I was desperate. I needed someone to vouch for me.'

'But what caused your outburst?'

'It—'

Bodil interrupted him. 'Now I think you should tell us who you are, beyond a name, what you're doing here and perhaps how we can help you.'

'OK. As I said to your husband when I rang – this is about your sister.'

'I've gathered that much. But you still haven't said what your job is.'

'Well, first off, I'm a private investigator and your sister commissioned me to track down you and your husband. She'd been trying to get hold of you.'

'Berit? Trying to contact us?' She furrowed her brow. Then she looked over at her husband. 'That's a bit of a turn-up, I must say.'

'Well, that's how it was put to me. So I've been trying to find you. I went to TWO, where I heard that your husband had quit his job.'

Again, there were sparks in her eyes. Clearly it wasn't just Garrido who had difficulty keeping a temper under control in this house.

'I've been to Hjellestad and Ustaoset. We talked about going to Barcelona. But I never considered going to China.'

'And why was Berit so keen to get in touch now?'

'She was worried about you, she claimed.'

'Worried? Berit? Don't make me laugh. There's some skulduggery behind this, if I know her.'

'Anyway, that's what she told me.'

'Then you'd better have another word with her and ask her for a more cogent explanation.'

'That ... will be difficult.'

'And why's that?' she asked, but I could see the reality was already beginning to dawn on her.

'Your sister's dead, Bodil.'

She stared at me, expecting me to go on.

Garrido was unable to restrain a reaction. 'Dead? Berit?'

'We found her in the sea at Hjellestad. She'd driven off the quay.'

A few seconds elapsed before she could take in what I had said. Then the reactions spread like ripples across her face. She lurched forward for an instant. Garrido stepped over to support her, and she pushed the baby into his arms. 'Take Therese. I…'

Then she pulled herself together. She walked over to the nearest chair and slumped down. Garrido was left standing with a helpless expression on his face, caught between his over-whelmed wife and the tiny creature in his arms.

Bodil Breheim stared at me with tears in her eyes. 'Just like…'

'Just like your mother, yes.'

'But was she alone? In the car?'

'Yes.' I waited a while before continuing. 'But there was another body up there.'

'Another? Whose?'

'You knew him well,' I replied, preparing her.

Again, she seemed to anticipate what I was going to say. Her pupils widened and went black; her oval, and initially so attract-ive, face began to spasm.

'Hallvard Hagenes,' I said then, and she burst into tears. She hid her face in her hands and sobbed uncontrollably. Her whole body shook, as though racked by hidden forces.

Garrido looked at me. 'Hallvard Hagenes? Who's he?'

'You didn't know him?'

'I've never even heard his name.'

As if in sympathy with her new foster mother, the baby in his arms started crying. For a moment his uppermost thought seemed to be to throw it down, storm out and leave everything behind him. The next, he looked at me. Without any further re-flection, his jaw set, he stepped forward and passed the screaming bundle over to me. As soon as I had the sobbing child safely in my embrace, he turned to his wife, walked over and sat on the arm of her chair, leaned down and hugged her, mumbling some inaudible words into her blonde hair. I was left standing there, as helpless as he had been, with little Therese Li in my care now, for God knows how long.

While Fernando Garrido consoled his wife, I rocked my arms reassuringly, made a few soft clucking sounds and did everything that occurred to me, apart from breastfeeding, to comfort the little mite. Slowly, almost in sync, they calmed down, the adult woman in the chair by the door and the infant in my arms.

When Bodil Breheim finally looked at me again, her eyes were red-rimmed and her cheeks wet. She had hectic, red blotches on her neck and looked unlovely and desperate. 'What happened?' she wailed.

'I'd like to know too,' I said. 'Are you ready to talk about it?'

'But I don't know anything.'

'Really?'

'No…'

I went over and gave her the child. She took her with a grateful smile. Therese Li had closed her eyes now and seemed to be sleeping.

'Let's take this one bit at a time. First – the breach of peace three weeks ago. I repeat my question: what caused it?'

'It had nothing to do with this. It was about Fernando and his job.'

'Bernt Halvorsen?'

'Yes.'

Garrido broke in. 'It's pretty simple, Veum. I'd decided to pack in my job. Halvorsen came out here to persuade me to stay. It ended in a furious row.' He raised both hands in an apology. 'My innate temperament, as I've said.'

'Just a minute, Garrido. You'd decided to pack the job in, you said. But my understanding was that you quit on the spot, without any notice.'

His eyes wavered. 'Well, yes. It came to a confrontation.'

'With Halvorsen?'

He hesitated.

'Or was it Kristoffersen perhaps?'

He met my eyes in a way that suggested I had hit the bullseye.

'Did you feel threatened in some way by Kristoffersen? Was that why you quit?'

'I…'

'He came here to your house to get hold of you.'

'Who? Kristoffersen?' Suddenly he looked frightened.

'Listen, Garrido. I know about the connection between Kristoffersen and Bjelland. The human trafficking via Utvik has been stopped.'

'What? Have they been caught?'

'I take it you haven't seen the papers yet?'

Bodil interposed. 'Fernando, what is this you're talking about? You didn't say anything about this to me. You told me—'

He brushed her aside with a sweep of his hand. 'Where's Kristoffersen now, Veum?'

'I hope he's given himself up to the police. If not, he'll be getting a visit from them. At any rate, he's finished with TWO as well. In his case though, he got the boot. And Bjelland's in prison. You'll lose nothing by laying your cards on the table.'

'What cards? My conscience is clear. That's obviously why I cleared off.'

'Can you tell me in simple words what happened?'

He met his wife's eyes. She was staring at him questioningly and nodded. Then he slowly turned back to me. 'Alright then. This is how it all started. By chance I came across a message from the captain of the *Seagull* to Kristoffersen. When I confronted him with it, he became very aggressive. He threatened to set this Bjelland on me. There was no limit to what he wouldn't do, and I have to confess I *was* afraid. The way I saw things, I had two options. One was to spill the beans to Halvorsen, and face the consequences, for Kristoffersen and me. However, with us about to leave for China, I chose the easier option. I chucked in the towel and quit without notice. When Halvorsen came to see us that Saturday, I tried to invent all sorts of reasons. But he didn't believe me, naturally enough, and so it ended in, well, you know how.'

'The breach of peace?'

'Yes. It's all so embarrassing. Halvorsen came out here, and we ended up having a furious row, with Bodil as an involuntary witness. Later, after Halvorsen had gone, I started drinking. I was so angry. I just had to … If I hadn't let everything out, I could've hurt myself, or others. Bodil lost her temper. First of all, she didn't like it that I was unemployed now that we … At last we were going to have a family after trying in vain for so many years. And then I caused all this trouble. She was also angry because I was drinking and it all ended in…' Once again, he looked at his wife, shame-faced. 'It was the worst row we've had since we've known each other, no?'

'And so loud the neighbour called the police…'

'Yes.'

'On Monday morning you went to clear your desk?'

'Yes, and again I was set upon by Kristoffersen. He thought that by leaving without giving notice, I'd alert people to the fact that something dubious was going on in Utvik. And, once again, he threatened me. With such aggression that when I got home…'

'Yes?'

'Well, we were going to change flights in Oslo anyway. We just packed our things, jumped in the car and drove over the mountains the same afternoon.'

'What made you react like that to what Kristoffersen was doing?'

'First, it was disloyal to the company and to all the rest of us, who were dragged into it without our knowledge. Second, it was morally questionable. He and Bjelland were making big money out of other people's misfortunes, abandoning them to their fates. What would happen to them?'

'Yes, what would?'

'I have no idea. As a foreigner myself, I just had to react.'

'But the other business in Utvik, you had no moral scruples about that? Not even as a foreigner?'

'You're referring to…?'

'You know perfectly well what I'm referring to. The toxic waste that was being shipped out of the country to the third world.'

'You're well informed, I see.'

'As well informed as I need to be.'

He looked down. 'No. I regarded that part of our activities as approved by the authorities. What could I do about it?'

'OK, you may be right about that.' I hesitated. 'Back to the Saturday when you landed in jail. This row you had with Bodil, it had nothing to do with Hallvard Hagenes?'

Bodil reacted furiously. But this time I was the object of her angry glare.

Garrido seemed confused. 'Hallvard Hagenes again. Who is he?'

I looked at Bodil. 'He visited you here in February, didn't he.'

She closed her eyes and opened them again, not that that helped to mitigate the irritation in them.

Garrido focused on her again. 'Bodil? Did he visit…?' His blood was beginning to boil – the veins in his temples were swollen, and his face was crimson.

She returned his gaze, irritably. 'Nothing happened. Nothing that can't be talked about.'

'So it's correct what this…' he waved his hands vaguely in my direction '…man says? He visited you – Hallvard Hagenes? You knew him?'

'Of course I knew him.'

'Was he your…? Were you two…?'

'Once, a long time ago. Long before I met you.'

'You met me long before February this year,' he objected, opportunely.

'But it wasn't … Let me explain.'

'I think that might be appropriate now, no?' he said crisply with a look in my direction.

She looked at me too. Perhaps it was easier for her too; having someone else to tell this to. 'Berit and Hallvard went out together. In the early seventies.'

How bored she had been that weekend. No one had invited her out. She had spent the Saturday in her room, with her record-player and a pile of magazines. On the Sunday she had been persuaded down to lunch, with difficulty, and there…

Berit had invited him home for lunch in Sudmanns vei, and he was so young – much too young for Berit. They didn't even shake hands, and he was much too shy to impose his presence. But she studied his hands as they ate, the way he held the cutlery: long, slim fingers, sensitive and nervous. She heard him timidly clear his throat when there were gaps in the conversation around the table. She listened to the bumbling answers he gave the few times Sara asked him a question. Her father didn't say a word. He obviously disliked this new element to their lunch routine, and her noisy half-brothers, they…

When Berit and Hallvard left, she had stood by her window on the first floor and watched them from behind the curtain. She saw Berit take his hand and smile at him, and she had been so jealous. It had all seethed and fermented inside her, the state of her excitement had been so great she had to … She locked the door, lay down on the bed and, with her fingers buried deep inside her, she swore: You will be mine, Hallvard. You shall be mine…

'But it finished, and for a while it was us two instead. Hallvard and me.'

'Did it finish or did you finish it?'

She looked away. 'We had a short affair, if you can call it that, when you're talking about two eighteen-year-olds. We went out together from July to September that year, and then it finished. Later I saw him only sporadically, *en passant*. And then once, in 1988, when Berit and he started again.'

I held up a hand. 'Wait a minute. What did you just say? This was in 1988?'

It had been around nine in the evening, one Friday in the middle of August. She and Fernando had been on top of Geitanuken watching the sunset. When they were almost back down, they took the short cut down to the sea behind a man she didn't recognise. But as the man turned off towards the neighbouring house, he had glanced behind him and...

She gave a start. Hallvard?

He stopped. With his easily recognisable, boyish smile he looked at her shyly: Bodil?

What are you doing here?

I...

She suddenly clicked. Don't tell me ... Are you and Berit ... Are you together again?

He shrugged and looked at Fernando with a strange expression. Then he raised a hand in a sort of goodbye and continued up to the house where...

'We met him briefly on the short cut here one evening. Fernando and I had been walking in the mountains, and he was on his way up to Berit's.'

'So that was Hallvard Hagenes,' her husband mumbled.

'Up to...?' I queried.

'Yes. She lived here as well then.' She nodded in the direction of the neighbouring house.

A new and significant perspective was slowly dawning on me. 'So, you didn't fall out because of Hallvard Hagenes? This was a classic row about property.'

'Yes, as so often happens, sadly. The inheritance settlement that goes wrong. That was how it was basically. Down here, where we live, there was originally a cabin from my father's family. For many years it just stood here because we had both Hjellestad and Ustaoset to go to. When Berit and Rolf got married, in 1978, they were allowed to build on half of the plot – up there. When Fernando and I were going to marry, five years later, we had Pappa's permission to demolish the cabin and build down here. But then Berit kicked up a fuss. There was no doubt that this part of the property was the most valuable, she said, and as she was older than me, she demanded the first choice.'

'So there wasn't a division of the estate in the will?'

'No, but Pappa had made his decision, so we applied for a building permit, despite Berit's furious protests. Then Pappa died, that summer. Later we barely talked.'

'But … she got the short straw?'

'Yes. They were terrible years. We couldn't start building until 1985. Early the following year we moved in, and in 1989 Berit and Rolf split up.'

'Because of Hallvard Hagenes?'

'It was a nasty, harrowing divorce on both sides. I haven't a clue what was behind it, but there was a lot of pent-up aggression, I can tell you. But it drew a definitive line under the property dispute. Rolf got the house and the plot, and Berit moved out.'

'And the relationship between her and Hallvard Hagenes didn't prove to be lasting, from what I've heard.'

'Wasn't it? Didn't you just tell me they died together?'

'Or separately.' I glanced at Garrido before turning back to her. 'When he was out here in February, didn't he say anything?'

'About what?'

'About Berit and him having got together, yet again.'

She shook her head. Her mouth was pinched, her eyes impenetrable.

'Would you—?'

She interrupted me. 'That was just a whim. We bumped into each other at Den Stundenløse, quite by chance. Fernando was away travelling. I felt alone. He came back here with me, we sat and chatted for a while, he played a few tunes on his sax...'

Garrido watched her, scowling. She turned to him and looked directly into his eyes. 'Nothing happened. We chatted, he played and then he left. I didn't see him later, and now I...' Her voice cracked and her eyes filled with tears. 'Now I'll never...' she said thickly, without completing the sentence.

'But when you were chatting – didn't you touch on what happened between Berit and Hallvard in 1988?'

'Yes, I suppose we must've done.'

They had sat in the semi-darkness. He had held his saxophone in his hands as if it were his own child he was protecting. She had looked at him, impatient to know, keen to understand:

What actually happened between Berit and you when you met again in 1988?

He wore a sad expression:

You know, the first time Berit and I were together, in a way we never got going because you came between us. You tore us apart, whether you wanted to or not. When we met again, in the summer of 1988, I was playing at Fossli Hotel on top of the mountain overlooking Måbø valley, for a weekend. She'd been hiking in the mountains for a few days and went to a hotel to enjoy a little luxury after all the hiking cabins. She'd planned to catch the bus home the following day, but I said if she stayed until Monday morning she could go back with me.

And that was all it took?

It was a reunion with what I thought I'd lost for ever, Bodil. We lived through an intense autumn and winter, until her husband began to have his suspicions and, in the end, there was a showdown. You know how it ended.

Berit and Rolf got divorced. But between her and you…?

I'm not sure. How much do you remember of what happened to your mother in fifty-seven?

Me? Nothing. Think about it. I was two years old.

Oh, yes, right. But Berit was what? Five? Six?

Six.

It must've had far more of an impact on her. Not least because there was so much that she wasn't told. For her, love between a man and a woman was for ever bound up with betrayal and pain, something no one would willingly be exposed to for a long time.

Meaning?

Things went up and down between Berit and me. She'd developed a sort of jealousy, which could assume the weirdest forms. If I'd been playing on a job and came home late, she would always wait up for me. Then she would cross-examine me. Who'd been there? Who was in the audience? Had I spoken to anyone? Why hadn't I come straight home as soon as we'd finished? That sort of malarkey.

I know what you mean. She could be very difficult.

It was just plain sick. In the end, it was unbearable. And so it died, like the last time. Without such an obvious catalyst as you, though. So perhaps it wasn't your fault after all, Bodil. It would've ended in the same way in 1973.

She looked at me. 'You probably met the official Berit. The professional, successful lawyer. But there was another personality behind the façade, Veum, which only her closest family saw.'

'But she'd managed to get married at least?'

'Yes, to someone who was ten years older than her and bore a vague resemblance to...' She paused.

'Your father?'

She nodded.

I looked out of the window, down to the sea, onto the quay where I had met Sjøstrøm the last time I was here. 'So that's who Berit married. I should've guessed.'

'You didn't know?'

'No. Now that it's too late, I'm beginning to realise there's quite a lot I didn't know. Have you seen anything of him since you've been home?'

'Who? Rolf?'

'Yes.'

'Just through the window. I mean we have no more to do with him than is strictly necessary.'

'OK, but it may be time for me to talk to him, for the last time.'

I got to my feet and looked at all three of them. I had a feeling the future wasn't going to be that easy for the little family of Breheim Garrido. They had lots of corpses to bury, both living and dead.

I had one more person to talk to. One who was still among the living, I hoped.

45

I leaned on the bell. No one came to open up. So I tried the door. It wasn't locked.

I stepped inside and shouted up the stairs: 'Sjøstrøm? Are you there?'

No answer.

I went up the stairs to the main floor and into the sitting room. Sjøstrøm was sitting by the window, well back, so that he couldn't be seen from outside. His gaze was directed outward and there was absolutely no reaction when I entered the room.

For a brief instant I was almost frightened he was dead, until a tiny movement of his hand, pinching an unlit fag, revealed that he was alive.

I walked in a circle around him, stopped in front of the window and stood like this so that he was obliged to look at me. He stared intently at the shirt behind my open leather jacket without raising his eyes.

I sighed heavily. 'You know what this is about, of course.'

He didn't answer.

'Your ex-wife's dead. Her lover – on and off – is dead too. Where were you when this happened?'

Slowly he raised his eyes. Even more than on the previous occasion he struck me as someone from whom life had departed; someone for whom all hope was gone. The half-furnished house, the bare patches on the walls, the abandoned aquarium; everything took on a new meaning now that I knew who had taken them with her: the furniture, the paintings, the fish.

'Me?'

'You're the person who set all this in motion. You rang the police and complained about the noise, so successfully that Garrido was arrested. You told me who used to visit Bodil, but maybe it wasn't quite as you described it. Bernt Halvorsen went there to talk to Garrido. Hallvard Hagenes was there only once. What was the point?'

He didn't answer. There was a gleam deep in his eyes, a kind of belated triumph at what he had achieved this time too.

'To make trouble? To maintain the agreeably unneighbourly atmosphere? Or something more profound, more personal?'

A twitch at the corner of his mouth was the only sign that he was present, that he heard what I was saying.

'You had a few accounts to settle, people whose lives you could do your best to make hell, and you had plenty of opportunity.'

Again, he raised his eyes to meet mine. And lowered them.

'But it was Berit you were really after. Berit and Hallvard Hagenes. How did you know they'd got together for the third time?'

'I…' His voice was husky and indistinct as though it was a long time since he had used it. He cleared his throat. 'She rang me and told me.'

'Berit rang you?'

'She hated me. And she was absolutely unbelievably jealous. I could barely cast a glance at another woman without her reacting with fury. Even after we were divorced … she could ring me in the middle of the night just to give me an earful. If she'd been difficult while we were married, it was no better afterwards. Anything she could think of to torment me, she did. And there was no end to it. She'd been at it for four years. Only last week she rang me to say: "Guess who's coming to dinner tonight, Rolf."'

'Last week? On Tuesday?'

'Yes, I suppose it was.'

'And why would she do that?'

'I've told you. She never gave up. She would keep doing it, all the time.'

'And you want me to believe that?'

'Why would I lie?'

'You've lied to me before.'

'Well…'

But now he wasn't putting up with it anymore. Four years ago, he had slammed her against the wall and said: You'll have to choose, Berit. Between me and … him.

'I used to travel a lot, when I was still working. The whole of Vestland was my area. From Møre to Ryfylke. Once, I had to leave my car in Førde because of an oil leak. I flew home from Bringeland and caught them by surprise. In there. In our own bedroom.'

The house had been so quiet. He hadn't suspected anything. In the sitting room he was surprised to see glasses on the table. Two of them. She must've had a girlfriend over … He opened the door to the bedroom. Thought she was talking in her sleep at first until he realised that was not how it was. She was talking to someone.

'Berit and this Hagenes.'

'There were reasons for you to be jealous too then, in other words?'

'Absolutely. The guy left the house head first, I can tell you, and he had to get dressed outside.' For a second a smile flickered on his lips; then it was gone.

'This was in 1989 or round about then, wasn't it?'

'Yes.'

'Right now, though, I'm more interested in the events of the last few days.'

'That's a matter for you. Didn't you say you were a detective?'

He had told him back then: If I see you with Berit one more time, I'll kill you.

'You were an odd couple, weren't you. You a travelling sales-
man – selling what?'

'Stationery.'

'She was a successful, young lawyer.'

'She must've loved me at one time. At any rate, she married
me.'

'She must've had her reasons. But enough of that. I don't
believe you're giving me an impartial picture of the relationship
between Berit and yourself. The jealousy was probably as bad on
both sides, I'd guess. I think you were still so embittered about
what happened four years ago that when you heard Hallvard
Hagenes and she had got together…'

'What did I bloody care who she was getting together with?
It was her who was jealous, Veum. Not me. Insanely jealous.'

'Sure?'

'Yes.'

He had rung her, in the middle of that February night: Ha *ha ha*
ha *ha.*

*Rolf? What is this? I can hear it's you. I'll call the police if you
don't…*

Guess who's visiting Bodil tonight?

Bodil? How should I…?

*Hallvard Hagenes. Isn't that his name? Your bosom pal from the
old days?*

Hallvard? What nonsense.

Nonsense, eh? Don't you believe me?

No, I don't. I know you're lying.

And how can you be so sure of that?

Because he's here.

At your house? Now?

Yes.

Then ask him who he was with earlier this evening.

There was a dark glow in his eyes now; another belated triumph to gloat over. 'She rang off, but the seed was sown. I knew her too well not to be aware how she would react.'

'In other words, that was probably why she became so uneasy when Bodil and Fernando disappeared. She suspected that the relationship between Bodil and Fernando was wobbly after the breach-of-peace episode, but she couldn't do anything herself. She wanted certainty before she ... I can see two love triangles overlapping here, Sjøstrøm, at least two. Bodil, Berit and Hallvard, once more. But that one was false. Berit couldn't know that, though. That was precisely what she wanted me to find out. The other love triangle was Berit, Hallvard and you. And that one was probably more real, definitely for one of you.'

'Oh, yes?'

'Yes.'

He had decided to find out where they were. He had rung around. Her house. Hagenes's house. He didn't get an answer anywhere. Accordingly, he drove to Hjellestad. There was a taxi in the car park, so he parked further out.

Hjellestad...

They had been there a few times while Berit's father was still alive. He had no problem finding the path through the forest, between the trees, to the cabin.

In 1989 the affair had come as a surprise to him. This time he knew what he would find. It was as sure as the pounding in his heart. Vaguely he wondered: wasn't this where her mother and her lover had...? This wasn't something she had ever spoken about, not properly, and he only knew fragments of the old story, but nevertheless...

When he stepped out from between the trees there was a moment when he no longer felt alone. There seemed to be others around him, on their way to the same side of the cabin, the same lit window. Shadows of the past, glimpses of destiny.

He went to the window and peered in. Through the reflection of himself he saw them inside. Her short red hair had glowed in some strange way. She was sitting on the edge of the table, naked, legs apart, like some whore. He was standing in front of her and holding her while he pumped and pumped and pumped. She was leaning back, staring blindly at the window. For a moment, they stared into each other's eyes. She had seen him before she realised what she was seeing, and he sprang backward as though he had burned himself on her hair.

When he tore open the door and stormed inside, she screamed as if in mortal dread. He set upon them. The naked man turned to him, defenceless in his nakedness. They wrestled on the floor. He wrapped his arms around Hagenes and squeezed. Hagenes hammered on his back with his fists. Far away, he heard sharp, metallic sounds he couldn't identify. Hagenes squirmed free. He rose to his feet, heavily, out of breath.

Berit was holding a shotgun in her hands, the barrel pointing at his chest. Don't move. Or I'll shoot.

Hallvard Hagenes had raised a hand. Don't. Think about…

He panicked, ran towards her and knocked the barrel to the side. At that moment the gun went off with a deafening explosion. Behind him, he heard a strange, foreshortened cry and the sound of a body staggering backward, a chair being knocked over and something rolling across the floor.

Berit let go of the shotgun: Hallvard, oh, Hallvard.

He quickly picked up the gun, aware that the second cartridge was still in the barrel, then stood waiting. She lay across the dying man, shielding him. They were as naked as new-borns. Her white backside was shaking helplessly; blood trickled between the two bodies to form an increasingly large pool around them. He stood watching, with the shotgun in his hand. Soon after, they left in the car, he and Berit.

'Berit did it.'

'Did what?'

'Shot him. Because of the business with Bodil. Then she rang me in desperation.' He imitated her voice. '"Oh, Rolf, you have to come and help me. Something awful's happened. You have to come up to Hjellestad." "Hjellestad?" I said. "OK …"' He looked at me with vacant, uncompromising eyes. 'So I did. I went up there. But I couldn't find them. Neither of them. All I saw was blood. That was when I realised what she'd done.'

'What rubbish. There was nothing at all between Bodil and Hallvard.'

'She wouldn't have known that.'

'She'd never have been able to drag Hagenes over to the well on her own.'

'Are you sure of that?'

'And then drive into the sea?'

'Like her mother in 1957 or whenever it was.'

'You're lying.'

'Prove it.'

She had got dressed as if in a trance. He had barely had to threaten her to get her in the car

But what about … Hallvard?

I'll take care of that.

He had sat at the back, with the shotgun beside him. She drove off with her foot jammed down on the accelerator and he called out: Stop! Stop for Christ's sake!

He opened the door and threw himself out as the car careered down to the sea. He used his hands to break his fall as best he could. When he looked up, he saw only the rear of the car before it disappeared from view.

'The cuts and grazes to your hands and there, on your forehead…'

Afterwards he had stood on the edge of the quay, looking down into the black water. Big bubbles rose to the surface. But that was all. Eventually there were no more.

'I must've fallen.'

There was a ring at the door. Neither of us reacted.

The bell rang again. We exchanged looks.

Then we heard the door open downstairs. Hamre shouted: 'Hello. Anyone at home?'

I walked to the door. 'Up here,' I shouted down to them. 'He's waiting for you.'

46

At the beginning of June, I received a strange telephone call.

The man at the end of the line had a marked foreign accent. 'Mr Varg Veum?'

'That's me. Who's calling?'

He hesitated, as though searching for words. 'That is not important.'

'Not for you maybe. Personally, I like to know who I'm talking to.'

Another tiny pause. I could have rung off, of course. However … there was something about the intonation that kept me interested. 'You were in Utvik, weren't you?' he said.

'If you're referring to … Have you read the series of articles in the paper?'

'Yes.'

'Then…'

'I am ringing on behalf of a group of people.'

'I see.'

'We have taken a decision.'

'Regarding what?'

'You did our compatriots an inestimable service, Mr Veum. If it had not been for you, they would all be dead.'

'Mhm. I wasn't alone. I was with the journalist who wrote the newspaper articles. It's her you should thank.'

'We already have.'

'In what way?'

'We sent her a list of names that could be useful to her. Perhaps there will be another article in a few months.'

'Interesting.'

'But we would like to thank you, too. The question is … Is there anything we can do for you?'

'No, I … What for example?'

'Nothing?'

'No, nothing. Thank you for the offer, but ...What was your name, did you say?'

'I did not say. It does not matter.'

'OK, but then—'

He interrupted me. 'Then we will do as we have planned, Mr Veum.'

'Planned?' I wasn't sure I liked the way this conversation was developing. 'And what's that?'

'You will find out in good time, Mr Veum. Read the newspapers. And do not forget that this is our way of thanking you.'

'But...'

'Thank you, Mr Veum,' he said in conclusion and rang off.

I sat thinking through what he had said. Then I tried calling Torunn Tafjord on the Dublin number she had given me. But no one answered. Perhaps she was out checking the names on the list they had given her, somewhere in the world where no one could reach her until she made her presence known. I didn't know anyone else to call.

A fortnight later I read in the newspaper: 'Famous Criminal Stabbed in Bergen Prison: *He died late last night in Haukeland hospital.*' From the body of the text I gathered that a prisoner with a foreign background was being interviewed by the police. For several weeks, rumours had abounded about racial tensions in the prison, but at the present time the police had no theories on the causes of the fatal incident.

I didn't need to contact the police to discover who had died. I had received a message: '*Thank you, Mr Veum.*'

On the first of July I tried Torunn's telephone number again. But there was no answer this time either.